# THE  SUITCASE

Written by Ruby Manuel

# THE SUITCASE

**THE SUITCASE**

**WRITTEN BY RUBY MANUEL**

**2013**

## THE MORNING AFTER

"How can I make the best of this terrible situation?' Jewel thought to herself as she rushed around the kitchen preparing to dye and perm her hair, over thinking every little detail.

Today was the day that the family was coming to see her and she had over slept and woke up with a slight hangover.

*"Step one, perm hair,"*

*"Step two, dye hair,"*

*"Step three, wash hair,"*

Jewel did everything in reverse;

*" Step one, washed hair,"*

*"Step two," perm hair,"*

*"Step three," dye hair."*

Jewel used ultra-blue hair lightener; one of the strongest hair bleach in the world. She read the direction but wasn't thinking with a clear head. She always had difficulties' comprehending what she read, so reading the directions wasn't really help for her. Sometimes when in a hurry she got things turned around in her head; just like back in school when she was a kid. Jewels' teacher Mrs. Washington would see her working diligently on a project, or at least the teacher though Jewel was hard at work. Mrs. Washington didn't have a clue how difficult it was for Jewel to make sense or complete the assignments' that she gave her to do.

When Jewel was thirty one years old she was diagnosed with a clinical disorder called dyslexia. For her to turn letters and numbers around was something that she did on a regular basics. She had to be really careful not to make errors. Lately she had been having more and more difficulties with remembering things. The way she was feeling now was different; this thing felt like it was connected to her in a sense; it had absolutely nothing to do with a hangover. This was something brand new. She was suffering every night and day with oceans of hot wave's, traveling throughout her body. She felt terrible about the disaster that she'd just created; she decided to called her family to let them know that today's outing at her home was canceled. She knew they would be upset, but there was no way she could possibly make today a happy day for any of them. Jewel, the Southern Bell was losing confidence in her decision making; she was becoming more and more insecure; this Southern Bell was an entrepreneur, a woman that allowed no one to tell her what to do; now she was losing control; which was very strange for a woman that had always been so sure of what she wanted out of life. She enjoyed living the single life, but when Jewel reached *thirty-four* she decided to get marriage. She wouldn't grow old, and live alone for the rest of her life. Jewel has been marriage less than eight years, but before John her husband she didn't want to be tied down. Now at *forty-two* her life was spiraling out of control. It was the beginning of her journey of forgetfulness, depression and a slew of hormonal unbalancing. Jewel had no idea how to regain control of her life after marrying John Dupree. "I have so much going on, how can I put my life back together?" So many things have happened since I got married. How do I start living again?" She asked herself. She wanted to blame it all on her slight hangover, but it had been too repetitive. All of her life she'd wanted to have a family and children, but to this day she had not been able to have her very own children. She and her husband had tried just about every trick in the book to conceive but no luck thus far. She was quite happy with her adopted son Ha-kin, he was a great son to her. He was a very loving and caring young man. Even though Jewel and her husband weren't able to conceive a child of their own, she wanted with all of her heart to make a happy life with her husband. She knew that life wasn't made up of apple and oranges; it just sometimes wasn't that simple. Whatever it took she was determined to make it work, marriage was until death do you part.

## CHAPTER ONE

## THE TAKEOVER

Jewel, a high spirited, country talking Southern Bell; a provocative masterpiece of chocolate sweetness; her beauty provoked a perceptual sensory experience of pleasure just by looking at her. She stood five feet six inch in height, a bowlegged statuette and when she walked her hips served the eyes, causing an arousing in men and sometimes even women. Her smooth rich skin, resembling that of cream, pouring from a milk and honey bar. Jewel wore beautiful light brown oval bedroom eyes that oozed sexuality from a glance and plump full glistering lips, which set her aside from all the other women in her circle. Now there were things happening in her body, but she couldn't quite put her finger on the problem. Something was taking over and she couldn't stop it. The really odd feelings of rushing waves of heat started at her feet and traveled upward until it reached the top of her head. It was an intense hot slow burning stimulus which levitated into spiral-ling sequences of movements. As it accelerated upward she became more frightened. Jewel thought her life was over. *"What could it be?"* She asked herself while standing in front of a full length mirror checking out her body. She didn't feel like a complete woman anymore. Something was terribly wrong with her, she thought. She didn't have sexual or intimate feelings anymore; her body was becoming numb to the touch of her husband. The intimate feelings that she once had were slowly swiped away without her knowledge. Jewel felt like someone or something crept in her bedroom in the middle of the night and stole her most intimate feelings. *"Who am I?"* She thought to herself while standing in front of the mirror that hung on her bedroom wall; she couldn't imagine living in an empty shell of a body, there was nothing left. There were no exciting rushing feelings of ecstasy when thoughts of the opposite sex came to her mind. She became more and more agitated and depressed. While standing in front of the mirror thinking about her situation, her cell phone began ringing. It was her stepson Ha-kin calling to see how she was doing.

When Jewel told him how she was feeling Ha-kin suggested that she go see her doctor. Ha-kin came into Jewel's life when he was five. He was her first love's child. At *twenty-four* he'd just finish grad school; his work was related to execution of the law and conduct of public and National Affairs in which Ha-kin was top executive/Vice President. After a lot of convincing from Ha-kin, Jewel finally agreed to see her doctor; reaching for her cell phone, Jewel called and scheduled an appointment with her OBGYN. As she spoke to the receptionist she became overwhelmed yet again trying to explain her problem. Jewel tried to talk herself into feeling better by telling herself, "*At least now after I go see my doctor I will be able to understand what was going on inside my body.*" As hard as she tried, she couldn't get those terrifying thoughts of what could be happening to her out of her head; not knowing what to do next Jewel decided that maybe cleaning her house would help her stop worrying about the worst case scenarios. She rushed through her day cleaning house and preparing dinner, all the while regretting her doctor's visit on tomorrow. When she finished with her cleaning she decided to take a break and pray about it. She knew that prayer changed things; she asked God to prepare her for whatever she was about to go through. After praying she took a long relaxing bath in her Jacuzzi tub and went to bed. *"Tomorrow will be better,* she told herself."* Jewel watched television for a while before drifting off to sleep. She awakened to the most gorgeous morning, with the sunshine peeking through her bedroom curtains; it was amazing to watch the shadow of the sun as it danced on her bedroom curtains. *"Come on in,"* she said, sitting up in her bed; Jewel took a long stretch; getting up from the bed she walked over to her bedroom window. *"I truly welcome the sunshine with opened arms! This is going to be a beautiful day,"* she said as she stood watching the branches that hung from the big oak tree blow gently in the crisp morning air. Turning away from the window she reached for her cell phone to see what time it was. *"Oh my,* she said," *it's seven-thirty.* She sat on the side of the bed to collect her thoughts; she had a long day ahead of her.

*"John must already be up."* She could smell the aroma of brewing coffee in the air. Jewel loved the smell of coffee early in the morning. The aroma created a warm, peaceful and inviting environment for Jewel to relax and think while planning her day.

*"My husband is the coffee drinker; only on special occasion when I go out to breakfast with the family or my girls will I drink decaf coffee,"* she thought. *I guess I will get this day started. Where the heck are my slippers?"* She questioned herself as she peeped under her side of the bed,

*"Oh there they are!"* she said.

*"Honey is that you?"* Jewel's husband John asked.

John, a *thirty-nine* year old Electrical Engineer from Detroit, Michigan stood *six feet seven inches;* a tall, attractive well-built man, *oozing* in dark chocolate skin and deep sexy light brown eyes. He wore a small goatee that ran evenly around his chin; a beautiful smile that curled up and rest in the dimples that were hiding deep in the corner of his sexy mouth. He was very talented and knew how to do just about anything. He always had valuable information on just about anything; John knew how to repair anything that was broken. He was very popular with the ladies because of his skills. They were always needing him for one thing or another. Sometimes this bothered Jewel. She had trust issues with her husband because of the women. She could see him from the bedroom; he was seated in his old lounging chair in their living room with his favorite cup in his hand, sipping his steaming hot coffee.

*"Yes it's me; I have a doctor's appointment this morning!"* Jewel answered.

*"Do you want me to go with you?"* He asked.

*"Yes, will you please, I'm a little frightened!"* She answered.

*"Okay, let me get up and get dressed. I need to finish wiring Richard's garage first. It won't take long, I will meet you over there babe."* Jewel's husband promised her as he got up from his chair. Jewel knew that he really didn't want to come which caused her to feel neglected; *"yes,"* they had problems, and communications was only one of them." She really didn't want another battle with him; knowing he probably wouldn't show up anyway, so why fight about it. Lately he made excuses of why he did this or didn't do that. She was tired of them all. She would do this alone if necessary.

*"Okay, I will see you there,"* she said, just to be polite. As Jewel was getting dressed for the doctor the telephone ringed. She really didn't have time to talk to anyone so she ignored it. *"Let it ring,"* She said mumbling under her breath. *"It's probably only Ha-kin again,"* she thought. Her stepson was the only one that sometimes made any sense to her. He was passionate about her problems and what she was going through. Ha-kin a *twenty-four year old, five-foot eleven inched;* all muscled stallion. He was an unmarried entrepreneur, with a passion for his mother's wellbeing.

*"I will call him once I am done with the doctor. As for now I am going to get out of here before I'm late for the doctor!"* She said to herself as she grabbed a glazed donut and a cup of cranberry juice on her way out the back door. Jewels' car was parked in the garage alongside her husbands' big Ford *F one-fifty* truck. John also had an old fixer upper truck that he and his friend Nathaniel had been repairing that was in the garage.

*"Those two will always have something to work on. They have been repairing that old truck now for years, and it still need twenty thousands more dollars of work on it,"* Jewel chuckled to herself." Jewel started up her car, put it in reverse and proceeded out of the garage without looking first; onto the street she went just as a car passed by, missing her by a few inches.

*"What the hell is your problem?"* She yelled at the person in the passing car.

Jewel drove along Adam Boulevard, still very furious with the person that almost hit her; her anxieties high to the point of panic; she was upset at the traffic lights for taking too long to change. She was angry at the man who was driving in the lane next to her because at the prior stop light he looked at her, nodding his head saying good morning.

*" Why is he speaking to me? He doesn't know me this morning. I might just cuss his ass straight the hell out!"* She said to herself. She couldn't make any sense of her actions. Her head was hurting and it wouldn't stop. By the time she reached her doctor's office sweat was popping of her head like golf balls. Once inside the doctor's office she began to calm down. She felt like she had just been through a fierce battle with herself. After signing her name on the sign-in sheet she grabbed a chair and sat down. It took about thirty minutes or so before a young nurse name Queenly Le called her name. *"Jewel, Dupree."* She yelled once. Jewel remembered the day her doctor hired Queenly; it was during her routine visit at the doctor's office one Monday morning; when through the double doors walked the most beautiful pair of legs; they belonged to non-other than Queenly Le. She was applying for the nurse position that Dr. Borene had posted months ago. Jewel overheard the entire conversation between Queenly Le and the human resource personnel who hired her. *"Everything checks out, the job is yours, when can you start?* The woman in the office asked Queenly.

*"Right away, now today!"* Queenly answered with the quickness; Queenly Le, *a thirty-one year* old bi-racial girl; her father's Caribbean and her mother Hispanic. Her parents met while station in Iraq. They got married and had two children, a son and a daughter. Queenly was a *five feet, ten inch* figurine, an iconic of lusciousness; her body *adorned* with shapely legs; full breasts and curves in all the right places, which increased her beauty. She wore full lips that spoke their own language; her hazel eyes rest beneath her well-shaped eyebrows. Queenly, a Register Nurse who'd just graduated from UCLA was a beauty; she migrated to California from the

Caribbean's to get a better college education; She was unmarried and had one child; a seven year old son name Justin.

*"J e w e l, D u pree!"* Queenly yelled again, *please come on in!"*

*"That nurse spoke as if she spelled each letter of my name one by one, what the heck is her problem?"* Jewel thought as she got up from the chair she was seated in. She was so ready to see her doctor; she didn't have time to check the nurse about her conduct. She needed to get to the bottom of this sudden change that was happening inside her body.

*"Follow me, go in room #2 and have a seat; I will be right in!"* the nurse said sarcastically. Jewel noticed the nurse's attitude but went in room #2 and sat down to wait for the doctor. The nurse left the room and returned later to take Jewel's vitals.

*"I will need to weigh you. Will step on the scale for me?"* After weighing Jewel, the nurse made a sly remark about Jewel's weight.

*"You need to lose a few pounds!"* The nurse told her. Nurse Queenly Le's attitude took Jewel quite by surprise. Jewel wondered if the nurse was having a bad day.

*"Whatever day she is having, she really doesn't want to piss off this Southern Belle, and if she says one more ugly word, I'm going to knock the shit out of her!"*

*"Doctor Borene will be right in,"* the nurse informed Jewel as she turned the knob on the door to leave room #2.

*"Alright, I will be right here waiting!"* Jewel snapped at the nurse. She waited to see what the nurse would say; luckily the nurse went about her business. Dr. Borene was one of the most trustworthy gynecologists around. He was an Afro American doctor from Nigeria, Africa. He was very well known for taking great care of his patients; He stood about *five feet three inches* with very kinky hair. Dr. Borene wore bifocal glasses that made his eyes look

four times the normal size; his glasses hung on top of his very large noise. For some reason Jewel thought he was gay, which really made no difference to her at all. Regardless to his sexual preferences she still had a crush on him. Something about the touch of his hands made her melt; she sometimes had sexual exotic fantasies about him. Once while Jewel was waiting in his office she fantasized that she and the good doctor made passionate love, right there on top of his desk. Her body melted like *butter,* running down the side of the doctor's desk as they climaxed together! *"Just at the time of us climaxing together Dr. Borene called my name! "Jewel Dupree, he yelled!*

*"Yes Doctor, I said feeling quite embarrassed for having fantasies about him. Looking around, I wondered if the people in the waiting room could feel my embarrassment as well. If they could, would they even understand my feeling for the doctor? They probably would think I'm delusional or something.* Thinking back on this episode caused Jewel to smile, but still the process was taking a bit too long for her. Several minutes had passed before Dr. Borene popped his head through the door of room #2.

*"Hello Mrs. Dupree, I will be right in; I have one patient ahead of you."* Dr. Borene said. Finally Dr. Borene came back into the room. *"Good morning Mrs. Dupree, how are you? Can you tell me your age?"*

*"I am questionable!"* She answered sarcastically. *"He's asking me how old am I?"* Jewel thought that was a silly question; he had her medical chart and information right in front of him.

*"I am forty-two,"* she answered, at this point Jewel didn't care how she sounds. She really did like Dr. Borene, but this had been the roughest day by far for her; he certainly wasn't making it any better. Dr. Borene asked her about the symptoms that she was having. After she told him about the hot stimulating sensations and depression that she was feeling; he nodded his head like he was on to something.

"*Oh umm, yes I see,*" he said. Now he had Jewel worried.

"*What the hell does he see?*" She questioned herself. Dr. Borene ran a series of test. When he'd finish, he left the room. She waited for a while, he still hadn't come back. She got up from the table and went to the door and peeped out. Jewel could see Dr. Borene in the hallway discussing something with the nurse. He looked up from the chart that he was holding, he waved his hands toward Jewel, acknowledging her and said, "*I will be right in.*" Jewel went back inside room #2 to wait for him. Everything about this day was upsetting to her. From the time she left home nothing was going right. "*Now here I am sitting, waiting for Dr. Borene to tell me God knows what.*" Just as she was thinking the worst Dr. Borene came into the room. He pulled up a chair, sat down, put his bifocals on and began reading very slowly. His actions worried Jewel; she wanted to throw her chair at him right about now. Inside her thoughts she screamed,

"*Come on slow ass man, I know you can see!*"

"*Now Mrs. Dupree, I went over your test; the ones that I am able to do here in the office, that is. Your blood pressure is a tiny bit elevated; your sugar is great and your cholesterol is good. We will have to wait for your ultra sound and blood tests to come back from the lab before we know why you are experiencing those symptoms. I will forward your test to Dr. Dorie; I want you to go see her next week.*"

"*But hold on Doctor Borene, I need to understand what is wrong with me now! I don't want to wait for nobody's lab; I'm going through pure hell!*" She said loudly.

"*Now calm down Mrs. Dupree, you shouldn't be getting yourself all worked up like this; everything will be okay; you are probably in the beginning stages of menopause. Just let me get the results, as soon as I get them I will call you right away. It shouldn't take any longer than a few days.*" Dr. Borene told Jewel as he got up to leave room #2.  Jewel really didn't understand why he couldn't tell her anything right away; *"hadn't he been in this business long enough to know when a woman body was changing,"* She thought to herself. Just as Jewel was getting ready to leave room #2 her husband John walked in.

*"You done?"* he asked her.

*"Yes I am!"* She answered with an attitude.

*"Well what did the doctor say?"* He asked.

*"Not a damn thing!"* She said.

*"What do you mean?"* He inquired.

*"What I mean is Dr. Borene didn't say anything, he has to get my test results back. He said in a few days he would know something!"* Jewel was already disappointed that John wasn't at the doctor's office with her. She understood that he had to finish what he was doing, but he could have put it off until later. This was very important to her; she needed him here with her.

*"You ready to go?"* Jewels' husband asked.

*"Yes,"* she answered him.

Just when John asked Jewel if she was ready to go, out walked Queenly, she dropped her chart on the floor in front of John and bends over very slowly as she picked it up. Suddenly John was ready to leave Jewel at the doctor's office.

*"Oh my goodness, I forgot one thing that I need to do, I will meet you at home."* He said as he hurried out the door. He was in such a hurry he didn't even open the door for her.

*"Why the hell did he even ask me the question? Oh my God what was that all about? He asked, then said see you at home. Something is seriously wrong with that man! Our relationship and marriage becomes stranger and stranger as the days past."* Jewel said to herself.

John's actions lately humiliated Jewel. What the hell was he thinking? Even a stranger would understand what she was facing if she told them. Why was he in such a hurry? Thoughts of infidelity flooded Jewel's mind. John had been acting strange the last few months; at this point in her life she refused to be thrown into a mass of confusion, and humiliation, wondering what the hell was going on. She has too many things on her plate already.

As Jewel left the office she was thinking; *"my personal style is, if anyone doesn't want to be bothered with me, then just say it; all these games that he is playing is going to come to an end one day!"*

When Jewel walked out to the parking lot; John's truck was still there, but where was he? She reached into her purse for her car keys only to find them missing; realizing that she didn't have them; she hurried back inside the doctor's office to retrieve them. Once inside room #2 she looked around everywhere for her keys, but didn't see them. She went to the front desk and asked the receptionist, but no one saw them. She tried calling John's cell phone, but no answer. She walked back to the parking lot and look around, but her keys wasn't anywhere in sight. She went back to room #2. She looked under the bed, in the trashcan, but found nothing. As Jewel was looking for her keys nurse Queenly came in with the keys in her hands saying, *"You left them on the table Mrs. Dupree!"* Jewel felt violated, knowing that someone else had her keys for such a long time, but was very grateful at the same time.

*"Oh thank you!"* Jewel said with a huge smile on her face, she was so relived.

*"You are welcome, have a nice day."* Nurse Queenly answered.

're

*"You have a blessed day!"* Jewel told the nurse as she left out the door. She was grateful that she didn't have to catch a cab home. Even though John had another set, but where he was God only knew. The mere thought of going next door to the locksmith, and paying for another set of keys to her *two-thousand, and fourteen* BMW would have been a monstrosity amount. She had to pay a *five-hundred dollars* deductible just the other day for a partial tune-up. *"I have no more money to spend on this car.* "She said to herself. Jewel headed back to the parking lot; as she was getting into her car she noticed that John's truck was gone, *"I wonder what that was all about?"* She thought to herself as she buckled her seat belt; started her car up, she settled in for her ride back home. On her way home she stopped at Food for Less. She needed to get food for the house. For one reason or another she was craving pork chop which she didn't even eat. She knew that she couldn't be pregnant; she figured it was just her hormones going crazy. By the time Jewel reached the grocery store her appetite had changed to wanting sea food. She was on some kind of craving thirst, like that of scavengers; she was having a quenching taste for a fiesta of crab legs. She was craving food that she didn't even usually eat. Jewel just didn't like too many things that crawl or swim the ocean. Now red snapper was a great fish. That was about it though. She just never really liked any of the other little creatures that swarm along the bottom of the ocean. *"They always told me that fish were scavengers; I don't care, nothing but death will stop me from eating my red snapper,* Jewel said to herself, *you know us humans; we will kill for our food, and we will eat just about anything."* There was a horrible smell coming from the aisle where they kept the lobsters, crawfish, scallops and the rest of the seafood; it smelled as if the seafood had spoiled, like something was rotting. Jewel quickly lost her taste for seafood, at this point there was nothing in this store that she wanted. The smell killed her craving for eating anything.

*"I lost my appetite, not my mind; I still need to get milk, eggs, bread and personals stuff for the house. The store isn't so crowded this time of the day, if I wait until*

*evening I will be in trouble."* Jewel thought to herself. Jewel hurried along the aisle, getting the few things that she needed and to the check-out register she rushed. After paying for her items, she asked a security guard who worked for the store if he would take her things to her car for her. *"I will give you a tip!"* Jewel said to him. The young man was approximately *six and a half foot tall;* with a beer belly and rugged mustache; the name Rusty Maxwell was on the tag attached to his uniform. He wore dark shades as if he was hiding behind them. The security guard told her that he would be happy to assist her. When the young man finish putting Jewel's groceries in the car she offered him the tip, but when he accepted the tip she became rude with him, saying how disrespectful it was to accept money from a woman.

*"Didn't your mama teach you anything?"* She asked.

*"My mother always taught me to do the right thing, and accepting tips is the right thing lady! If you didn't really want to give me a tip, that would have been fine too. Now that you have offered I will accept it,"* the security guard said shaking his head as if he couldn't believe what he had just encountered with Jewel. He put the last bag in Jewel's car and the money in his pocket and walked away. *"I only gave it to you this time because I said I would! I think it's rude though to take money for a job that you are already getting paid for!"* Jewel said pointing her finger at the young security officer.

*"Whatever lady,"* he said as he turned away to leave; he stopped walking, turned around and flipped her off, giving her the middle finger. Jewel got in her car, started it up and drove away. She reached to turn the radio on. She needed something to settle her mind. She was consumed with emotions and dark thoughts of doom. Her mind was racing forty miles an hour. She needed to go away and relax on an island somewhere.

*"After I find out what's going on inside my body I am going away, far away,"* She said to herself as she turned into her driveway; she made it home in a

matter of minutes, she sat in the driveway for a moment trying to remember the route that she just took; shaking her head she laughed at herself and said loudly, *"get it together Jewel."*

As she was getting the groceries from her car her husband John drove up; one arm hanging outside of his truck he pulled into the driveway with music blasting like some kind of crazy delusional teenager. John's loud music really bothered Jewel, but she tried not to speak on it, so she didn't say anything. John parked his truck at the far end of the driveway and got out; he had a huge smile on his face.

*"Hold on baby, I will take those things in for you!"* He yelled to her.

*"Oh, okay thank you honey!"* She happily answered. There was no way she wanted to carry all those groceries into the house by herself. *"Right now isn't the time to have something nasty to say to him, I need my husband! I wish he only knew how much!"* She confessed to herself. Today has been full of mishaps along the way. She hadn't accomplished much of anything; this was racking her nerves. She wanted to get to the bottom of this scenario one way, or another. Not been born with patience was one of Jewel's downfalls, and now she had to wait for answers from the doctor.

*"Oh God, the waiting is killing me slowly."* she thought to herself.

*"My mama use to say all the time, Jewel patience is a virtue; you just got to have it!"* Jewel never learned how to wait, and it made her life so much more complicated. This problem was not going away so now she would have to deal with whatever the problem was. *"I am going to pray about it and with God's help I will walk right through it,"* Jewel thought to herself as she enters into the kitchen from their garage. As John was bringing in the rest of groceries, the phone started ringing. It was Jewel's adopted son Ha-kin calling to see how things went at the doctor.

Jewel answered the phone, *"hello son."*

*"So how is things mama?"* He asked her. She sometimes resented his imputations. He always said that she blows things way out of proportion. Personally Jewel sometimes thought Ha-kin made this statement because he didn't have the time to care what she felt one way, or another, and he was sick and tired of her complaining, just like John.

*"I don't have any answers yet."* She told Ha-kin.

*"Why is that?"* He asked her.

*"Well, because I have to wait for test results."* She answered him.

*"So, Dr. Borene didn't have any news for you at all?"* He asked.

*"The only thing the doctor told me is that my blood pressure is good. I have to wait for the other results to come back from the laboratory."* She told her son.

*"That is great; I mean your blood pressure, and all!"* Ha-kin said with hope in his voice.

*"Yes, it is great son, but I am still a little confused that Dr. Borene didn't know more."*

*"It's okay mama, it won't be long before you will have your answers, and then you won't have to wonder anymore. I know how you worry, and I don't want that for you. Just chill out, it will be fine."* Ha-kin said.

*"I will try my best to be patience,"* Jewel answered Ha-kin.

*"Mama, you don't have a choice! Either you condition yourself to be strong and secure or not. There aren't two ways about it. I know you can do it, just tell yourself this over and again, "Whatever is going on I will be strong for myself. To have perseverance is to live through your problems; and not give up!"*

Ha-kin stop talking about it.

*"I know you are right son. I will use this affirmation that you have given me. I love the way that it makes me feel when I say it to myself. It makes me feel stronger, thanks, son!"* She wanted Ha-kin to stop talking about it.

*"Just remember always to pray mama, God will hear you! You only need to believe that what you ask of him he will do!"* Ha-kin told her.

*"I know baby, I know and I will pray to God. He is my only answer; I have no clue as what to do. It does frighten me when I think of getting older."* Jewel said to Ha-kin.

*"Mother, don't think for a minute that I don't understand because I do. I want the complete best for you; this is the reason that I want you to stay calm."* Ha-kin told his mother Jewel.

*"I will try very hard to pull myself together baby,"* Jewel answered Ha-kin.

*"You will have to do more than try mama, if you have never worked hard for what you need or want in your life, now is the time!"* Ha-kin said.

*"What do you mean by that remark?"* Jewel asked her son.

*"I didn't mean to sound as if I was personally attacking your character, but you tend to give up especially since you got married. You sometimes stop going after what you want mama, and you know it!"* Ha-kin said.

*"Alright son I will do this, there will be no stopping me, just watch and see!"* Jewel answered Ha-kin.

*"Ok mama, but you say that all the time."* Ha-kin answered.

*"Why do you keep repeating those same words Ha-kin? I have heard them over and again and again for years now! I don't want to hear your put downs anymore!"* Jewel yelled at Ha-kin.

*"I am not trying to upset you; I just want you to take this serious mama."*

"*I am taking it seriously; it is my job to take my health seriously! Don't you take your job seriously, making sure them foreigners get to stay in the United States?*

"*Now why you have to bring my job into it mama?*" Ha-kin asked.

"*Because my job and your job isn't any difference; I don't harp on you every time I see you as if you are not capable of doing your job. You always talk down to me like I am your child, and I don't like it one bit!*" Jewel answered.

"*What in the world is going on in here, what have you all excited?*" John asked Jewel.

"*I am just speaking with Ha-kin; he is trying to lecture me once again that's all,*" Jewel replied, as she put her cell phone on speaker.

"*Hey Ha-kin, don't be getting my wife all upset, and then I will have to sleep in the doghouse!*" John yelled through the phone to Ha-kin.

"*Man, I don't know what is wrong with my mama, she be bugging out sometimes. You alright though, she will not put you in the dog house tonight!*" Ha-kin told John. They both begin laughing like little boys; Jewel personally didn't find any of this amusing, she threw the phone at John and stormed out of the room. She was not going to stand there and allow those two degrade her. She was no one's fool. After speaking to Ha-kin, Jewel began to think about all the mishaps and unfortunate incidents that she had stumbled across in her life time.

"*Surely I will be able to handle this! I can just about handle anything!*" There is a reason I'm still here in the land of the living she thought. The Lord knew good people just like he knew who the bad people were in this world. For the most part, I have a great heart. I'm considered of others; I do my best to be a good person, and I have great morals.

"*Just the other day I gave the woman at the Post Office money to buy food,*" Jewel said loudly as she sat reminiscing back to the day of the post office incident. "Reminiscing" Jewel had just finished mailing letters at the Post Office and was on her way back to her car when an elderly woman approached her asking for money. The woman's story was that her children didn't want her around anymore once they found out that she had a rare contagious lung disease. They were afraid of catching the disease; so they put her out into the streets with nowhere to go. She had suffered a major heart attack three weeks ago and had just got released from the hospital and now the streets were her new home. Jewel felt horrible for the elderly woman. She gave the woman a ten dollar bill; the woman looked at the ten dollar bill and started to cry. Jewel felt even worse after seeing the woman in tears; she asked for the ten dollars back and gave the woman a twenty dollar bill. The elderly woman cried even harder, with snot and green mucus creeping from her nose.  Even though, the sight of the woman's nose made Jewel sick to her stomach, she gave the woman the ten dollar bill back; the old woman now had thirty dollars, but she kept crying. The elderly woman's wailing and moaning came from deep in her belly. Jewel started to cry too. Jewel told the woman that she could only give her seven more dollars, which was all the cash she had left after her purchases at the post office. That old ass woman took the rest of Jewel's money, said thank you and walked off to another car. Jewel felt like she had just been screwed in plain daylight.  Jewel sat in the parking lot watching the old woman begging and taking people's money. She watched the elderly woman for so long it angered the old woman. The old woman turned to Jewel and gave her the middle finger, took off her old grey wig and the awful dirty coat that she wore; throwing them both into a trash can right in front of Jewel. It wasn't even a woman; it was a man. He pulled his bike from behind the Post Office, jumped on it and rode off down Denker Avenue with an ass pocket full of money. Jewel was shocked that she didn't notice that it was a man acting as if he was an elderly woman.

*"He got me good, but it won't ever happen again, this I promised myself. That's why she kept crying and tearing up so she wouldn't have to keep talking for fear*

*someone would catch on to his voice! Well, at least I didn't give her/him all my money!"* Jewel thought to herself.

After the initial shock wore off Jewel managed to drive from the parking lot. *"Some people will do anything to get what they want. I guess his parents didn't teach him morals like mama taught me.* "You will reap the benefits of the seeds that you sow, that what Mama always told us kids.

While Jewel sat reminiscing; her cell phone begins to ring. The caller's number was a very familiar one. "Conifa Barkman was the name that appeared on the caller ID." Conifa Barkman; *a forty-three year* old short haired, small-breasted, dark skinned; Afro-American police officer. She hide behind dark slanted eyes; being very heavy and round in the middle section of her body caused her to wear the shape of a basketball with tiny legs. She lived in Baldwin Hills; her monumental ten thousand square foot home was located at the east end of Sunset Avenue, it was trimmed with Italian double doors and dressed in a beautiful color of soft tangerine; it was simply gorgeous. This area of the city is where relevant Afro-American was said to live. Conifa married her first husband Ralph Barkman, a Real Estate's Broker twenty years ago; Ralph died in *two-thousand and ten* from food poisoning. Ralph's family didn't like Conifa's evil manipulating ways, but dealt with her unbalanced life because Ralph loved her. She was a force to be reckoned with; either way what could the family do about it? They had to love her for peace sake; she wasn't going anywhere anytime soon. After the death of her husband, his family completely stopped socializing with Conifa. They thought she had something to do with it but couldn't prove it. Conifa would host the most elegant parties at her home; her social network of friends was the mayor, some celebrities and pro- basketball players. She didn't have any children because she had complications with ovarian cancer in her early *twenties.* Conifa was always the one that corrected everyone's language.

*"Oh no for God's sake, that is not proper English!"* She would tell the ladies. She was a wanna-be white girl. Conifa loved to control everything and everyone. For the most part, she and Jewel were friends; however, there were times when their friendship was compromised to say the least.

Jewel answered her cell phone,"

*"Hello Conifa,"*

*"Hey, what are you doing?"* Conifa asked.

*"Awww nuttin' girl, what's up?* Jewel asked.

*"Well, the girls and I have been talking about this trip to Jamaica and New York; you think you may want to go? It is a huge convention that's sponsored by Barkman Associates. You only need to pay seventy-five dollars for registration fee."* Conifa told Jewel.

*"That sounds nice! When is the trip?* Jewel asked Conifa.

*"It's in September, around the 16th or so."* Conifa answered.

*"Oh, ok count me in. Sounds like fun!"* Jewel said.

*"I will get everything together. We are going to be away for seven days. They will only pay for the three days in New York, and we will pay the other four. Is that cool with you?"* Conifa asked.

*"That's cool; I have always wanted to go there! Excitement began mounting inside Jewel's chest. Oh, how she had dreamed of one day going to New York, and now she had the chance of a life time,"* She thought as she held the phone tightly to her ear.

*"Okay, so let's make plans for some tours in Jamaica and New York! The only thing is we will have to attend all the meeting in New York, or they will not pay for our tickets."* Conifa informed Jewel.

"*Okay girl, give me details please,*" Jewel said.

"*Oh, I forgot to tell you the details; there will be seminars on prostate cancer that we have to attend. Ralph's organization pays for our tickets, but we must attend all of the meeting and seminars.*

"*That's fine,*" I *have quite a few relatives with this disease. I can bring awareness back to them about how important it is to get tested for Prostate Cancer before it's too late. I have always wanted to speak to the representatives, maybe they can find a cure or something; this would be a great time to bring awareness about this disease!*" Jewel said.

"*Alright girl let's make this happen!* Conifa said with excitement in her voice.

"*I'm ready; I just have to get this blood test back from Dr. Borene in two weeks, I need to find out what been ailing me,*" Jewel told her.

"*What is the matter with you?*" Conifa asked.

"*I don't know; I have been going through something. I get these burning sensations all over my body. I'm having terrible mood swings. Sometimes I even feel suicidal, very depressed and angry, emotions all over the place girl!*" Jewel told her.

"*It sounds like menopause to me; I went through that already. I'm in post-menopausal now, at least that what my doctor told me. Going through menopause is terrible girl. I even started to get fibroid tumors on the wall of my uterus. I told the doctor to take all that shit out. I wasn't going to be bother with it; I'm barring; I wasn't ever able to use it, so why would I keep it when it was only giving me problems!*" Conifa said.

"*Yeah, that makes sense. I thought about removing my uterus, but doesn't that leave a woman with a big dark empty hollow hole up in there, and when you have sex you don't feel the penis?*" Jewel asked.

*"Girl, hell naw! I'm just as I have always been. Sex is still good, and I am not burning like I'm on fire."* She said as she gave Jewel a high-five handshake. "Now this is the real Conifa," Jewel thought.

*"I'm going to speak with Dr. Borene when I go back for my next appointment about getting my ovaries taken out of me. Honey anything to help, as long as I don't have these problems anymore. Now when these hot sweats and burning sensations starts happening, they are here to stay. Back in the day I would get a pain for a day or two, after that it would go away, not now!"* Jewel said loudly.

*"Yeah, this is something we as women just have to get use too!"* Conifa said.

*"Conifa, do you know why women go through menopause and not men?"* Jewel asks.

*"Girl bye, shit men go through it too, but they will never tell. Just as some women won't tell, it's a secret; fear of getting older and losing control of our bodies I guess!"* Conifa said.

*"Yeah, I guess you are correct. I have asked so many women if they had any idea what menopause is, and each of them said no. The only person besides my stepson that has ever said a word about it is you and my doctor. What the hell is the problem?"* Jewel asked in anger.

*"Well, at least now you will have some answers, so after you see your doctor let me know for sure if you want to go."* Conifa said.

*"I don't have to wait until I see my doctor; I already said I want to go! There is no way I'm missing out on a great vacation. I going to Jamaica and I get to go to New York. Maybe we can even go to Niagara Falls; isn't it in New York somewhere? Girl you better put me on that list to travel."* Jewel yelled through the phone at Conifa.

*"Okay girl, calm down, it's going to be alright, just let me make all the arrangements and I will let you know, okay."* Conifa answered.

## CHAPTER TWO

## STILL HERE

Jewel sat on her couch salivating after speaking with Conifa. It had been really great having this conversation. She felt so much better about the possibilities of things getting better; she believed in her heart that Conifa tried to be a positive person. Of course she had problems like everyone else. Conifa suffered from bipolar; she would change up on a person in a split second. As long as she got her way, everything was cool, but the minute someone else had an opinion that was different from what she thought she would sparrow out of control.

*"Hell sometimes I am not too much different than Conifa,* Jewel thought to herself, *especially right now with all that is going on in my life. I always had a way about myself. I want things to be in order all the time; otherwise I find it very difficult to function. Quite often Conifa and I bump heads on certain issues; however I still adored her; hell we all go through something one time or another!"* Jewel said loudly as she got up from the chair.

*"Are you alright?* John asked?

*"Yes, I'm fine; I'm just having conversation with myself."* Jewel snapped at her husband John.

She was still very angry with him for leaving her hanging earlier today.

*"Honey I knew you were not feeling well this morning, so I thought it would be better for you to see the doctor alone."* He said.

Jewel had to turn around to get a good look at this man who called himself her husband. She couldn't believe what she just heard. She had to make sure that John was speaking to her.

*"What kind of moron husband allows his wife to go to the doctor alone when he knew darn well she was having unexplainable problems? Wouldn't he want to be*

*there to comfort his wife, wouldn't he want to know what was wrong with his partner, his love till death do them part? This dude is completely out of the zone, he done lost his mind!"* she thought to herself.

Of course, she was not going to tell him the way she really felt, there was no need of discussing this topic any further. Discussing it any more would only cost more confusion. She was too excited about the trip to Jamaica and New York; this would be the trip that both her mind and body needs right now, she thought to herself.

September was only a few months away, and she couldn't wait to start planning and packing for this excursion.

When she was a young woman, she used to dream about these awesome places to go. She always wanted to travel the world. Niagara Falls was on her next to do list.

Jewel's husband John pranced back and forth in front of Jewel with his left hand in his pant pocket. He was still waiting on a reply from her.

*"It is okay honey, maybe when my results are in you will come with me. I want you to be there with me for support."* She eventually answered.

*"What did the doctor say about your condition?"* He asked.

"Dr. Borene said for me to wait until he has more information about my tests. My blood pressure and cholesterol are fine," Jewel answered.

*"Oh ok, that's great news, right?"* John asked.

*"Yes it is honey,"* Jewel answered.

*"I know you want to get to the bottom of the problem honey, but you will have to be patience,"* John told Jewel.

*"I know, but that the problem! The waiting games! You know how impatience I am."* She laughed.

*"Yes I do, but right now you need to understand what's going on with your body, so if patience is all you need, then you need to learn patience,"* John said.

*"I don't need you lecturing me; I know all too well about my problems!"* She snapped at him, even though she knew he was right; she just didn't appreciate him talking down to her.

*"See, you are getting upset right now, that's what I'm speaking about, when you are calm we can finish this conversation."* John said.

*"I'm not getting upset; it has been a very long frustrating day that's all. It has nothing to do with you."* Jewel lied; the day had been long and very frustrating, and it had everything to do with him.

*"Okay, I will chat with you a little bit later; I got to run to the gym right now,"* John said.

*"Okay honey, I love you."*

After he left Jewel realized that she had forgotten to tell him about the trip that she and Conifa were planning in September.

*"Oh well, I will tell him the next time we talk,"* she said to herself.

It was time to relax; take time for her; she needed to think about lots of things. She seriously hoped that John would prepare dinner when he came back home. John did most of the cooking. People always bragged about how great his food was, and he loved putting on a show for them all, especially the ladies. It was chaotic when they had house parties. Jewel had just thrown a birthday party for her youngest sister's Stacy thirty-second birthday the other weekend. Stacy, who was ten years younger than Jewel, and was the youngest of Jewel's siblings; she was darn near a carbon copy of Jewel except she weighed one hundred and twenty pound, forty pound smaller than Jewel. Stacy divorced her husband Brandon two years ago. They have two children, a daughter named Empress and a son name Brandon Jr. whom everyone called little Brandon.

After their divorce, Stacy and her children stayed with Jewel for the first year; it took that long for Stacy to get on her feet. Jewel and Stacy were close but had problems sometimes communicating. For whatever reason, Stacy couldn't understand why Jewel didn't want her sitting on John's lap. One afternoon not long ago they had heated words regarding the situation.

*"You are a grown ass woman, don't ever let me catch you sitting remotely close to my husband again; if I do there will be problems."*

*"So what you were trying to say, Jewel? I know you are not trying to imply that I want John, are you?"*

It wasn't long after their argument Stacy and her children moved. Jewel and Stacy remain cordial; fervent toward each other, but never as close as they were before. Jewel planned this birthday party as a way of telling Stacy that she loved her no matter what. Jewel had been planning since January and it was now time to have fun.

John worked his butt off that weekend. He prepared the entire dinner, barbecued ribs, steaks, hot links and chicken with his homemade barbecue sauce. As soon as one of the ladies would ask for anything, John ran as fast as he could to get it. He acted as if he was the only host; this was one of the reasons why Jewel was still a little teed off; he never treated her that way. Whenever she asked for anything at all, it was a long wait, and most of the time his face was frowned up like Chucky. Of course, she loved his cooking; it was one of the reasons why she married him, his cooking, love making and his sense of humor. It had been a backyard boogie-down kind of day, just plain ole fun for everyone. The children played on the teeter-totter, and they bounced back and forth on the trampoline. The grownups ate and drank good wine, played spades and dominoes. Of course, John was at the head of the domino table. John love playing dominoes and thought he was the best at it. It pissed John off when he played domino with Jewel because she beat him every time. Most times Jewel wouldn't play with John for fear of him getting angry and throwing the game.

Jewel began reminiscing of the first time she met her handsome husband that day at the San Diego Festival. In most cases upon first glance she would have run the other way but there was something about John that made her pay attention when he said hello to her. While walking to the bathroom with a co-worker from her job, Jewel ran into an old acquaintance; a man name Nathaniel. He was a bi-racial, attractive well-built gorgeous hunk of a man who dibbled and dabbled in medicine; she noticed him when he walked through the doors of Dr. Borene's office. Jewel struck up a conversation with him. He appeared to be a nice gentleman. They exchanged phone numbers, met up for dinner a few times and dated a few months, but nothing serious ever came out of their relationship. Now months later here he was at the San Diego music festival. Nathaniel was happy to see Jewel. He introduced her to John Dupree

*"John this is my friend Jewel that I have been telling you about,* he said as he reached for Jewel's hand. She and I met at doctor's Borene office over there on La Brea a couples years ago. *She is a beauty, isn't she, and she is single!"* He winked at John, how fortunate for you."

*"Jewel I want you to meet my best friend John Dupree!"* Nathaniel whispered in Jewel's ear as he introduced them, *"you need a man in your life and John is a hell of a good man Jewel!* Jewel and Nathaniel parted ways on a friendly note; she knew he was a playboy; she didn't have time for his out of control partying ways, but they decided to remain friends. Jewel knew what Nathaniel was up to when she saw him coming. He had this big grin on his face like he had just won a million dollars. Nathaniel had been spoken to Jewel about his friend John once or twice after their relationship ended. His complete agenda was to hook her up with John. He had mentioned once before that they would make a great couple; all he wanted was for his friend and Jewel to live a happy life together. John and Jewel fell hard for each other and got married quickly. She wasn't ready to get married, but she was getting older; *"this may be my last chance,"* she thought to herself when John asked her to marry him. They had a small wedding in Vegas.

Jewel didn't believe in large weddings. She thought that it was a waste of time, as well as money that could be used to buy more property later on, or just save it for a rainy day. Their weekend stay in Vegas was that of lovemaking, gambling and shows that consist of girls dancing in skimpy outfits. Jewel never liked this type of dancing, but she wanted to satisfy her newly found husband, so she went along with it. She wondered why John needed to spend their quality time looking at other women dancing instead of giving her all of his attention. Jewel was sure that this was going to be a problem for them. There would be no way in hell she would continue this new way of life for long. She hoped that this was a one and only time she would experience this type of partying with John. Jewel would have rather went sightseeing or touring the city of Las Vegas. She knew that there were many other types of shows that they could attend instead of these practically nude shows. She told herself, as soon as they got home she would let him know that she really wasn't into lap dancing or pole dancing. She would tell him that she only did it to please him that one time. The newlywed couple spent the last night of their honeymoon in Las Vegas on the strip. They rest underneath the stars on the roof of the Flamingo Hotel. Their bodies masked together making love until the wee hours of the morning. It was heaven; lips locked; the pounding of their hearts, the squeezing and rolling of her inner thighs; John penis clinging into her depths. It was like a still overshadowed sea with pulsating tremors as their bodies climaxed together. It was the best lovemaking that she had ever experienced in her life. John's lovemaking was difference from any other. The mere thought of his penis probing her love nest made her body thirst for more. He had opened up avenues of lovemaking that she had never known or felt before. "*Yes he was a keeper, nude girls and all,*" Jewel said at that moment in time. The weekend in Vegas was over; it was now time for them to go home. Jewel was tired from the weekend and didn't feel like helping John drive the distant back to California. John drove the entire way home. Jewel felt a tiny bit guilty for not helping him. John told Jewel not to worry about it, "*it's better that you don't help me if you are exhausted, we don't need to be causing accidents and killing everyone. I will take us home, no worries* baby."

"*Ah, next time I will help baby,*" Jewel said before falling asleep.

They stopped at State Line to grab a bite to eat and do a little gambling. "*The food at Buffalo Bill's is pretty tasty,*" Jewel thought as she sat at the one dollar slot machine putting in three dollar bills at a time. She had one hundred dollars to lose, but she was hoping that she would win a huge pile of money. Jewel played for a while when all of a sudden, bells, and ringing noises came from the machine that she was playing on. Jewel had hit the Progressive Jack Pot in the amount of *two million, eight hundred and twenty-nine thousand dollars.* Overwhelmed from winning all that money, Jewel passed out on the floor. The casino personnel took Jewel to their office; they gave her water, and made sure she was stable enough to leave. John took care of all the business so far as getting the money transferred into a trust account. After they were done transferring the money into a trust account, John came to check on Jewel. She was doing much better. They both were over joyed at the turn of events. They were richer; they decided not to tell anyone just yet. They would sit on the money for at least a year before deciding to spend any of it.

"*Babe we can live off the interest alone!*" John said.

"*Yes honey, you are right. We already have a nice home; we have no need for anything right now.*" She totally trusted her new love's opinion.

The four-hour ride from Vegas home was exhausting for the both of them. Once they reach home, John pulled into the driveway. He put his truck in the park position; turned off the motor and reclined his seat, laying his head back on the headrest. He took in a deep breath and released as if to say, "*damn we finally made it* home." Jewel's home was a beautiful four bedroom three bath dream house sitting on twelve acres of land on the west side of Los Angeles. Jewel was fortunate to purchase seven and half acres of land back in the *nineteen-eighty-one after her father died and left her million of dollars.* She had her home built on the land *twenty years ago* in her crafty taste. Jewel inspiration and design for the home was gorgeous; a one stop destination. When family or friends came for a visit, they didn't want to leave. Jewel incorporated flowers large and small; from lilies to bird of paradise that she planted alongside the curb and the front gate. Everyone that passed her home stopped and looked saying, *"oh what great curb appeal."* She had three water falls in the front yard as well as the back yard. Jewel loved designing and making her home a beautiful, comfortable and serene place to be. Jewel's four bedrooms home is where the newly marriage couple would live, out on the west side. John's place was entirely too small for them. He had a one bedroom apartment, and lived on the south side of Los Angeles. John had seven brothers and five sisters. They were a very close family. His parents were deceased; they passed away back in the early nineties.

*"To this day I still haven't gotten over the death of my parents. They were traveling to New York when their car was hit head-on by a big rig truck. My parent never saw it coming; they died on impact. It was fortunate that the me and my sibling weren't in the car with them."* When Jewel heard this she had so much empathy for him; she could relate because she lost both of her parents with-in two weeks apart a long time ago. Jewel took John's hands in hers; she kissed him gently, letting him know that she would always be there for him.

*" You will always have me babe; Jewel told her husband. I know how hard it must be for you, losing both your parents like that."*

*" I know you understand Jewel, John said. It had to be difficult for you also; you were only a kid when your parents died."*

*" Yes I still think about them,"* Jewel answered.

*" It will be alright babe; we will make it together!"* John told Jewel.

John moved into Jewel's home. Jewel didn't mind one bit, she never intended moving in with John, she always knew that her home would be where she would live with her husband. Jewel reminiscing brought back happy moment with her husband; now it saddens her when she thought of those times.

*"Back when we first got married John kept me laughing, nowadays all we do is fuss and argue about everything. I can only wish for those days again. Even though, John was very busy there were so many things that we could do to enhance our love life, but as usual John find reasons to create distant between us."*

Jewel felt like she was hanging on by a thread sometimes; she, who everyone called super-girl, was feeling a tiny bit weak these days.

*"John said that my menopause is the reasons. I'm not sure, I sometimes think he has another woman tucked away somewhere. When I come back from my trip, I intend to find out about everything; right now I have bigger fish to fry!"* Jewel thought to herself. Jewel didn't want to create even bigger problems; she was only looking for love. She sometimes thought that if she said anything about the way that John treated her he would leave her. Whenever she thought of him leaving she panic, *"what will I do at my age?"* She asked herself. Just recently when she spoke with Stacy about the way she was feeling Stacy told her to stop with the pity parties. *"You are not the only woman in the world that has problems Jewel; you are such a baby."* Stacy said.

*"You will see how this feels when it's your turn, just wait,"* Jewel laughed.

*"No baby, I will never have me any; what did you say that is again?"* Stacy asked. *"Girl you don't even know what I said; and you are talking smack."* Jewel laughed again.

*"Well, I never heard that before you started talking about it. So don't you even laugh at me; you the one forty-two,"* Stacy said smiling at Jewel.

"*I know you are younger than me sweetheart, but only by ten years,*" Jewel answered. "*Yes, and ten years is a bunch of years if you ask me,*" Stacy said.

"*Yea, whatever you say Stacy, I don't have time for you right now. Get out of my house, go home girl,*" Jewel said. "*I will go home, at least in my home there is peace and quiet,*" Stacy said.

"*There is peace and quiet in my house,*" Jewel said. "*Okay Jewel, I'm leaving,*" Stacy said. "*Goodnight Stacy, I love you. Kiss the kids for me,*" Jewel said.

"*Goodnight big sis, I love you too!*" Stacy answered Jewel.

Stacy may have been a brat, but Jewel loved her younger sister. She had another sister who was older than her name Jacqueline who lived in South Carolina with her husband and their four children. She was in LA visiting Jewel a few months ago. Stacy and Jewel were closer than Jewel and Jacqueline. Jewel couldn't stand the sight of Jacqueline because she was always in her business. Jewel was happy when Jacqueline moved out of town. She only started drama whenever she was around. Stacy looked to Jewel for support in just about every area of her life, but Jewel made sure not to get in Stacy's business unless she asked her specifically to help her and the children. Jewel had no idea how long she had been asleep. She must have drifted off while she was reminiscing about her and John's marriage and adventure in Las Vegas. John was standing over her yelling: "*Wake up baby, are you hungry?*" he asked. Slowly opening her eyes Jewel said, "*No I'm not!*" "*Well, don't wait until I make my plate and think you are going to eat my food!*" He said.

"*John, I don't want your food, and, by the way, yes I'm hungry!*" Jewel said.

"*I knew it!*" John said with a huge smile on his face.

"*You knew what? Jewel asked.*"

"*That you would be hungry.*" John answered.

## CHAPTER THREE

### FIRE

As John was preparing dinner Jewel decided to talk with him about the trip that she and Conifa were planning in a month to Jamaica and New York. Now was a good time to talk about it, it's not like John would care if she went or not. However she wanted to try one last time to see if he gave a damn. She needed him to take the time to look at her, to listen to her needs and desires. It would have meant the world to her. Even though, she had come to accept his ways, it still hurts deeply to be in the same house with him and not be notice. He showed his love by cooking and doing other things like working on her car. Jewel thought to herself, "*Shoot; I need this man to touch my body, rub a leg or something!*"

As she sat thinking, John approached her with a big delicious plate of food. She secretly wished John was on that plate; she would suck him through a straw like he was a caramel frappe from Starbucks.

"*Oh, thank you for being so sweet honey,*" she said.

Jewel was ready for this great food; collard greens with smoked turkey, macaroni and cheese, candy yams and cornbread.

"*Oh my God, this man can cook!*" *She said.*

"*Is it good honey?*" he asked.

"*Yes baby, your food gives me that warm back home feeling. Its cause me to think of my mama's cooking.*" Jewel told him.

John loves when she complimented his cooking; he had the biggest smile on his face. It was all true. He was great at it.

"*Thanks hon, I love cooking for you!*" he said with excitement in his voice.

"*Hey John, is this a good time to talk?*" She asked.

Jewel could see his entire expression change at the thought of having a serious conversation.

*"He must think that I am about to get on his case about something or ask him to show the balance sheet for our combined trust account."* Jewel thought to herself as she waited for his answer.

John had spent so much of Jewel's winning on his Electrical business ventures with Nathaniel; she needed to know how much money they had. The apartment building they brought together was thriving rather well. That income along was more than enough for their future, if only she could stop John's spending they would be alright.

*"Don't look at me like that John, it's nothing you have done, I'm not angry about anything. I just need to discuss a very important topic with you."* Jewel told her husband.

*"Well, I guess so, as long as I don't have to hear that bullshit!"* He said.

*"Bullshit? Why do you have to take it there?"* she asked.

*"Because on some level I get blamed by you for one thing or another; you say one thing and be meaning another, then blame me for the outcome."* he said.

*"Okay, hold on a minute, lower your voice please; this isn't even where I'm trying to go with this conversation! We have gotten off on something entirely different from what I'm trying to talk about John!"* she said raising her hands up, motioning for him to be quiet.

*"Alright, what is it?"* He asked.

*"Today Conifa and I had a long conversation about us girls getting together for this trip to the Jamaica. We were discussing making a stop on the way back in New York; and check this out babe; we will only pay seventy-five dollars for a round trip ticket. How cool is that? What do you think babe?"* Jewel asked.

*"Oh, that sound great, but why would you get a cheap ticket for seventy-five dollars? You don't have to do that, not with all the money we have; you can pay for whatever you want."* John asked.

*"Well babe, I don't see any reason to spend extra money when Barkman's & Association is going to sponsors us. Each person will get a chance to speak to the representative of their state about Prostate Cancer. The Foundation pays for the round trip tickets and a three-day stay in New York. Now the punch line is we must attend all of the meetings or we will have to pay thousands of dollars back to the company. So we figured we would pay a little extra money on the ticket; leave a week earlier so we can spend a week in Jamaica and a week in New York."* Jewel said.

*"Well, that sound nice I guess; I just haven't heard of anything quite like it before. If you ask me, it sounds downright crazy for anyone to buy free tickets for a whole bunch of peoples to go trolling off somewhere, but I see you are excited about it. I think you should go if that's what you want to do."* John said to his wife.

*"Yes, you know how much I'd talked about getting my story out on Hepatitis C; this will be a good time as any,"* Jewel answered.

Jewel had contracted Hepatitis C. from getting a tattoo a year ago which caused her to be extremely tired and exhausted most of the times. She also had to watch what she ate or drink on a daily basis.

*"Yea, you had been talking about a cure for Hepatitis C since we got married. How did Conifa find out about this?"* He asked.

*"I'm not sure how she found out, but I'm glad she did!"* Jewel replied.

*"That woman knows about any and everything!"* John said.

There was a fire inside Jewel's bones at the thought of finally going to these places. She was getting excited about the trip all over again. John could see the excitement on her face and heard it in her voice as she told him about

're

each event they had planned. They finish their conversation on a good note. It was decided that she was going. After dinner John went to his favorite spot. Jewel was along once again with only her thoughts. She didn't really care tonight if John spent the rest of the night in his office or not. She was too excited. Jewel put the dishes away, turned off the television in the living room and went into their bedroom. She thought about watching her pre-recorded reality shows before getting her bath, but knew if she stopped to relax for a second she would fall fast asleep. Instead of watching television she got her bath first; Jewel towel dried her body; gently rubbing her favorite Channel lotion over her curves. As soon as her head hit the pillow her mind wander on a cloud o'er vales and hills to some beautiful destinations she'll be traveling in a few months. Her first stop was Niagara Falls. Jewel had successions of images; she saw herself standing at the bottom of the waterfall looking up in complete amazements; the water flowed flawless and copiously, it seems to be spewing out of heaven.

*"Oh the wonderful wonders of our creator. Only he could create something so beautiful, so strange and mystical!"* In her dream Jewel prayed, asking God to fill her up with his spirit, his love, kindness and goodness. She asked the Lord to help her find her way. To give her the strength to overcome any obstacles in her path, *"remove them Lord I pray."*

She also asked the Lord to give her peace in her home, and bring joy to her lonely heart. The shaking of the bed woke her up, it was John coming to bed. She rolled over and looked at the clock to see what time it was. It was five a.m. in the morning. This was no different than any other morning. When it was time for her to get up, John would be coming to bed. Jewel remained in bed beside John thinking of the excuses that he made to keep from being with her sexually.

*"They say women make more excuses when it comes to having sex with their spouses. We are told that we use, "I have a headache bullshit; hell my husband use*

*all kinds of excuses. Some I have heard before and some I have not. I really believe there is another woman somewhere. I have not seen her, nor have I heard of her yet, but I'm nobody's fool. Sorry Lord, it's too early in the morning for this. I haven't even opened my eyes well yet and already I'm having a negative morning. I know this can only change if I change it. The cold part of it all is John claimed he doesn't understand why I am angry at him."*

Jewel got up from her bed. If she continued to stay there beside him it would have angered her more, and she wasn't going to allow anything to gain possession of her mind and power this morning.

*"I am going to have a wonderful day, I'm blessed by God. He told me so in my dream last night. I only need to allow him to guide me. I really try hard at being a nice person, but honey child let me tell you, sometimes I feel like throwing something on someone!"* She laughed at her thoughts, *"girl get a grip,"* she told herself. Before she even left the bedroom, John was snoring loudly. She wondered how he could stay up all night, get in bed at six a.m. in the morning and get right back up after three or four hours of sleep. *"He will be up in a little while installing electrical wires somewhere; I hope he doesn't cause electrical fire damage to anyone's home,"* she thought as she prepared for her day.

*"Oh well so much for this, on with my morning and what a beautiful morning it is,"* she thought as she stood peeking through a half opened curtain in their bedroom. As she peeked outside she could see that there was a UPS truck in her driveway. Jewel wondered why the UPS driver was coming so early.

*"Why is he here so early?"* She questioned herself quietly under her breath; she didn't want to wake John up. The UPS man ringed the doorbell once; before she could get to the door he was already back in his truck. When she opened the door she discovered a priority package had been placed inside the gate. She reached down, picked the package up and inspects it. She found a note saying that they had attempted to deliver the package four

times. Each time there were no answer; she then realized it was the package of exotic toys she ordered for a business venture with her niece a while ago. Jewel had forgotten all about the shipment; she stood at the door for a moment or two thinking to herself;

*"I have been going through so much lately with this menopause stuff, I had forgotten all about this."*

The forgetfulness was one of the things that really bothered her. She picked the package up, rushed into her office; sat down at her desk, grabbed a pair of scissors and opened the package. Inside was everything that she ordered.

*"This venture is going to be fun. Mostly everyone like exotic toys, even the ones who say they don't; behind close curtains they are doing all types of sexual favors.* Jewel laughed to herself just thinking about it; *maybe I could even try some of these toys on John. I better do something before I become like that lady "what's her name? The one that cut her husband dick off and threw it in the field! "Maurina Babbit," or something like that. How dare a man lie in bed next to his woman for days, months, even years and torture her like that. That kind of shit will make a woman cut his dick off. I swear I understand, I'm not saying it's the right thing, but hell I totally get it!"* Jewel said loudly. It was time for her to get a move on, the morning was passing by and Jewel hadn't even brush her teeth. Jewel was still angry with John. However, she was not going to allow the thought of him, or the way he treated her shame her into thinking she was no better than a piece of meat that he didn't want or need. He only wanted to keep her and her money tucked away for a rainy day, at least that's the way he acted sometimes. She loved her husband, she always told him whatever he did in the dark was going to come to light one day; God was going to shine a light from heaven on one day on his behind. She knew that her God wasn't going to keep her in the dark for too long. Once Jewel was dressed for the day, off to the kitchen she went to make coffee. The smell of coffee early in the morning made the house so warm and inviting. Before

she could make a cup of coffee the phone ringed. It was Conifa, *"why is she calling so early? Maybe she too is excited about our trip."* Jewel thought as she answered the phone.

*"Good morning Conifa,"* Jewel said.

*"Hey girl, what's up? What did John say?"* She asked.

*"Oh yes, it's a beautiful morning,"* Jewel answered, knowing full well that wasn't what Conifa wanted to hear.

*"Girl will you stop playing! Did you speak to John yet?"* She asked.

*"Yes I did, we talked about it during dinner last night,"* Jewel answered.

*"Okay, so what did he say?"* She asked.

*"You know how John is; he couldn't care one way or another!"* Jewel said.

*"Girl please, John really does love you. He is just into himself most of the time. Shit you knew that when you married him, didn't you?"* Conifa asked.

*"I know, but every once in a while I need his attention; I mean I need to feel like he loves me. He never does anything special for me anymore besides cook,"* Jewel said.

*"So how did the conversation go about the trip?"* She asked once again.

*"He told me to go and have fun,"* Jewel told her.

*"Well that's good, right?* Conifa asked.

*"Yes and I'm excited about it!"* Jewel answered.

*"Okay, so let's make plans!"* She said in excitement.

*"That's fine; just tell me when and where."* Jewel answered her.

*"I will talk to the other ladies and let you know later today,"* Conifa told Jewel.

*"Okay, I will be home most of the day. I just have a few things this morning to do. Wait a minute; I forgot to tell you that my exotic toys came early this morning by UPS. We need to get the women together for an exotic toy party!"* Jewel told her.

*"Girl your package came, are you excited?"* She asked.

*"Girl yes, everything that I ordered came,"* Jewel said.

*"When can I come over and see what you have?"* Conifa asked Jewel.

*"Anytime is fine."* Jewel answered her.

*"I will be over there around four, this after-noon,"* She told Jewel.

*"Sounds great, I can't wait to see you, talk to you soon!"* Jewel told her.

*"Okay, we will talk later,"* Conifa said.

Jewel called several of her close friends to invite them over to her house for drinks and some fun. She told them to be there around *four-thirty*, and to bring money because she was having an exotic toy party. Of course, she wasn't drinking hard alcohol because of her Hepatitis C. disease, but Jewel sometimes had a glass of white wine on special occasions or over the holidays. She was so excited to show off her toys to her friends. They were middle aged women and could all stand learning new ways of enhancing their love life.

*"It is okay that we have to succumb to toys to fulfill our needs sometimes. We know better than anyone what our needs are."* Jewel laughed out loud just thinking about it.

It was getting later by the minute. Jewel needed to go out, run a few errands. Lord knows she didn't want to be out in the crowd. Today she had a doctor's appointment with her primary doctor; this Jewel hated. The doctor's office was always over crowded. It appeared that Dr. Dorie's patients' and their entire family was all sick at once, and needed the doctor's care daily. Dr. Dorie was also from Africa; she was one of the best family doctors around. She showed concern for her patients; she was kind, and understanding. This alone made Jewel very comfortable and happy that Dr. Dorie was her doctor. Jewel knew today was the day that she had to tell Dr. Dorie what her gynecologists Dr. Borene said the last time she saw him, she regretted this. What and how was she was supposed to explain to Dr. Dorie her diagnosis, she was no doctor.

*"I guess I will say it like this, oh excuse me Dr. Dorie, but Dr. Borene told me to check in with you. He wanted me to update you on what was going on with me, which seems very strange to me. Isn't Dr. Borene supposed to do that, isn't that his job?"*

Nevertheless whatever she thought or felt about it she still had to do it, so she may as well get a move on it, she thought.

*"This day isn't waiting on anyone, at least not me,"* she said out loudly.

Jewel could hear John stirring around in their bedroom. She thought she heard him say something to her, but wasn't sure until he repeated himself.

*"Honey is you still here? I thought you had a doctor's appointment or something this morning!"* John yelled out to Jewel.

*"Oh shit, let me get the hell outta here before I see this man!"* Jewel said to herself.

*"Hey Jewel,"* John yelled again.

*"Yes John, I am still here, I am on my way out the door! What do you want?"* she asked.

Jewel thought to herself, *"Now I know this man doesn't want to start talking to me again about a damn doctors' appointment as if he is concerned. We just went through this shit. I have nothing to say to him about it. He just like the sound of his voice when he ask me questions. I know he is not concerned about me. He is too selfish, he only think of himself. I remember back when we got married he told me when he was a young man I wouldn't have liked him; he said everyone called him ruthless. Shit his ass is still ruthless! He will wait a person out to see what they are eventually going to do about any given situation. He will not move an inch to fix a problem if he doesn't want to. I tell him how I feel about the distant between us. You know what he tells me? "Those are your feeling, what do you want me to do about them?" I tell myself one day I will leave him.*

"*I didn't want anything,*" John eventually answered as he stood there staring at Jewel.

"*I will see you later,*" Jewel said as she went out the back door. She didn't even want to see his face this morning. She was afraid it would spoil her entire day.

"*Have a nice day, I will be here when you get back; I have some work to get done over on the other side of town. I know your doctors' office is going to be crowed as hell*" John yelled.

Jewel wanted to kiss him goodbye, and tell him that she loved him but she knew her love wouldn't be reciprocated so she didn't say or do anything. She waved goodbye to John, grabbed her car keys from the coffee table, and hurried out the garage door. She moved so quickly; she forgot that she left her car parked in the driveway the night before. On weekdays, Adams Blvd was always crowded. Too many stops lights; also now that it was time for the children to go back to school, people would surely be out and about school shopping. This she had no time for; she took the back way, through the neighborhoods. When Jewel reached Dr. Dorie's office, to her surprise there were very few people there.

"*Wow, this is amazing!*" Jewel thought to herself.

After signing her name on the roster she found a seat and sat down. Jewel reached inside of her purse and took a brochure from her recent order of exotic toys. Just maybe she would see something that she wanted, or better yet maybe she could sell some toys right here in Dr. Dorie's office. The thought of selling exotic toys in the doctor's office was funny as hell, so funny Jewel laughed out loud. The lady seated across from her turned around to see where the outburst originated from; this cause Jewel to laugh even louder. As hard as Jewel tried to contain her laughter, she couldn't.

"*You okay?*" The noisy woman asked Jewel.

"*Yes, I am, are you okay?*" Jewel questioned the noisy woman.

Jewel only did it to be funny because she felt like the woman should mine her own damn business.

"*I thought I heard you crying!*" The woman yelled and rolled her eyes at Jewel.

"*Excuse me lady, why in the world are you yelling, and what makes you think you heard someone crying when clearly it was laughter!*" Jewel asked.

At this point Jewel realized the woman was just being messy for one reason or another; then again maybe she really believed I was laughing at her, Jewel thought to herself.

"*Lord knows people are crazy as hell. One thing for sure she is in the right place for a medical or mental problem. I will have Dr. Dorie take good care of her by sending her straight over there to Norwalk. They will put her crazy ass in that padded room in a strait jacket if she messes with me,*" Jewel sat quietly in her seat thinking to herself while the woman kept staring at her. It was a good thing that the nurse called Jewel in right away because that lady was a fool. Jewel had already told herself before she left home she was going to have a beautiful day. She couldn't wait to see the doctor and get back home. Conifa was coming over and Jewel wanted to be there to greet her and the others. Jewel was excited at the thought of making money and having fun at the same time. When Dr. Dorie came in the room to see Jewel, she smiled and extended her hand in greeting.

*"How are you Mrs. Dupree?"* she asked Jewel.

*"I'm doing well except for a few issues that has me concerned,"* Jewel answered.

*"What issues are those?"* The doctor asked.

*"Well, I went to see Dr. Borene because I keep having these hot stimulating sensations in my body and crazy mood swings; he wanted me to follow up with you. The doctor said he would be sending you my lab reports,"* Jewel informed Dr. Dorie.

*"Yes, I received some of them; sounds like you may be in menopausal stage. I went over the lab work that I received, but to be sure, we will have to wait for the other results to come. However, I do believe that you are well on your way,"* She told Jewel.

*"I'm well on my way, what do you mean by that? I hope not o the funeral home!"* Jewel yelled at the doctor.

*"Calm down!" Mrs. Dupree, It will be okay, it's only menopause. All women one day or another will face this time in our life. You are going to have to change a few things: such as the way you eat! Instead of dairy products you will need to use soy. No caffeine, no sugar, no red meats, no pork, you understand?"* She asked.

*"Wait a minute! Why do I have to change all of that? I'm going to starve to death?"* Jewel told the doctor.

*"Well, let me give you some history on menopause, and the changes that it takes a woman through. Some of these changes are hot flashes, night sweats, difficulty sleeping, vaginal dryness, atrophy, incontinence, osteoporosis, and heart disease. During the menopause period, fertility completely leaves but is said not to reach zero until the last day of menopause. So with all this being said Mrs. Dupree I just want you to know some facts, things to avoid at all cost."* Dr. Dorie told Jewel.

*"So do men go through menopause?"* Jewel asked the doctor.

*"Yes they do, but they would beg the difference,"* Dr. Dorie told Jewel.

Dr. Dorie started explaining again; all Jewel could hear was *blah, blah, blah.* The doctor kept right on talking, even though she knew that Jewel was ignoring her. *"The use of sugar, caffeine and diary product will make your journey through menopause unbearable. Each one of these product will more than likely power your mood swings and hot flashes into full effect. I know it is difficult to adjust to; but that's life just as everything else we go through. When life circumstances changes then we have to change with it. There is nothing that we can do about it but follow the protocol. When we women go through the change of life, we lose progesterone, we lose our hair, and some even lose memory. Just follow the guidelines that I will be giving you today; you will do just fine."* Dr. Dorie said. Jewel didn't believe the doctor; she sat there looking at the doctor trying to figure out what the hell she just said to her. The only thing she got was that she was going to keep burning the hell up every day and night for the next eight years or so. The kicker was Dr. Dorie said that men also go through male menopause. Jewel couldn't wait to tell John. The mere thought of him going through menopause with her made her feel so much better. Jewel laughed at the thought, she secretly wished at that moment that she could give it all to him. She sat in the doctor's office thinking to herself.

*"I know those people in the waiting room heard me and the doctor conversing on the subject of menopause. I just refuse to believe all the things Dr. Dorie is telling me. I am not even old enough; this is for women in their eighty or something. My mama never told me about none of this craziness. I wondered why mama never said a word; older women in my family were afraid to tell the younger women about personal stuff like this. It was embarrassing to them, a hush subject, not for us to know. Now that we are adults we have to figure this out for ourselves. That's not even fair,"* she thought as she got up to leave her doctor's office."

*"Okay Mrs. Dupree, I will need to see you in September, will the first be okay?"* the doctor asked as Jewel rushed out the front door of her office."

*"Yes whatever, after all that information you just gave me, I don't need to see you for a year or two,"* Jewel said under her breath. She felt like having herself a good ole pity party, but she knew that wouldn't do her any good. She was taking this matter to heart; she knew that it wasn't the doctor's fault, but she wasn't ready to admit it to herself yet;

*"I have to blame someone, might as well be Dr. Dorie, right?"* she laughed, which made her feel a tiny bit better. Instead of having a pity party Jewel quietly prayed. She knew she needed to get out of her feelings and in touch with God; she needed to accept the changes that were happening to her.

*"I have to go through the process of life just as any woman. Getting older is supposed to mean becoming wiser, and I plan on making the rest of my life beautiful, filled with joy and harmony. Now is the time to look ahead, to plan, to make the best out of my life and this is exactly what I will do. Life for me has only just begun. No more whining or complaining, God has always been good to me and he isn't going to stop now. I will keep pushing forward regardless of my body changing. Just like the doctor said, every woman goes through this at one time or another in their life time; I am no different than the others. The Lord will give me the power to deal with it; he will help me to take care of myself as I go through this change in life. He will give me the tools that I will need to hold my head up high; there isn't much else that I can do. I can't go around yelling and screaming at everyone because of my present situation. I will keep praying that with time it will get better; I need to feel better in my soul; I pray that I will eventually feel like a woman again, in Jesus name, Amen."* Jewel went to God in prayer when times were unbearable for her. She knew that the only way to conquer her fears was to allow her Savior to work it out. She had always been a praying woman. When she was a kid, her mother had prayer in their home all the time. Jewel was taught to pray.

*"Make sure you give God his time,"* Her mother would say.

*"I know mama, I know, and if I don't I am going to hell!"* Jewel answered.

*"Not only will you go to hell, but you will burn in hell forever,"* Jewel mother said.

*"Come on now mama,"you are scaring me!"* Jewel said to her mother.

*"Okay, you will see one day,"*Her mother said.

*"Mama, I do pray, I pray all the time!"* Jewel finally gave in.

*"Make sure that you do."* Her mother told her.

Jewel finished with the doctor earlier than she expected, she felt better now and could get on with the rest of her day.

*"Now I have time to stop by the store and get more chips and dip, and I will have time to prepare dinner. I love to host and make sure everyone has a great time whenever I have anything at my house, "you are my guest,"* She said to herself. Now home and all done with the food shopping it was time for Jewel to finish preparing dinner, relax and enjoy the rest of her day. Most of Jewel friends were on their way over in the next couple hours.

*"I am so glad that I did my cleaning earlier, now all I had to do is get ready for the festivities at hand. So many will have something negative to say about me having adult parties, but I don't care; I love making money. John and I are pretty damn comfortable, but I still need another way to make a cash flow. No one is going to give me money to do the things that I want to do or to live the lavish lifestyle that I want to live. I have to pay for the seven fifty BMW that I drive. Everyone may as well mind their damn business."* She thought as she prepared trays of delicious finger licking food for her guest to eat. As she went about her way preparing entries for her guest she suddenly began to panic and second guess herself. Jewel insecurities start to set in.

*"What if this doesn't go the way that I expect for it too?"* she questioned herself. Jewel knew that there would be a few ladies that would have something very ugly and negative to say, especially those three from

're

church. They were the same ones in the church choir that generally brought a gushing wave of negativity when the director wanted them to practice singing for Sunday afternoon service.

"Anne and her groupies always complained,"

*"Why do we need to practice so much? Everyone already knows those same ole songs."*

The women and Jewel attend the same church. Anne, a heavy set fifty five year ole Caucasian woman from Canada who played the piano at the church had stage four breast cancers; she had just recently moved to California. Anne told the ladies that Canada was too cold; she wanted to live the rest of her days in the beautiful sun shine state of California. Whatever Anne said her two friends from church Sophie and Maggie followed in anticipation as if Anne words came straight from God himself. Jewel tried to give Anne the benefit of the doubt, but she hoped that Anne didn't come to her naughty girl's party in a negative way.

*"I just simply won't have it today! This is my business venture, and I will not allow anyone to mess it up for me."* Jewel finish cooking and arranging the food on her beautiful table for her guest. She made a seating chart because there were a few of the ladies that she didn't want seated together for fear there may be problems. Conifa and Sophie didn't really like each other even though they pretend they did. Jewel had been around these ladies long enough to know who like who. Jewel chuckled to herself thinking about the confrontation Conifa and Sophie had the other Sunday at church. She didn't know why or what happen back there in that kitchen, but Conifa and Sophie were supposed to get the food together for dinner after church. The fight was so bad the Pastor had to come down out of the pulpit and separate them. Some of the folks at church said the fight was about something that Sophie did. They said that she spilled food on the floor and didn't want to clean it up. Conifa had something smart to say about it,

which led to a catfight between the two. It was so out of order the people in church could hear the entire fight while service was still going on.

*"Our Pastor was so disappointed with both of them, she sat them down; they couldn't participate in anything at church until Pastor told them they was off restriction. Pastor said that she wasn't going to tolerate his sheep's "so to speak," getting lost along the way! He said that he was responsible for leading all God's flock to heaven. This is what God has called me to do; there will be no interference from this congregation,"* Pastor yelled to the congregation. Jewel was so deep in her thought about that Sunday she didn't even hear the knocking at her front door until much later when Conifa started yelling out her name.

*" Who is it?"* She yelled.

Conifa didn't even give Jewel time to get to the door before she was already inside. She sure is in a hurry Jewel thought.

*" What is going on?"* Jewel asked her.

*" Girl I got to go, I need to use your bathroom."* she said.

*" God only knows what would happen if and when I had to go in a hurry."* Jewel laughed.

Conifa hurried to the bathroom, as she was going in there was another knock at the door.

*" It's open, come on in,"* Jewel said.

> *" It was Miss. Prissy and Dolly,"*

Miss. Prissy, a retired sixty something year old College Professor; she was the sweetest woman ever. She lived in Hollywood Hills, in a mansion with her husband Professor Henry Tolbert. They both taught at Cal State University. Miss. Prissy was a cool little lady that basically kept the same personality. She stood about five feet tall five inches tall, and had the cutest little shape; round hips that she loved to roll when she danced. She was brown complexion with full thick lips and dark brown eyes. She was an elegant woman; she always tried her best to make sure everyone was okay. Jewel admired Miss. Prissy so much, even though she just met her, it felt like they had known each other all their life. Dolly Madison, a distinguish unmarried woman from Paris France, and had not long moved to Los Angeles. She was corporate manager for Macy's department stores. Dolly travel where and when corporate needed her. She had high self-esteem; she sometimes differentiated, pointing out the qualities of things that Conifa ever said, or did. Conifa would say that Dolly thought she was superior, and she tried to express power over others. Jewel didn't think so, she thought Dolly was nice. Jewel loved them both, they were the sweetest women. Jewel knew that they would grow to love each other the minute they all met. Jewel met Miss. Prissy and Dolly through Conifa. Even though, she introduced them, Conifa didn't like their bulging friendship or the closeness that they shared; she was very territorial when it came to her friends and her space. This was something that Conifa would have to deal with. Jewel has never been a person that allowed anyone dictating to her who to be friends with. She did her own thing and if someone didn't like it, then oh well, that was their problem! There will always be a few girlfriends in their circle that had problems with the one or two of the others, as for Jewel she tried to get along with each of ladies; however if it became a situation of bickering and fighting and no one could solved their issues then the group would get together to vote that person out. When Conifa came out of the bathroom and saw Miss. Prissy and Dolly, there was instantly a change in her demeanor. Jewel watched to see what she would do next. Jewel thought about the conversation she and Conifa had earlier that day when they were on the phone. *"There will be no problems at my exotic toy party,"* Jewel told Conifa and Conifa agreed.

*"Miss. Prissy and Dolly will always be my friends. We can all get along if we try, but you will never get me to turn my back on either of them; they have been too kind to me,"* Jewel told Conifa.

Jewel seriously thought they were all cool until the day when Conifa blew up on Dolly; something about Dolly saying that Conifa was always trying to run everything. Conifa did always want everything to go her way. Jewel usually just ignored Conifa. She knew something was off about her, but she had unconditional love for her.

*"There are three ladies here, so we may as well get this thing going,"* Jewel thought. She had invited ten ladies; Jewel still needed to get the rest of the toys out on display before the others arrived. She went into her office and brought out more adult toys.

*"I had big ones, small ones, toys for everyone!"* Jewel said loudly.

By the time Jewel got through placing all of the adult toys on display mostly everyone was there. There was excitement in the air as the ladies discuss what had been happening in their lives. Jewel was excited to have them all under her roof at the same time. She love hosting, it didn't matter what, and as long as she was able to host and enjoy her friends she was happy!

*"Okay ladies, come on in and grab a seat. One of the reasons we all are here today is because I have some interesting stuff to show you! I need for everyone to gather around so you can hear what I am saying about my new business venture!"* Jewel told the group of women.

*"She is going into a business venture selling adult toys; you ladies will be surprised at the things she has to show you, I don't even believe that Jewel has the nerves to really do this."* Conifa said in a sarcastically voice.

At that moment Jewel really didn't believe that Conifa just talked down about what she was trying to do. She was being too faced again, a very jealous soul; it has always been that way.

*"She and I had already discussed this venture of mine! Jewel told her friend Miss Prissy. I am not going to allow her to be a Debbie Downer on my party. In the past Conifa, usually, waited awhile before she got started, but for some reason today she is in quite a hurry to bash me."* Jewel looks at Conifa as if to say, *"don't you start, not another word out of you. I think she understood the clear message that my eyes sent her way,"* Jewel told Miss. Prissy.

*"So what is this all about?"* Miss. Prissy asked Jewel.

*"Yeah, what do you have going on here?"* Dolly asked.

*"Okay ladies, simmer down. I will explain everything to each of you when everyone gets quiet, so I will not have to keep repeating myself,"* Jewel said.

Jewel needed to regroup herself. After watching how uncomfortable Conifa was acting threw her off her game. Conifa sat there in her chair squirming around like her ass was on fire. She knew she needed to try some of these toys; she hadn't had a man in damn near four years, or so she said. As Jewel was getting the ladies together, the doorbell ranged, it was Tara, Jerry, Brenda G. and Mary.

*"The last of the Mohegan has come together,"* Jewel smiled and nodded her head at them as they walked passed her. They seated themselves directly in front of Conifa.

*"Maybe now we can get started,"* Jewel said, and she began to tell them about her new business. She explained the way each of the adult toys worked. Most of the women were excited and ready to place an order except for two of them. It was shocking for Jewel to see Conifa and Mary acting as if this was a disgusting venture. They had lots to say about Jewel idea to make money. The main thing that upset them both was the vibrating panties.

"*Who in the world would walk around with this on?*" Conifa asked everyone.

"*Well, it is to each person taste Conifa; no one is trying to make anyone do something that they are uncomfortable with,*" Jewel replied.

"*Yes, but you already know that Mary goes to church; she shouldn't even be here right now,*" Conifa replied.

"*But how is that any of your business? Besides we all go to church, what does that have to do with anything?*" Jewel asked.

"*Wait a minute, I can speak for myself, and I seriously do not need help Conifa. You only are including me in your conversation because you can't or won't stand by yourself in your true beliefs. Conifa you told me that you did not want to be involved with such evilness, so don't be acting as if it's all me.*" Mary yelled.

"*What are you saying Mary? Jewel asked. Conifa and I talked about this earlier today. I asked her to call and invite everyone and she said yes,*" Jewel turned her attention to Conifa and told her,

"*If you had problems with this why did she agree to help me?*"

"*That is not what I told Mary, she is adding her little extras on it,*" Conifa said.

"*Yes you did say that you didn't want to be involved with this because you felt that God put man and woman together to enjoy each other, not with all those nasty toys!*" Mary yelled at Conifa.

"*Okay, it doesn't matter,*" Jewel said. *I will not keep fussing back and forth. Who want to purchase something? That is all I want to know. The smaller vibrators are excellent toys.*" To Jewel's surprise the toy party sales went very well. Each of the women bought an intimate surprise for their significant other.

Conifa purchased a few very intimate toys also, while paying Jewel for the order, she said, "*Oh, by the way, this is for my friend; she has a birthday coming up soon.*"

*"Yeah right Conifa, like anyone believe that load of crap."* Jewel really didn't care who it was for as long as she made the sale. *"I am a business woman, making money, never mind me who uses it."* Conifa should have been embarrassed; *she talked all that shit about the toys, then turned around and bought the vibrating panties."* Jewel laughed out loud as she thought about it. She couldn't hold it in any longer. Dolly witness the entire transaction; she also overheard what Conifa said about the purchase. She couldn't wait to blast Conifa to the other ladies; she wasn't going to allow this chance to embarrass Conifa get away. She yelled loudly,

*"Conifa, all that talking about them vibrating panties, you mean you are buying them! Girl somebody needs to call the police on you for being a big ass fake, and what you gone do with them? You know damn well you will be wearing them panties!"* Dolly said. She was laughing so hard at Conifa she nearly peed her pants. All Jewel could do was stay in her chair, and keep her laughter to herself. She didn't want to make matters worse than they already were. Jewel knew Conifa wanted the toys; she just didn't want the other ladies to see her buy them. Jewel whispers in Miss. Prissy's saying,

*"I don't know why she just didn't get what she wanted earlier, before everyone got here. She is just stupid that way. I guess she wanted to be the center of attention. No one even care about the way she was acting until she brought them vibrating panties! We all knew that she was bi-polar."*

It tickled Jewel pink when Miss. Prissy told her that Conifa was just a silly moron and that she need to get her life. Dolly was big in making Conifa miserable; just as Conifa was trying to cause problems for Jewel.

*"Come on Dolly it is okay, you making bad business for me,"* Jewel finally said.

*"That right,* Miss. Prissy said, *whatever Conifa wants to buy is her own business. You just get what you came for and let eat,"* She said with a huge laugh.

*"Okay everyone it is time to eat some of that finger licking good food that Jewel has prepared for us,"* Mary said. Jewel was quite surprised that Mary even came to her adult party. The thing that so funny about it was Mary and Pastor was so close.

*"I guess Mary didn't care if Pastor got wind of her coming to my naughty girl's party. Mary knew that as soon as Maggie and Sophie found out about it they would run straight to pastor and tell on everyone. Sophie already said she wouldn't be caught dead at something like this. She and Maggie were totally against this type of partying. That is why I asked Conifa not to invite them, they would go gossiping all over town about us being cougars and wanting young boys. They are old fashion; they don't know how to change with the times, they both are stuck in the nineteen-twenties. I don't care girl, I know my age, I am only forty-two. This is my time to shine, travel and have all the damn parties that I want! I have one stepson who is all grown up and John cooks for both of us. He is not a man that requires a woman to care for him like that, he is hands on. John can take care of the outdoors as well as the indoors, so I will do whatever I want to, and when I want to, unless it bothers John, or God tells me it is time to lay down and sleep forever!"* Jewel finished preaching her sermon to Miss. Prissy.

*"Wow, honey baby, she got you all worked up; don't allow her to do you that way sweetheart. You are so much better than that. I think she intentionally does things to make sure she messes up everything for you."* Miss. Prissy told Jewel.

*"Yes, I think you are correct Miss. Prissy,"* Jewel answered.

*"Just stay calm, I'm not used to you getting that worked up behind what someone say,"* Miss. Prissy told Jewel.

*"I'm not getting worked up Prissy, I'm just stating facts."* Jewel replied.

Miss. Prissy was glad that Jewel was finally quiet; all that talking about Maggie and Sophie was giving her a head ache. She would have rather not go with the ladies herself but was not going to say anything about it.

## CHAPTER FOUR

## LATE NIGHTS TOYS

Jewel had many thoughts were running through her head, she had to get a grip. Jewel was a little apprehensive because of the confusion, but this wasn't the time to become involved in stupidity; it's time to handle business and have fun. Jewel's past experience with these ladies was cost effective; they usually had a blast when they all got together for a trip or a day out at the movies or the beach. They either car pooled or every one chipped in on gas. Jewel didn't want anything to stand in the way of them having a grand time on their trip. Now that Jewel had all the ladies in one place, she would discuss the trip. In order to get the ladies moving Jewel had to have direct induction of her idea. Conifa and Jewel had discussed it before, but since Jewel couldn't trust Conifa to bring it forth without more drama she decided to do it herself.

*"Yes, let us wrap this up so we can have dinner!"* Jewel said with intuition.

Transitioning the ladies from the living area to the dining room went smoothly. Jewel's lay-out was beautiful; she use her creative taste of elegance. She brought out her best China and silverware; she had delicious foods which were assembled on the dining room table. Jewel placed yellow, white and pink long stem roses along the center of the table next to the wine glasses. She had a passion for beautiful flowers; they brought sunshine into a dreary room. She had previously made a seating chart; this was also done to keep the peace. Jewel place name tags alongside the plate where each of her guests would sit.

*"No exception,"* she said to herself while decorating. *"I know there will be a few that does not like where they will be seated, nevertheless they will still have to sit where their name is placed!"*

Thank God there was no fighting getting the ladies seated, things were going smooth.

*"Just the way I like it,"* Jewel thought to herself.

After the ladies were seated Jewel asked Mary to say grace. Mary was delighted, and as usual she went on and on with one of the longest prayers in history at the dinner table. Jewel had no idea why she even asked her.

*"I guess I must have forgotten for a minute how Mary gets when praying on any occasion,"* Jewel thought.

After Mary finally finished saying grace everyone race for the food. They couldn't wait to load their plates of Jewel's home style cooking. Jewel was also hungry and wanted a taste of everything. She knew the food would be delicious, and have a special taste, because while Jewel was at the doctor, John took his time and prepared some of the food. He was her helper; she loved his way around the kitchen.

*"Who did the cooking Jewel?"* Conifa asked.

*"Why is that any of your business helfa?"* Brenda G. asked.

*"It's okay, and yes John helped!"* Jewel said. She knew the ladies would ask.

As they ate dinner Jewel told everyone about the plans for this big trip. Everyone except for a few of the ladies was excited about it, and wanted to go. Conifa agreed to make all the arrangement and the ladies agreed to allow her to do it. They knew what an enforcer Conifa was, however all still agreed to let her make the plans. Jewel really didn't care who made the arrangements. She had not been anywhere in such a long time; she didn't have a clue what to do in Jamaica or New York, so far as planning tours. She knew New York had been widely extolled and she wanted to see what it was all about. Conifa had traveled the world, she knew what tours to take, she knew where the great restaurants were, she knew all the exciting things happening in each place they would travel. After the discussion the ladies left for the evening. It had been an exceptional day even with the tiny but of confusion. Jewel couldn't wait for John to get home so she could

're

tell him about her day with the ladies. John said that there would be confusion, he knew how Conifa and a few of the others ladies were. This wasn't their first time disagreeing about one thing or another.

*"John called them the fighting cougars!"*

Jewel told John, *"whatever you think is fine with me it doesn't matter, we fight and we make up! That's just the way our cycle of life does its thing. I have no control over what others think; only God has control."* Jewel could hear John's key as he unlocked the front door. She was so glad he'd finally made it home. *"As much as we fight I truly missed him when he isn't around. I can't get to sleep at night without his presence in the house. He always came to bed late but I still need him, he makes me feel complete."* Jewel thought to herself.

*"Hi babe,"* she said as she reached to kiss him.

*"Hey you,"* he replied and kissed her on the lips.

*"How did your day go?"* She asked him.

*"It was okay. I had a couple jobs that felled through, what about your party?"* He asked.

*"It went very well, dinner was great! Thanks for helping with the food babe; the ladies spent lots of money. I filled eight orders!"* Jewel told him.

*"Wow, that's great! Did I hear you say everything went fine?"* John asked his wife.

*"Yes everything went fine!"* Jewel said.

*"I find that a little hard to believe!"* John replied.

*"Why?"* Jewel asked him.

*"You know why, because of your friends. They aren't always the nicest people!"* John said.

*"There was some conflict but it's not a huge problem. We worked it all out and I made money. What else is there to discuss? I know you want to hear the low down, so here it goes John. Conifa and Mary had words which upset me. I eventually got things back on track and continued on with my business as planned."* Jewel told her husband.

*"Whoa, don't get upset with me, I didn't do anything!"* He said loudly.

*"I am not babe, just really had a long day. I am so glad you are home honey!"* Jewel told her husband; she didn't want to fight with him.

*"Me too baby, it had been a long day, I've missed you,"* John said.

*"I missed you too! Did you know babe that I can't sleep very well when you are not home?* Jewel asked John.

*"I know babe, and I don't sleep well when you are away. I'm really tired tonight babe, maybe I'll get some sleep,"* John said to Jewel.

*"So does this mean no nookie tonight, and what about dinner?"* Jewel asked.

*"Let me get my shower first, and then we will see, and no I'm not hungry. I ate some of the food that I cooked earlier. I saw your toys too,"* John laughed.

*"Oh, so you were in my toys, and why can't you answer me right now?"* Jewel asked.

*"Babe please don't start with me right now, I am exhausted!"* John answered. Sometimes they didn't touch each other for months. Jewel never liked it, but they both were very stubborn people. They sometimes were at a stand-off so to speak. If they went to bed angry at one another it became, *"If you touch me here then I will touch there you kind of thing."* Their bed was a cold lonely place for Jewel to be in.

*"John, may I ask you a question?"*

*"Sure, as long as you are not trying to pick a fight!"*

're

*"A fight; who is picking a fight?"* Jewel questioned, John.

*"Come on now Jewel; just ask the damn question please!"* John said.

*"Do you still love me?"*

*"Of course, why would you ask me something like that?"* John asked in disbelief.

*"Because you never show me you love me anymore,"* Jewel answered and turned her back to John.

*"Whatever, I can't ever satisfy you!"* John said to Jewel.

*"You could satisfy me if you try, I'm not that damn hard to please. You never do anything special for me anymore like you use too,"* Jewel said.

It was one of the coldest nights of the year. The weatherman said it was going to be fifty-six degrees; Jewel didn't care about the little argument she and her husband just had. She snuggled very close to John to keep warm. For some reason, he was feeling himself and snuggled back; this was very nice, especially since it rarely ever happen in their bed. Things were different, but Jewel was not complaining. John had a hard on the size of California. Not only did he have a huge package, but he knew how to work it. The way that he made her body feel inside was like warm rivers of water, dripping slowing, overflowing gently into the sea of love, until gigantic waves erupted, taking her breath completely away. *Now that was the man that she married!* Jewel thought as she cuddled in her husband's arms. *"I will not even think of interrogating him about why the change, I just appreciate the attention. I have a good husband and one of these days I will learn to appreciate him for his worth, for what he does, What if I was in Conifa's shoes and completely lonely,. She doesn't have anyone to care for her like John does me since Ralph is gone on to heaven. I sometimes feel very sorry for her losing Ralph like that. They had a great relationship. He was so loving and considerate to her,"* Jewel thought silently to herself.

## CHAPTERFIVE

## KISS GOODBYE

Jewel looked over at John who was now fast asleep. Sometimes he was a perfect gentleman; she thought to herself. She secretly wished that he felt the same way about her. Jewel couldn't help the way she felt; she had trust issues and misplaced anxieties that stemmed from her adolescence years. She said that she would stop bickering with John and learn to trust him, but so far it hasn't happened. She would get better at trusting him, she just knew she would. She also knew there weren't any perfect peoples in this world. To expect a person to come even close to being perfect is completely dumb, inconsiderate and completely out of the question. She awakened the next morning to the sound of raindrops tapping lightly against her windowpane. She felt so special after her exotic romantic night of passion with John. Every time she pressed her legs together she could feel the stimuli pulsating in her vagina muscles from their lovemaking. Jewel eased her body from the bed and slipped quietly into her slippers; into the bathroom she went. The bathroom was a one stop for her in the mornings; her morning ritual was; "brush teeth, take shower, dry off and put on make-up. Do everything before she exited the bathroom. When she came out, she was ready for the day; this was Jewels' daily routine. She went into the kitchen to prepare breakfast and make coffee for John. Whatever he wanted today he could get. He had rekindled the fire that had been shut up in her bones. Jewel guessed the sex toys that John saw last night turned him on.

*" I will have more of them if that's the case! What better way to explain to the other ladies how valuable it is to have sex toys around."* Jewel thought to herself. Jewel put on a pot of coffee; the aroma of John's good ole fashion Folgers coffee would wake him up. Just at that moment she heard John, stirring around in the bedroom. Something inside of her wanted to go and climb right back into bed with him. When she wanted to be with John there

're

was sometimes that feeling of insecurities' which made her feel unattractive. According to her doctor, she was supposed to have abnormal hormonal imbalances the rest of her life. This Jewel didn't want to think about. She tried to refocus her mind. She needed to think in a positive direction, one that would make her feel better instead of the scary feeling that came along with getting older.

*" I deserved to have intimate moments with my husband. Nothing but death should be able to take that away from me!"* Jewel told herself.

John walked into the kitchen and kissed Jewel tenderly on her lips.

*"Good morning baby!"* John said. Jewel detected a little excitement in his voice as he spoke.

*"How are you feeling this beautiful morning babe?"* She asked while flirting with him.

*"Girl you ready again?"* He asked her with this huge grin on his face.

*"No, I am not, but I do feel pretty damn good from last night episode! What has gotten into you?"* Jewel asked him.

*"What got into me, babe? You got into me my love; I wanted to spend some quality time with you!"* He said.

Now Jewel knew something was off, or maybe something was back on; either way there was a difference;

*"Why was he acting so differently than before the party?"* She asked herself. They hadn't spent quality time together in months. She wondered if the women being there and the sex toys had anything to do with it, but she sure as hell wasn't going to say anything about it. She would just trust his word and for once believe in him.

*"Okay babe, if you say so."* Jewel finally replied.

*"Well, okay babe, a little bit of both, the toys and you!"* He finally admitted, all the while smiling like he had something else going on in that mind of his.

*"Wait a minute; do I need to take your temperature? Are you alright?* In all the years that we have been married I have never seen you act this way, well not recently,"* Jewel said to him.

*"That is because you are always angry at me about something. How can a man make love to an angry woman?"* John asked.

*"John, please don't start with the blame game, there is enough blame to pass around till next year! So let's stop before this conversation gets out of hand. Last night was too beautiful! Can we please just remember the best times and not the worst times?"* Jewel answered.

*"Sure you right babe!"* John said.

Sometimes Johns' personality was the cutest; the way that he articulated his words; when he laughed it progressively spiraled from the central point of his belly. He would start with a tiny chuckle that continuously got deeper and louder until he was rolling on the floor; which always had an impact on her. The next thing Jewel knew she would be laughing and rolling on the floor right next to him. After hearing him just now say,

*"sure babe,"* brought back the sweetest memories.

She remembered back to the night when she was sitting alone in the living room watching television and John walked in and said,

*"Hey babe, I have something very special for us to do! Do you want to know what it is?"* Jewel was somewhat taken back and very surprised. She wondered what on earth it could be.

*"Planning a surprise for us was something that John hadn't done in a very long time,"* She thought.

*"Hell yes, I want to know! What is it babe?"* Jewel asked in excitement.

John was standing there looking sneaky as hell; he looked as if he had the hugest secret ever, and he couldn't hold it any longer. It had weighed him down, now it was time to spill it to her.

*"Damn John will you please tell me!"* Jewel yelled at him.

*"Okay babe, look at this right here!"* He said showing her a pair of tickets.

*"Look what I have for us! I know you love Reggae music, Bob Marley, and all, so I got us front row ticket to the Reggae Festival next week in the city!"* He was as happy as he could be as he talked on and on. Jewel was happy too and caught up in the moment; John had her fantasizing about this event. She had dreams of going to an event such as this one and now she had front row tickets.

*"Oh babe, you are the sweetest one ever! When did you have a chance to get these tickets?"* She asked John.

*"That's my little secret; a man shouldn't tell his wife everything; if he does then he won't be able to surprise her like this!"* He said as he turned and looked at her in that sexy way that made her body ache for him. Jewel melted right into his arms, hugging, kissing and thanking him for being such an awesome husband. The day before the concert John gave Jewel money to get her hair done; he also brought them matching outfits to wear. Since it was a Reggae Festival, they dressed in Rastafarian attire. Jewel wished that she had dreadlocks to go along with her outfit, but instead she had her hairdresser whip her up a freeze this time around. She wanted something different than what she was used to wearing. Her hair turned out fabulous; she felt like a million bucks. When John saw her hair all done up, he was just as excited as Jewel.

*"That's a different look babe; I like it!"* He told her.

*"Oh thanks babe, I thought I would change it up this time.* Jewel said winking at him. *"Alright babe, lets' get on the road before it gets too late."* John said. Once they reached downtown L.A. they went straight to the Hyatt Regency; a hotel that John had reserved for them near the Dodger's Stadium a while ago. The room was elegantly tailored just for them. Their bed was covered in red rose buds. There was a beautiful vase with flowers on the table nearby with her name on it.

"Jewel was so elated; she started to cry,"

The Festival was everything she had ever dreamed off. Reggae music filled the air; the sweet aroma of incense burning alongside each venue. The quaint voice of the Rasta's' was hypnotizing.

*"Incense for sale,"* the Rasta said to them as they passed.

Jewel had always been attractive to the Rasta's' and admired the tone in their voices. She found it to be quite charming.

*"John knew how much I would love being in this environment. Enjoying this culture and the people; that's why he brought me here,"* she thought to herself as they walked along hand in hand. It was one of the most fabulous weekends of her life.

*"Lord those were the days back then, Jewel thought, and to think that it may be possible again gives me hope for a better relationship with my husband. There is no way I am going to spoil whatever triggered this reaction from him. I will do everything in my power to make sure we kept this going."* Jewel was so into her thoughts she didn't even see John standing over her breathing down her neck. When she turned around he was right there in her face, with that same huge grin.

*"Yes my husband is on one,"* Jewel thought.

*"You sure you don't want to go back and knock this on off?"* He asked her.

*"Tonight babe, I promise!"* Jewel told him.

Jewel wasn't in the mood anymore. P.M.S. and the aftershock of last night, even though it was wonderful was still in effect. It was like a five-point quake in her head right now. Jewel could do no more thinking or talking about it, so she changed the subject fast.

*"John, I need to discuss with you about the trip,"* Jewel said.

*"What is it babe?"* He asked.

John acting concerned shocked Jewel as much as his performance the night before.

*"Well babe, the clock is ticking and I need to get a few things for the trip with the girls. Everyone is going except for a few of the ladies. I need to pay my registration fees.*" Jewel told him.

*"Go ahead and pay it then. What exactly is it that you want me to do?"* He asked.

*"I want you to give me the money, I don't want to go into our trust account, and I will need at least five thousand dollars!"* Jewel said chuckling under her breath.

*"You have all the money. Everything I make I give it to you!"* He said.

*"No, you don't, you give me what you want me to have, and lie about the rest,"* Jewel said.

*"That is not true!"* John said in his defense.

Over the years, John had become so secretive. He had grown accustom to putting issues on the back burner, away from the mainstream of their everyday lives. They both felt like if they didn't discuss it then maybe it would just go away. Last night was a single instance that only periodically turned romantic. Jewel needed to hold on to this feeling, and so with this epitome and the encapsulation of her reality she became the nice wife once again.

*"You are right John; I apologize for making that statement,"* She said after a long silent and lots of thought. She needed to be careful in the way she spoke to him to keep the peace.

*"I love you babe; I want you to have fun on your trip with the ladies. Do what you need to do to make it happen,"* He told her.

*"Okay babe, I will do it today, thanks for understanding!"* Jewel answered.

*"Not a problem babe, oh yeah, thanks for breakfast and coffee,"* John said as he went down the hallway and out the door to the garage. He had to get started with his day.

*"You are welcome my sweets,"* Jewel answered in her sexiest voice.

Jewel knew when he went to the garage; the next thing she was sure to hear would be his music. John would be in the garage for the rest of the day unless someone call or came by with a job for him to do. Jewel headed for the bathroom; she had to freshen up, it was time to get her day started too. She finished getting dressed and made a few phone calls. One call she made was to Conifa. Jewel wanted to let Conifa know that she was about to take care of some important thing that had to do with their trip.

When Conifa answered the phone her voice was different.

*"Hey girl, how are you?"* Jewel asked her.

*"Girl it feels like I am trying to come down with something!"* Conifa replied.

*"Oh no, you appeared alright last night, what happen since then?"* Jewel asked her.

*"I probably caught something from Mary's ass last night. You know I dropped her off at home. She had a bad cough,"* Conifa answered Jewel.

"*No woman, I didn't hear Mary cough one time while she was here at my house,*" Jewel replied.

"*Well, she coughed all the way to her house. I even had to let my window down,*" Conifa said in a sarcastic tone.

"*I sure do hope you feel better. What are you doing today?*" Jewel asked, changing the subject.

No one wanted to hear Conifa's negative talk this morning. She was the only person that could create a problem when there wasn't one and Jewel was not going to add to her ugly demeanor.

"*For sure if she kept putting all that negativity out there into the universe it surely would surface again,*" Jewel thought as Conifa rattled on about how she caught this nasty cold from Mary the night before.

"*Conifa was probably was still upset about the toy party and was making up stuff for attention again,*" Jewel said to herself.

"*Blah, Blah, Blah* was all that Jewel heard out of Conifa's deceiving mouth."

Another one of Jewel's philosophy on life was if people want positive reinforcements to come, then positive words and vibes need to go forth into the universe.

She told herself, "*I am not the most positive person but I try to be better than I was the day before.*"

Jewel had a conscious that reminded her each day of how great God was. She was happy that God was installed into her heart during her adolescent years.

"*Mama molded and prepared me for this journey. Every Sunday morning she took us to church; she fast and prayed for her family, and God answered her. She said this was the only way that she was sure that God would take care of us. She made a believer out of me that is for sure,"* Jewel thought to herself.

*"Are you there?"* Jewel kept hearing Conifa's voice say. Jewel had totally forgotten that she was even on the phone. Daydreaming was one of her avenues to ignore someone when she didn't want to hear what they were saying. No one liked it when she did it. It was a connection to the writer in her. It was a place where she went for peace and tranquility. It was her secret place, and no one else was welcome, which was a good thing and it was all hers.

*"Oh girl, I am sorry. I just went on one, you know how I get,"* Jewel laughed.

*"What the hell were you thinking?"* Conifa asked.

*"Shoot girl, now I have forgotten,"* Jewel answered.

Jewel was lying to Conifa, but no one was welcome in her private thoughts unless she allowed them in.

*"Okay, so what were you saying?"* Jewel asked her.

*"No you were saying something along the line of taking care of business today,"* Conifa reminded Jewel.

*"Oh yeah, I will be paying my registration fees for the trip today. Will you be paying today also?"* Jewel asked.

*"Oh yeah, that's cool. Do you want to go together later?"* Conifa asked.

*"That isn't necessary; we can just do it over the computer, right,* what is your problem? *You were the one that told me to do it on my computer. I guess you just want to come over,"*Jewel answered.

*"I wanted to come and do everything with you. Maybe we can all meet at Starbucks and figure this out! I will call the ladies. How about we meet at eleven-thirty?"* Conifa asked.

*"That's fine Conifa; I will see you at eleven-thirty,"* Jewel said.

*"Alright girl, see you then!"* Conifa said.

At this point, Jewel could detect enthusiasm and excitement in Conifa's voice. Jewel started to feel excited too, it was about to go down!

*"Oh, my freaking goodness; we are going aboard; I wish we were going to the White House!"* Jewel yelled at the top of her voice. *"Maybe I will get to see the President and his lovely wife Michaela; I want to see her garden. I heard she planted collard greens and okra in the garden that was designed just for her."*

When thinking about Michele Obama's garden Jewel thought about her days as a child; growing up in the country their garden was full of squash, collard greens, turnip green, corn and okra. They have the best fruits that grow from their very own fruit trees and her family plants watermelons each year during planting season. Everything their entire family ate came from their very own garden.

*"Shoot, Michaela know how to live so far as I am concerned,"* Jewel thought to herself. Time wasn't waiting for her to sit and think, Jewel needed to get moving. She grabbed her purse and car keys. She had to stop at the mailbox on the way out; she had a few birthday cards to mail. For one reason or another everyone in the neighborhood mailboxes were on the corner. Jewel thought that was the craziest thing ever.

*"Mailboxes on the corner, what will they do next? When I first moved to Los Angeles, I looked for mail for two weeks and nothing came. Even though, there was a mailbox attached to my house, nothing ever came, not even junk mail. I became suspicious after weeks of not even receiving any junk mail. Who doesn't get junk mail? One day I went across the street to Mr. Marshall's, my neighbor's house and asked him if the mailman came on our street. Mr. Marshall said yes; he told me that he does come but leaves the mail in the mailbox on the corner. That is when I discovered that my mailbox was at the end of the block. My mailbox was*

're

*overstuffed with two week old mail, and the mailman had returned some of my mail back to the post office."*

Jewel said her morning affirmations; there was no way she would start her car up this time without first praising God for his love, mercy and protection. She knew without the protection of God's hands she wouldn't make it from day to day. As she proceeded out of her driveway Jewel noticed that the gardener hadn't come. Today was his day to do the yard. For the most part he was a great gardener, a little costly though. She wondered why he hadn't come yet.

*"Oh well, he will probably come later,"* she thought as she left her driveway.

Jewel stopped at the mailbox and mailed the birthday cards. It was almost time for her brother's birthday. Jewel wanted to make sure that he received his birthday gift and card in time. Lately, she had been late or had forgotten to send anything. Jewel's brother was always prompt when it came to birthdays and Christmas. Mr. Marshall was already at the mailbox getting his mail. Jewel candidly spoke to him. She had hoped that he wouldn't start a long drawn out conversation. He always wanted to chat about all sorts of things, but this particular morning she was in a hurry.

*"Good morning Mr. Marshall,"* Jewel said.

*"Good morning Jewel, where is John?"* Mr. Marshall asked.

*"Oh, he left earlier Mr. Marshall. If he calls me I will let him know you were asking for him,"* Jewel answered.

*"Alright you have a nice day,"* Mr. Marshall replied.

*"You have a nice day too Mr. Marshall,"* Jewel said.

Jewel mailed the cards; then continued on her way to Conifa's house. It, usually took Jewel about twenty minutes or so to get to Baldwin Hills. Conifa has one of the most beautiful houses in the county Los Angeles,

're

Jewel thought as she drove along La Brea Avenue. Conifa was fortunate to own a mansion; it was so beautiful.

"*I am not jealous or anything because I could buy one like that if I wanted to. I admire her tenacity. She is a go-getter. When Conifa went after her dreams and aspirations she, usually, accomplished them!*" Jewel said to herself.

Once Jewel reached Conifa's house she remembered that they were supposed to meet at Starbucks. Jewel was one of them people that got sidetracked if she didn't stay focus. That was her dyslexia acting up once again. Jewel turned her car around and went back to Starbucks, which were only a few minutes away. Once she got there, she saw the others ladies sitting outside with Starbucks cups in hand waiting patiently for her. After parking her car, she made her way through the doors of Starbucks; Jewel waved to the ladies as she went inside; after standing in line she placed her order.

"*May I have a caramel frappe?*" She asked the server. Jewel loved Starbucks' Carmel Frappe's; she couldn't wait to order it. The ladies had been waiting for a short while for Jewel and Conifa made sure to let Jewel know.

"*What happen to you Jewel?*" Conifa asked.

"*Excuse me,* Jewel said as she hurried past Conifa. *Will you please give me time to grab a seat before you ridicule me! Don't be so contemptuous Conifa! You would have something to say, about any and everything, but shield all of your faults and mishaps from us. Conifa you are great at calling everyone else fault's out, but no one better call your fault out, you would blow a fuse, just like a time bomb that has been ticking forever and is ready to explode!*

Jewel ignored her; she wasn't going to get the best of her today. Jewel knew that Conifa needed her friendship. The bad part about it was Conifa didn't even know how much she needed Jewel's friendship. Conifa tore every relationship and friendship to threads. Jewel couldn't ever figure out why Conifa acted that way.

*"She always said she wanted friends; but how in the world did she expect anyone to keep putting up with her sarcastic remarks? She speaks badly, saying awful things about everyone behind their backs. She doesn't even know what kind of friend I really am; if she did she would treasure our friendship as I do. One day her friends will disappear one by one if she doesn't stop being such a bitch to everyone."* Jewel thought to herself as she grabbed a chair right next to Miss Prissy. After seating herself, she then turned to look in Conifa's direction. Since Conifa wanted information Jewel would give her some positive feedback to her question. She will not like it, but it will be the truth.

*"Aye Conifa, now let me answer your question as to why I'm so late. It's funny you should ask me that question because the craziest thing happened on my way here. I went to your house instead of coming straight to Starbucks. My one track mind got all turned around once again girl. I was sitting there in front of your house admiring how beautiful it was and I remembered that I was at the wrong place for the meeting. Isn't that the craziest thing?"* Jewel asked Conifa.

*"You were at my house?*" Conifa was confused; with raised eyebrows, she questioned Jewel.

*"Yes, I was at your house; didn't you hear a word I just said?"* Jewel asked her.

*"Oh, ok you were at my house,"* Conifa repeated again in disbelief.

Jewel didn't understand why it was so hard for Conifa to receive the words that she said to her. People make mistakes; Jewel didn't have any hidden motives for going to Conifa's house; what the hell was Conifa hiding? But then again Jewel knew it wouldn't be easy for Conifa to hear the truth or anything positive for that matter.

Jewel thought to herself, *"maybe next time Conifa will think before she tries to make a fool out of me. They always said when a person points a finger there is always a finger pointing back at them."*

*"Jewel, did you see a blue car in my driveway?"* Conifa asked.

*"I seriously don't remember, like I said earlier I was daydreaming and admiring your house when suddenly I remembered I was at the wrong place,"* Jewel told Conifa once again.

*"Oh, it is okay, I thought perhaps you notice,"* Conifa said.

*"No girl, I didn't pay any attention. I would have been mad as hell if I've gotten out of my car, walked up that long driveway to your front door, and then realized I wasn't supposed to be there. I would have been standing ringing the doorbell like like booboo the fool,"* Jewel said with a chuckle.

This comment broke the ice, and everyone started to loosen up. It took long enough. It had been a huge pink elephant in the room, and everyone was afraid to say,

*"Hey there is a pink elephant over there,"* Everyone had been sitting there holding their breath; which angered Jewel.

Jewel wanted to tell each of the ladies, *"please everyone, stop being so afraid of Conifa's big mouth; I wasn't trying to make her feel better; I was only telling the truth."* Of course, she wasn't going to say anything out loud because she didn't want to cause any more confusion. Jewel would just allow them to think it was funny so they could get this meeting off the ground.

*"So okay ladies it's so great that we are all here,* Jewel said. *As you know Conifa, and I have been discussing this awesome trip. I think Conifa has already brief everyone about it, right?"* She asked.

"The ladies all nodded their head saying yes,"

*"Okay great,* Jewel continued speaking, *"we want to include all of you ladies, and we need to make plans right away. Isn't it exciting to be able to do this trip?"* Jewel asked.

*"Yes it is,* Miss. Prissy answered, *"and the thing about it is we don't even have to spend a great deal of money to have a grand time. We could all pitch in and take*

care of the hotel accommodations in New York. The Foundation pays for everything else. I mean the entire round-trip airfare and hotel stay while in New York; I did this trip last year!" She excitedly informed the group of ladies.

"Oh really, Dolly said. I didn't know all that. Wow, that's awesome girl! So when is the trip?" She asked.

"The trip is scheduled for this September," Conifa replied.

"Count me in," Dolly said.

"Me too," Miss. Prissy said.

"I will make all the arrangements. I will go online and see what type of tour packages we can get for Jamaica. I will also find out what they have going on in New York," Conifa told everyone.

"Girl yes, please do, I have never been to either place, so I am ready!" Jewel said loudly.

"Calm down, don't get your blood all worked up," Conifa told Jewel.

"I'm okay; I just got a tiny bit excited!" Jewel laughed.

"So Conifa; when do you think you will be letting us know about the prices of the tours?" Dolly asked.

"As soon as I find out you will be the first to know Dolly," Conifa replied.

"I have been to New York; I already know lots about what is going on there," Dolly said sarcastically.

"So do you want to plan it Dolly? Conifa asked; if you do you can."

"No, you go ahead since how you took the lead and agreed to do it all," Dolly said to Conifa.

're—

*"Well, I didn't take the lead, I was sort of voted in as the arranger of the trip. Anyone that wants to do the planning is welcome to do it."* Conifa stated.

Conifa waited to see if anyone wanted to take over, but not one single rebuttal came from any of the ladies.

*"I guess everything stands with me coordinating and planning the trip,"* Conifa finally said after waiting a moment or two for an answer.

*"Okay, so when do you ladies want to get together and discuss what Conifa has planned for us to do on our fabulous trip?"* Jewel asked.

*"I think the 1st of September would be great. That is exactly fifteen days before departure day. We already know that we have to register. The registration cost is seventy-five-dollars. So go ahead everyone and register today. I will get back to you with the price of the hotel in New York by email. We will be better off doing the AIR-BNB instead of those other expensive hotels in New York. AIR-BNB is online places that we can rent for a week. Let's just say, for instance, I owned an apartment in New York; well I would rent it out to you for much cheaper than those hotels in Time Square. We will talk again when I find out more information on this subject. The next time we meet you ladies can give me the money for everything. Is this okay?"* Conifa asked.

*"That sounds great!* Who wanted to second this motion so we can close the meeting?" Jewel asked.

*"I second the motion!"* Miss Prissy said in her high pitched voice.

*"Okay ladies, I will see you all a bit later!"* Jewel said. She was so glad to get away from these ladies and get home to her husband. She still had him on her mind. Jewel had already planned dinner; something special for John. She had not been in a romantic mood in forever. She wanted to show John that she truly did appreciate him and all that he does to help their home run smoothly. Jewel rushed to the parking lot; got into got her car as quickly as she could. She didn't want to talk anymore with Conifa.

*"These females were a bit too much today for me to handle,"* Jewel thought to herself. Once Jewel reached home she could see John's truck still park in the driveway. That was a good sign; he was still at home. Once inside she headed straight for the bedroom, put her purse down on the side of the bed and took off her shoes. As soon as she began undressing in walked John, he stopped and stared at her and asked, *"You were getting ready for me?"* He had the same big grin on his face as he did earlier that morning.

*"John, what is going on with you? I was only changing my clothes babe!"* Jewel answered.

*"Oh okay, I thought you wanted more of the same from last night!"* He said smiling.

*"What in the world has you so excited and full of lust?"* Jewel asked him.

*"You have me excited and full of lust babe!"* He said.

*"I think it is my toys that have you excited, would you like to try one of them?"* Jewel asked him.

*"I don't know anything about that stuff!"* He answered.

*"I can show you how this one works!"* Jewel said as she handed him a vibrator.

*"What about that other thing over there? How does it work?"* He questioned.

*"Oh, you mean the penis vibrator? I will show you tonight how it works, is that okay with you?"* Jewel asked her husband.

*"No, I mean that thing that looks like a vagina; can a man put his penis in there?"* John asked.

*"Oh, ok babe, so that why you are lusting? Yeah John, a man can put his penis in there and screw it all he wants!"* Jewel said; she was becoming angry at John. *"Was that all he was thinking about, the massaging vagina?"*

're

*"Yeah, that is cool, tonight it is on!"* He said with that same big grin.

*"Something has change in my husband attitude,"* Jewel thought to herself.

Jewel had a sneaky suspicion it was the toys. *"Has he been trying toys on other women?"* She questioned herself. Jewel had a suspicious mind and John wasn't helping the situation. He was like a panting dog in heat! Initially, she wanted to be with him when she first got home, but John was rushing her a little too much. It was simply too much for Jewel. What was wrong with her husband, he was in a hurry which caused Jewel's bipolar to kick in; not to speak of her dyslexia that killed her passion for lovemaking; if she did it now it would be just plain ole sex. Jewel didn't want to come off as ungrateful, but her insecurities always took over. As hard as she tried to fight it, she was still suspicious of John's every move. John tried to soothe things over by saying, *"All I need is you babe, I wish you could just accept what I am saying without trying to find a reason I say everything!"* Jewel understood how John's feeling could have been hurt by her actions. She promised him that she would be okay by the end of the day. She didn't want him to feel unwanted and unloved. She knew that feeling all too well. She had felt the same exact way since she was a child. Landing John had been a blessing for her. The other relationships had been disastrous in one way, or another. The worst off all were the emotional put downs from the men in her life. The first man to level her insecurities was her father. She looked for love in men everywhere but never found love until John; she didn't by any means want to cause pain to anyone else, especially not John. She loved him with all her heart and wanted to be a great wife to him. *"I'm sorry John; I know sometimes I make it difficult for you because of my insecurities. I promise you that things will get better,"* Jewel said softly to John.

*"Its okay babe; I married every inch of you; I love every inch of you!"* John told his wife. *"The reason it's so hard for me to believe you is because of my past relationship, and yes I know I should have never allowed my past into my future*

with you. I am sorry; I just don't like rushing into lovemaking, it causes me to feel insecure sometimes," Jewel said.

"I understand how those times could haunt you, don't worry Jewel, you have all of my support. I am very happy that you felt comfortable enough to tell me about your past. It is very understandable how traumatized you must have been. All little girls depend on their father to love and protect them." John answered.

"Yea I know, but in my case it was the other way around, but I promise this will be the last time I allow it to interfere in our marriage," Jewel replied.

"That's my girl!" John said.

"Yes I am yours, I am all yours. We will fix this babe; I promise," Jewel replied. "I know, don't worry, it's okay. We will try again in a few hours," John said, as he looked deep into Jewel's eyes, he winked at her and smiled that sweet smile of his; which cause Jewel to love him all the more. He was a good man and nothing would cause Jewel to stop loving her husband. With each passing day she loved him more and more, but John didn't know how to take no for an answer. The more she said no to him, he pushed harder to get whatever it was that he wanted from her. The only thing Jewel would never give up was her father's money which made John very insecure about their relationship. He couldn't understand why his wife was holding the money so tight, but Jewel promised her father that she would never allow anyone to come into her life and take the money that he left from her and Ha-kin. She had many men that only wanted her for her wealth. She was aware that people would try to steal from her and her son. She rushed into a marriage with John, but she wasn't going to make any more bad choices. "Not saying that my marriage was a bad choice, but it was sudden," Jewel thought to herself. "If anything I will invest my father's money in real properties that would enhance our lives, not bottom us out. Lately my husband has been coming up with investment ideas that surely would cost me my fortune and more, and that will never happen!

## CHAPTER SIX

## A TRIP ABROAD

Today was the first day of September; Jewel was lounging across her bed relaxing while thinking; the day had finally arrived for the ladies to get together for the last time before their trip; Conifa had kept in touch with each of the ladies letting them know exactly what was going on. She informed Jewel that Annie, Sophie and Maggie would not be participating in their venture, which wasn't very surprising to Jewel. She knew all along that neither of them would go. The two ladies had already been bashing Jewel since her naughty girls party/toy party.

*"It was enough dealing with them in my front yard, why in the world would I want to spend fourteen days abroad with them?" Jewel thought to herself.* Jewel was very happy that those funny style old women wouldn't be going. She made sure Conifa knew how she felt.

*"That's right, Jewel said, please let them stay at home, I don't want them to go! They are Debbie Downers; they complain more than you or I, and they are absolutely no fun,"* Jewel replied.

*"I understand why you feel this way Jewel, but please don't be so harsh!"* Conifa said.

Annie, Sophie and Maggie were each close to sixty years old. Jewel being only forty-two thought they were ancient complaining women that wouldn't be able to keep up with the group.

*"Harsh? Girl bye! You know we wouldn't have any fun with those two ole farts,"* Jewel said.

*"So here is the list of people going, Conifa changed the subject. You, me, Miss Prissy, Dolly, Tara, Jerry and Brenda, Mary decided not to go with us this time. Mary said she would try and make the next one,"* Conifa told Jewel.

Today was the day that each of the ladies finished paying for their trip; this was the final meeting; Conifa had to get all of the money together for the tours. She had done well planning their trip, getting discounts on every tour. Jewel loved the way that Conifa cut corner, saving them all money. As usual they would meet at Starbucks; this was Jewel favorite place to spend quality time on any giving occasion. *"Starbucks has free wire-fire and great coffee, what wasn't there to love?"* Jewel thought. Jewel and John said their goodbyes at their front door. They both had early a.m. appointments; they needed to get going. Jewel had to be at Starbucks at ten a.m. She also had one other important appointment to take care of and she didn't like rushing, but lately she found herself rushing for everything. Today was also the day that she would find out the results of her other blood work. She drove the back way to her Doctors office. She had no time for traffic today. Entering Dr. Dorie's office, her nerves got the best of her. The palms of her hands became wet and clammy, her mouth was watering, and she felt faint. She made her way to the first chair she saw and sat down.

*"What the heck is wrong with me?"* She asked herself. Jewel waited for thirty minutes or so before the nurse came out and called her name.

*"Hello, Mrs. Dupree, will you come this way, please?"* The nurse made a motion for Jewel to follow her. Jewel stood up; her knees were wobbling, she felt sick inside. She was overwhelmed with worry; she felt panic and her belly was tied up in knots.

*"What if I have something and can't get rid of it!"* She thought to herself.

*"Are you alright?"* The nurse asked Jewel.

*"No, I am just a tiny bit nervous about hearing my results!"* Jewel told the nurse.

*"Don't be, you will be okay, Dr. Dorie is the best in her field,"* The nurse said with such confidence, as if the doctor had the ability to save the world.

're

*"I know I am just a little taking back from all of the waiting; now that it's time for the results I'm emotional,"* Jewel said to the nurse. As Jewel and the nurse walked down the hallway together, Jewel began talking to her about the results of her blood tests.

*"Have you heard of menopause?"* Jewel asked the nurse assistance.

*"Of course, I have,"* The nurse assistance told Jewel.

*"Oh wow, and then you may understand my dilemma!"* Jewel said to the nurse assistance.

*"Of course I do. I have been Dr. Dorie's nurse assistance for many years. I have seen women come and go out of this office with the same questions as you have. However, I can't make any assumptions as to your results; only Dr. Dorie can do that. I can tell you that your blood test results were emailed over from Dr. Borene office."* The nurse assistance wanted Jewel to know that she wouldn't be losing her job because she gave her information that she wasn't supposed to.

*"I totally understand, thanks for listening!"* Jewel told the assistance.

Jewel was now in a much better mood. Something the assistance said calmed her down. She calmly waited for Dr. Dorie to see her.

Dr. Dorie finally entered the room, *"how are you Mrs. Dupree?"* The doctor asked Jewel.

*"I am blessed, thanks, Doc. just anxious to get my results."* Jewel replied.

*"It is all right here; the doctor told Jewel, let me just pull up a chair. Just allow me to go over my reports again; I have to make sure I don't give you the wrong information"* Dr. Dorie said. *"This is the second time today that I have heard someone mention, the wrong information, first the assistance now Dr. Dorie! What the hell is going on?"* Jewel thought to herself. Dr. Dorie could feel the tension in the room; she tried to comfort Jewel by saying, *"don't worry, it*

're

*will all work itself out. I told you before this is normal for women all over the world, you are no difference Mrs. Dupree, so don't worry. You're going to make yourself ill with all of that self doubt,"* Dr. Dorie told Jewel. As the doctor looked over her report, she questioned Jewel about how everything else in her life was going; her questions irritated Jewel to the core. She didn't want to talk about anything other than her results. The doctor finished looking at her report; looking over her glasses she turned to Jewel and said, *"Well just as we expected, you are in pre-menopausal stage 1. Most of your tests were fine except for the blood test that shows your viral load. You know you have hepatitis C; you have to eat more vegetable Mrs. Dupree. That's one way to help your body stay healthier which will also prevent less toxic in the liver. Stay completely away from sugar, because sugar, dairy products, caffeine, process meats and potatoes cause toxic in your body that cause your liver to work extra hard to detox. Now Mrs. Dupree, all you need to do is eat like I told you last month, you will be fine. I will give you a prescription for hormone pill. You will need to take them every day to help balance your hormones and your system, okay. Do you have any questions Mrs. Dupree?"* Dr. Dorie asked.

*"Yes I have a few questions Dr. Dorie. How will this affect me in my future? Is this going to make me have bad mood swings? Will I still be able to make love?"* Jewel asked the doctor.

*"It will cause some changes, but nothing as drastic as you are probably thinking. Women don't always have a hard time going through the change. Just follow the instructions that I gave you, you will be alright,"* The doctor said to Jewel.

*"Yes I will, by all means, and thank you so much Dr. Dorie for the pep talk. I do feel better,"* Jewel replied. Jewel took the news of her stage one menopause really well; it wasn't as bad as she had thought. In her mind she had imagined every negative thing could be wrong with her, from Cancer to a blood disease. She had been waiting so long for answers, now to finally get the answers about her condition felt like a huge weight was lifted from her shoulders. Jewel had so much to celebrate today; *"One down and one to go,"*

're—

she said to herself as she got into her car. Just thinking of the meeting that she was about to encounter with the ladies gave her instant gratification. The thought of her leaving for a vacation was uplifting all by itself, now the news from the doctor that she wasn't terminal, she was on cloud nine. She couldn't wait to share her news with her friends during lunch. Entering Starbuck Jewel went directly to the table where the ladies were seated. She sat down quietly, she didn't want to make a scene, she was already late, and that would only open up a can of worms for Conifa to act silly. After seating herself, she spoke to the ladies. *"Hello Conifa" "hello Dolly," "hello Tara," "hello Jerry," "hello Brenda, and "hello Miss Prissy."*

Jewel turned her attention to Conifa and said, *"Sorry I'm late girl, I just left Dr. Dories. I got my result back, and everything is just as we suspected, ole menopause has caught up with me."*

Conifa laughed, sounding like a hyena calling her mate. *"It's all okay girl, no worries! I'm so glad it's only menopause and not all them other things you created in your brain."*

*"What the hell is so funny?"* Jewel thought to herself, but she said nothing. She didn't want to spoil the moment by feeding into Conifa's craziness.

*"So can we start the meeting now?"* Dolly asked.

*"Yes we can, I was just waiting for everyone to get settled,"* Conifa said to Dolly.

*"The only unsettled one is you Conifa,"* Dolly replied to Conifa.

*"Okay Dolly, I am settled now, anything else?"* Conifa said and rolled her eyes as if to say don't mess with me today. Seated around the table were the seven ladies that were going on the trip. The looks of excitement in the ladies' eyes were mental images of the journey ahead of them. The journey was about to enlighten their universe. They had planned to spend seven days in Jamaica, and seven days New York, and then they would return

're-

home. Conifa asked the ladies during the meeting if they would mind if she stayed over an extra night in New York. She said that she wanted to eat at this quaint little restaurant called Betsy's. *"Oh my God, I just love eating at Betsy's! Does anyone want to stay over and have lunch with me?* Conifa asked. *They have good Caribbean food."* When Dolly heard that Conifa wanted to stay over an extra night; she became angry. She was livid at the nerves of Conifa wanting everyone to go out of their way just so her selfish behind could eat.

*"How is that fair to the rest of the group?"* Dolly asked.

*"Now Dolly, don't you remember when we first discuss this everyone was on board. I just need to get clarification now. That's why I am asking again,"* Conifa said.

*"I'm in,"* Jewel said.

*"Well, I guess it is okay with me too,"* Miss Prissy said, but all the while she was watching to see what Dolly was going to say.

*"It is okay with us too;* Jerry and Brenda G. said simultaneously. We all agreed to allow Conifa to make all the arrangement, so now what is the problem?" Jerry a beautiful sixty year old Defense Lawyer was as friendly as all outdoors; she loved to party every weekend. She had many men friends, but she chose carefully who she dated. She was a smart, educated woman with a master's degree in criminology and six years of law school. Her favorite saying was, *"the only rat that I ever loved was Mickey Mouse,"* rats are what she called men. Sometimes Jewel could barely keep up with Jerry, and she was only forty-two. Brenda G. and Jewel had been friends since they were in their early twenties. Jewel had only known the other women for about five years except for Miss. Prissy and Dolly. Brenda G. was high in stature; her thickness was top proportioned; she wore long skinny legs that knocked a little at the knees. When she was angry the tone

're

of her voice was a note or two higher pitched than Miss Prissy; this was a problem, it sometimes irritated Jewel.

*"I am fine with it too,"* Tara answered after thinking about it for a while. Tara, a talker, but was never too quick to answer questions. She always had to think things through first. She was the Vice President of National's Insurance Company, was a beautiful dark skinned, Afro-American woman; she wore a huge derriere and shapely legs that carried her from coast to coast. She loved traveling and yes she could afford to. Tara's a people's person; everyone loved her personality. Even though, Jewel loved Tara, she hated her acting like a floozy at times. The entire group knew how Tara was; they kept a watch out for her inter-actions around their men; it was almost as if the women had to sleep with one eye opened. Jewel laughed at the thought of watching Tara's behavior. *"Maybe like me Tara didn't get the love she needed when she was growing up; that's probably why she felt that way."* Jewel sometimes believed that if Tara didn't have a man, she felt empty inside. The most important thing was that Tara believed in God; she was a Christian; she had a good heart, and that's why Jewel loved her.

*"I am not trying to cause friction;* Dolly said. *I only want what fair. I don't understand why we all have to pay an extra one hundred and fifty dollars so that Conifa can have lunch at that stupid restaurant. It is just not right!"*

*"I always wanted to travel, wherever we go is fine with me. We all sat right here and told this girl to make the plans. Don't tell me now it's a problem!"* Jewel yelled; she was beginning to get frustrated with Dolly.

*"Since everyone wants to go, I will go too, but it still isn't fair!"* Dolly said with an attitude.

*"So it is settled; as you all know we leave on the sixteenth of September; I will give you the entire itinerary package at the fly away,"* Conifa said.

*"Hey, now ladies, here we go,"* Jewel yelled. *You ladies know we are going to have a blast, dancing and partying in New York."*

*"Yes we will,"* Miss Prissy and the other chimed in; they sound like a musical bell, all harmonizing together. Jewel laughed; she thought their voices sound funny.

Conifa laughed and said, *"Miss Prissy, you ladies sound like you were all singing a song together in a choir. I will see you all later this week."* She got up from her seat and headed for the exit door.

*"I will call you later Jewel,"* Conifa said as she walked passed Jewel.

*"Alright girl, we have so much to talk about. I will be home in about an hour; first let me grab me a frappe! You know I got to have my caramel frappe girl"* Jewel laughed and gave a friendly wink at Conifa.

Jewel went to the counter and placed her order. She couldn't wait to sip the caramel frappe through the straw. It was the best.

*"Starrbuck should be ashamed for making something so delicious, so highly pleasing to all my senses and at the same time has my brain cells on freeze,"* Jewel thought after taking a huge swallow of the frappe. As she walked to her car she waved goodbye to Miss Prissy and Dolly, *"see you'll later,"* she yelled. The drive home was exasperating and annoying for Jewel. There must have been an accident up ahead, Jewel thought as she sat in traffic waiting for the cars to start moving; this was totally unexpected; she needed to get home and start planning her trip. The police were driving past fast on their motorcycles, one by one. All of a sudden an ambulance with sirens blasting went past Jewels car. The noise from the ambulances siren was so loud it caused Jewel head to pain. Jewel could hear the police officer speak over the bullhorn saying, *"Pullover to the right lane, pull over now!"* everyone started pulling into the right lane. There had been an awful traffic accident on the Santa Monica freeway and everyone was getting off onto Santa

're

Barbara Avenue. Slowly Jewel inch over to the first lane. Jewel made a right on Dalton Avenue, a street with less traffic. *"I hope and pray that whoever was in that accident lives. That was all bad,"* Jewel said to herself. Jewel was elated to get home in one piece. John was there waiting for her. She loved the fact that he had been so responsive to her needs lately. He was the man that she married, the man that she loved, her lifelong partner.

*"Hi babe,"* Jewel said as she hugged her husband.

*"Hey, Muffin how was your day baby?"* John said. He called her Muffin when he was in a sexy mood. He said she reminded him of a golden brown muffin.

*"Just great, we ladies had a fun filled day discussing the details of the trip. We had our meeting at Starbucks."* Jewel answered.

*"Oh, okay that's great, and everything went smooth?"* John asked with a questionable look on his face.

*"Well, not quite,* Jewel answered. *Dolly had some issues with the suggestion that Conifa had. We did work it out, and everything is good to go,"* Jewel told her husband.

*"So what suggestion did Conifa have that Dolly didn't like?"* John asked.

*"Conifa wants to stay over one extra night in New York so she could patronize a restaurant called Betsy's. She wants the ladies to pay an extra one hundred and fifty dollars to stay with her. The problem was Dolly didn't feel that was fair for us to spend extra money just so Conifa can have dinner at Betsy's Restaurant."* Jewel answered John.

*"I can't understand why Dolly feels that way; that's not too much to ask, is it?"* John questioned Jewel. *"Yeah, yes it was, however we got it all straighten out. We finally got Dolly to agree to it. As for me I don't care one way or another. I just want to go!"* Jewel reiterated again.

*"Yes I know babe, you only want to leave me here all alone,"* John smileed as he spoke to Jewel. He had his sexy on again.

*"No, I never want to leave you babe, not ever; this is only for fourteen days, and I will be home to you. I just need to get away for a little while. I will miss you every day while I am away."* Jewel said.

*"I know I miss you already, and you have not even left yet; just the thought of you not being here is too much for me,"* John said.

*"John sometimes you say the sweetest words, I love you babe,"* Jewel said to her husband.

*"I say these words because they are true babe; I am not use to being without you. You know we, usually, travel together,"* John answered. Listening to John carry on about how sweet she was caused Jewel to feel a little strange. He was being so sweet, which made her wonder what he was up too. He was too excited at the thought of her leaving, but why? Was it because he had a side chick? Jewel mind race with thoughts of infidelity. Jewel's insecurities and trust issues began to set it. She always had thoughts of John possibly cheating on her. There had been time when he didn't come home for days. When she inquired of his where about he always said he was working overnight at some building, repairing the electrical system. *"Yeah right, someone's electric system alright!"* Jewel thought. She had been letting things slide because she just couldn't deal with the thought that John was cheating. It did no good to accuse him; he would only deny everything. Jewel decides to not make a big deal about what she was thinking; she didn't want to start a commotion about something that may or may not be the accurate. Jewel decided to wait until she got back from her trip; then she would get to the bottom of it all.

*"Babe, are you ok?"* John asked.

*"Awe yeah, I am fine, just got carried away in my thoughts,"* Jewel said.

*"Wow, whatever you were thinking about had you in a daze,"* John said.

*"I know babe, I am sorry. You know how I daydream,"* Jewel answered.

*"Yeah, I know. Hey, did you want to do anything special before you leave?"* John asked his wife.

*"Yes babe that would be nice,"* Jewel said, still wondering what was happening between her and her husband.

*"Okay, so we need to plan something sexy and romantic!"* John answered.

*"Sexy and romantic, is this man I married coming back to life?"* Jewel asked John. Even though, she had reservations, there was no way she was going to jeopardize a sexy romantic escapade with John. It was obvious that he had plans for them. It wasn't often that he planned a wild or exciting adventure. It was all beginning to sound mischievous and carefree; Jewel was starting to feel excited about what John had planned for them.

*"Babe, hello, are you in there?"* John asked Jewel as he stood over her shaking her.

*"John, yes I am, I just keep getting carried away at the thought of being in your arm,"* Jewel answered.

*"Being in my arms, is that all you want?"* John said in a flirting way.

*"No babe, I want all of you each and every day, which is why I married you!"* Jewel answered. She wanted John to know that she loved all of him.

*"I want all of you, my sweet Muffin!"* John said as he passionately kissed Jewel on her lips. His love and attention were all that Jewel ever needed or wanted. She felt weak in her knees at his touch, and her body slowly melted into his electrifying kisses. John drew her closer to him, parting her lips, he search for her tongue. John's kisses were assorted flavors of chocolate; so sweet and delicious. Jewel eagerly kisses him back, deep and

slow; as John pressed his body against Jewel's body she could feel his penis growing, bulging to the point of release.

*"Come babe, let take this to the bedroom,"* John said to Jewel.

*"Okay babe, okay!"* Jewel replied, it was so difficult for her to tear herself away. All she wanted right then at that moment was for him to explore deep into her tunnel and down her lover lane. Jewel's body was on fire; *"someone call the fire department in a hurry!"* She thought as they enter their bedroom, his arms tight around her waist. John and Jewel fell onto the bed; there they made love for hours. At this moment, Jewel knew she had rekindled her love affair with her husband. It had been so long since they had a passion for each other. Now finally after all this time she could feel the passion in John's love making. She could see the fire in his eyes; this was the man that she married all those years ago. He was the man that made love to her on top of the Flamingo Hotel when they first got married. After their lovemaking was over they cuddled for a while. They held each other tightly as John whispered tenderly into Jewel's ear,

*"I love you babe!"*

*"I love you too my sweet babe,"* Jewel mumbled as she kissed John suckling lips. They enjoyed each other for a few more moments before Jewel suggested that they take showers together. Their master shower was also a steam room; which got very hot and steamy in no time at all, as the couple went for another round of hot steamy love making. Jewel held tight onto her husband huge arms as the thrusting of his penis against her g-spot sizzled into flames. They executed a series of orgasms, interchanging climaxing and melting to the beat of each other's hearts as their lovemaking slowly came to a still. John and Jewel finished their steamy hot shower in a dramatic ecstasy. After putting on his silk pajamas, John went into the kitchen. He removed two microwaveable dinner from the refrigerator and put them into the micro-wave; neither of them wanted to cook, they were exhausted from their wild and sensuous encounters. After

're

dinner, they cuddled and watched television until they fell asleep. Jewel slowly opened her eyes the next morning, looking around in bed for John. Instead of John, Jewel found a beautiful red rose on his pillow. Jewel smiled and picked up the rose, "*my sweet man*," she thought to herself as she sniffed the rose. At that moment she thought the world of John. All the while she made breakfast for herself, she thought about how sweet John had been to her. She still didn't quite understand why he was being so nice; "*maybe he is beginning to fall in love with me again*," Jewel thought while eating her breakfast, at least she hoped so. Through-out the morning Jewel noticed that she wasn't feeling well, but she figured it was just a bug or something simple, so she ignored it. She was on a high and nothing would bring her down. She scattered around most of the morning packing for her trip. There were so many things left to do, and she only had a few days left before her big trip. She needed to do some personal shopping. Jewel decided she would shop at Wal-Mart, there she would find the personal items she needed for her trip. It was still early; she could get in Wal-Mart before the crowd. Jewel knew where all the items she needed were because she shopped at there all the time. Jewel had called Conifa before she left home to let her know that she would be stopping by after going to Wal-Mart.

"*Which Wal-Mart, you know we have several?*" Conifa asked.

"*Why did she ask that question?*" Jewel thought about the question for a second or two before answering Conifa.

"*I will be going to the one by my house; your neighborhood is too expensive for my taste. When I am finish shopping, I want to come by and show you a few things that I brought. I need advice from a fashionista's such as you!*" Jewel laughed. At the last minute Jewel decided to shop at the Wal-Mart in Conifa's neighborhood, it would make her drive to Conifa's home quicker. When Jewel finished her shopping, she decided to call Conifa first before just popping up at her house. No one ever knew what type of mood this woman would be in; Jewel picked up her phone; dialed Conifa's phone number and waited for an answer. Finally, Conifa answered the phone.

"*Hello,*" Conifa answered.

"*Hey girl, this is Jewel,*"

"*I know, I saw your number, you know we have this thing called callers ID,*" Conifa said with a chuckle.

'*Yeah okay, I know. Hey, the reason I am calling is to let you know that I am on my way,*" Jewel replied.

"*It's okay, come on ova! I will make us some lunch!*" Conifa answered in great dimensions of enthusiasms. Jewel wondered why Conifa was so happy, but she dared to ask. Conifa had so many different personalities; today was no difference, Jewel thought to herself.

"*Okay girl, I will be right over,*" Jewel answered.

"*Alright, I will see you in a few,*" Conifa replied.

Jewel hung up the phone, put her car in the driving position and headed down La Brea toward Conifa's house. She was happy that she decided to shop in Conifa's area, now she was closer to her house. Jewel turned onto Conifa's street; Jewel could have sworn that she saw John's truck on the block over from Conifa's house.

"*No, that couldn't have been John. Why would he be over this way?*" Jewel questioned what she thought she saw. "*That has to be someone else with a truck, like Johns,*" she thought as she pulled into the driveway alongside Conifa's red Mercedes.

"*Such a pretty car and a beautiful house to go along with it, some people got it made in the shade!*" Jewel thought as she walked up to the huge gated double doors and rung the doorbell; she could hear the bells chiming inside like a downtown Cathedral Hall.

*"I am coming!"* Conifa answered.

*"Okay,"* Jewel replied.

Conifa opened the door wearing a sexy negligee. Jewel wondered why she was dressed like that; *" she knew I was coming; Conifa has other clothes to wear. Why in the world are you dressed like that?"* Jewel asked.

*" Girl, I was just chillaxing; watching the movie on how Stella got her groove back."* Conifa answered.

*" Okay, but what about lunch woman?"* Jewel asked.

*" I made lunch, you know it doesn't take me long to do anything,"* Conifa answers.

*" How you make lunch that fast, I only call twenty minutes ago; girl whose man you got up in here?"* Jewel asked in a suspicious tone.

*" Why would you even ask me that?* Conifa asked with a frown on her face; this was weird to Jewel, she was only kidding, why was Conifa taking her kidding around so serious?

*"Girl I was only kidding, why so serious?"* Jewel asked.

*" I don't know, just sounds like you think I'm lying or something,"* Conifa answered.

*" You are wearing a skimpy negligee in the middle of the day. You have tits and ass hanging out everywhere! What else would anyone think?"* Jewel said in an angry tone.

*" Well, as you see I am alone!"* Conifa answered.

"*I want to see what you are taking on our trip. I just left Wal-Mart; there were a few personal items that I needed.*" Jewel told Conifa.

"*Oh girl, I am still packing. I have five suitcases, and still I am not done!*" Conifa answered.

"*Yeah girl, I did most of my packing last night before me and John's wild passionate night of love making. I can barely breathe right now just thinking about it all. Girl it was like nothing before! Wow, what a night!*" Jewel told Conifa. Jewel noticed the change in Conifa's attitude when she mentioned her wild night of passion with her husband. Jewel knew that Conifa had a jealous spirit and was very lonely living in this big ole house all alone.

"*This had to be the loneliest feeling in the world; maybe that's why she has the sudden attitude change. Maybe Conifa was only trying to feel better by dressing sexy. I know that sometimes dressing sexy has helped me when I am depressed. Conifa needs to find herself a man; maybe while we are on our trip she will meet someone special,*" Jewel thought. "*I hope that I didn't hurt your feeling before,*" Jewel told Conifa.

"*Oh no, you didn't, everything is cool girl!*" Conifa answered.

"*That's great Conifa, what you prepare for lunch girl?*" Jewel asked.

"*We are having Chef Salad, and a fruit bowl; nice and healthy!*" Conifa laughed.

"*That's cool, exactly what I needed,*" Jewel replied.

"*Come on, we will have lunch on the patio!*" Conifa said as she rushed past Jewel with a tray of sandwiches in one hand and Chef Salad in the other.

"*Have a seat right here girl,*" Conifa said to Jewel pointing to a chair nearby.

"*Oh, okay thanks,*" Jewel answered.

Conifa went back inside; when she returned she had a pitcher of lemonade and a pot of coffee.

're

*"Which one would you like?"* She asked Jewel.

*"Neither, I will just take water,"* Jewel answered.

*"Water, oh okay, let me get you a glass,"* Conifa said as she went back inside. After ten minutes pasted, and Conifa hadn't returned; Jewel peeped through the sliding glass door that led into Conifa's huge kitchen. Jewel noticed that Conifa was on her cell phone in a deep conversation with someone. As Jewel watched, she saw Conifa leaning up against the stairs that led to her second floor. Conifa appeared to be in dreamland; it was as if the love of her life was speaking to her on the other end of the telephone. Conifa's body language changed the minute she noticed Jewel watching her. Jewel could hear Conifa tell the person on the other end of the phone,

*"I gotta run now dear; I will see you later on. Oh Jewel, that was my insurance man. Girl he is always calling me for one thing, or another. I don't know why; my insurance bill is not due until next month!"* Conifa told Jewel.

*"Yeah, that does sound a little strange, but nowadays a person never knows,"* Jewel answered.

*"Okay, let us break bread together and eat,"* Conifa said; she had an extraordinarily enormous smile on her face. Jewel's antenna's was picking up signals; she knew something was off with the way Conifa was acting, but she didn't have time to figure out Conifa's brains, so she ignored the awkwardness of Conifa's behavior. Lunch would have been great if Conifa wasn't acting so strange, Jewel thought as she sat at the table. She was trying to have a decent conversation with this woman; but under the circumstances Jewel felt it was best to talk at another time. *"Maybe this girl is having a strange day but I'm sure as hell not going to allow it to change my positive temperament or disposition. Today Conifa is truculent in her spirit, and she is going to remain this way if she doesn't change. So what are you wearing to the fly away Conifa, it a tiny bit chilly here, but that island may be hot as hell; it's better to dress warm and if need be take it off when we arrive."* Jewel said.

*"I have a few outfits that I am considering; do you want to see them?"* Conifa asked Jewel.

*"Hell yes, that why I wanted to come over; for a fashion show, I need some ideas!"* Jewel laughed.

*"Okay, are you all done with your lunch?"* Conifa asked.

*"Girl yes, I was filled to my capacity a while ago, but that Chef Salad was so delicious I continued eating!"* Jewel took a deep audible breath as she grabbed her belly, *"I'm stuffed,"* she lied. Jewel only picked at her food; she was too uncomfortable to eat; there was a half-naked woman sitting in front of her.

*"Okay, upstairs we go; oh girl, wait a minute! I forgot I moved my things into the downstairs bedroom yesterday,"* Conifa said. She appeared in a nervous state; anyone with ears could hear the crackling in her voice when she spoke.

*"Okay girl, don't even trip, we can do it at another time, it's not a problem. I don't want you going out of your way,"* Jewel replied.

*"Alright girl, let's do it on Saturday,"* Conifa answered.

*"That's fine, let me grab my things, but let it be known that I carried all these Wal-Mart bags in here to show you what I brought for nothing,"* Jewel answered.

*"They are all personal things aren't they? We all use the same things, don't we?"* Conifa asked.

*"You sometimes speak the most insane words that make no sense at all girl!"* Jewel laughed.

*"That's what they all say Jewel, don't take it personal honey!"* Conifa replied.

*"I try my hardest not to; it kind of hard sometimes, like now,"* Jewel answered.

When Conifa opened her huge glass double doors for Jewel to leave, Jewel noticed that Conifa had love bites on her neck. *"Oh yes, there is a man or a woman somewhere; maybe Conifa is secretly gay, in the closet and don't want anyone to know."* Jewel thought to herself. *"Ok girl, see you on Saturday,"* Jewel said to Conifa as she hugged her goodbye.

*"Bye lady, see you soon,"* Conifa said and they parted ways.

*"That was some strange shit,"* Jewel thought as she was getting into her car. *"I know that we women are sometimes strange, but this is a whole new strange!"* After putting her bags back into the car, Jewel drove away. All the way home she did nothing but think of how kind and sweet her man had been to her; he had articulated his love for her. He had the authority, the position and the power to bring her to her knees.

*"Now I am leaving him to go on this trip,"* she thought. On the drive home, Jewel remembered to stop at the corner mailbox. She hadn't checked it in a few days. As beautiful and updated as her neighborhood was Jewel still couldn't understand why the city placed everyone's mailbox at the end of the block. She had filed a petition to change it. As she approached her street, she could clearly see John's truck in the driveway of their home. Her heart raced a pace or two. Just the thought of his arms around her sent her body into boundless adrenaline that lifted her hormones three-dimensional. She knew at that moment that she would always love John. There was a slew of mail from previous days; she opened the mailbox and retrieved the mail. Jewel had been waiting for a letter from the State regarding her business; she had no idea why she hadn't checked the mail before now. The most important piece of mail was right on top; it was what she had been waiting for. *"Oh my God, here it is!"* Jewel nervously opened the letter; it read approved. Jewel was so elated that the long awaited mail had finally arrived, she forgot to get back into her car; instead she started to walk home. After walking a few foot she remembered;

*"Oh hell, I drove here!"* Getting back into her car, she drove the one block home. John was waiting for her at the front door with arms opened.

*"Hey babe, you all done with your business?"* He asked Jewel.

*"Yes babe, I am all finish with my shopping; I just need to finish packing my overnight bags, and get my camera's,"* Jewel answered her husband.

*"You need me to help with anything?"* John asked.

*"No, thank you babe, I have it all together!"* Jewel answered as she placed a thank you kiss on his adorable dimples. John winked at her and walked into the kitchen.

*"Are you sure babe?"* John yelled from the kitchen.

*"Yes I am sure,* Jewel yelled back.

*"Hey honey, guess what?"* She asked.

*"What?"*John replied.

*"I went by Conifa's house for lunch today; she was acting so weird I didn't eat my food. I'm a tiny bit hungry."* Jewel informed John, hoping he would offer to cook dinner,

*"She was acting weird, like what?"* John asked; he was more interest in what happened with Conifa; this pissed Jewel off!

*"Weird, like something was going on she didn't want me to know about, which was strange to me. I had just called her and ask if I could come by, she said yes, and then fifteen minutes later when I arrived there she is dressed up in this skimpy see through negligee and acting very nervous. Now doesn't that look and sound strange to you?"* Jewel asked John.

*"Well, not really, she could have just been in a sexy mood?"* John replied.

*"But for who is the question?"* Jewel asked.

're

*"That's that woman's business, just leave it alone!"* John advised Jewel. At this point, Jewel wondered why John was defending Conifa's action.

*"You know damn well that was uncalled for. Why in the world would anyone invite someone over to their home, and walk around half naked, unless they were going to roll around in the hay or something. I'm not gay, so what the hell was her point?"* Jewel said as John continued making his point.

*"Conifa isn't gay either, is she? After all, she was inside her home and not in the street. Don't you think it is okay for someone to be nude in their home if they want?"* John asked.

*"No not when you know company is coming over. And how the hell would you know whether she is gay or not?"* Jewel asked. *Sometimes you John lacked the ordinary keenness of a sound mindset. You will say senseless shit for the fun of it; like these words that were flowing so easily from your stupid mouth right now,"*. She was getting angry at John's nonchalant attitude. She was disgusted with John's comments; none of the things that he was saying made any sense. John noticed the change in Jewel's attitude and changed the subject quickly which caused Jewel to become angrier; she didn't understand why John was being so defensive of Conifa. She had never seen him this way about any of her friends before; he, usually, had her back in any situation. His reaction to their conversation was so strange and unusual, Jewel had to look twice to make sure she was talking to the same man she married all those years ago. Jewel was so upset at John she left the kitchen and went into their bedroom. She picked up her cell phone and called Miss. Prissy. She needed to speak with anyone that made sense to her. Surely someone knew when things were out of order. After a few second, Miss. Prissy answered the phone.

*"Hello,"* Miss. Prissy answered.

*"Hey Prissy, this is Jewel. How are you this gorgeous afternoon?"* Jewel asked. *"Baby doll I am wonderful, how are you?"* Prissy asked Jewel.

*"I am doing just fine, getting packed for the trip, and all,"* Jewel answered.

*"Me too, I am almost done!"* Miss. Prissy replied. Jewel, usually, talked to Miss. Prissy when she had things on her mind which she needed honest, solid advice on. Jewel had always felt that Miss. Prissy was a loyal friend out of the bunch of women. Miss. Prissy tried to treat everyone with respect and courtesy. Jewel totally believed that Miss. Prissy was a good woman with the fear of God in her heart. Jewel knew whatever she said to her friend would stay between them, and she didn't have to worry about Miss. Prissy gossiping to the other ladies.

*"I need to speak to you about something that happen earlier Prissy. Do you have the time to listen?"* Jewel asked Miss. Prissy.

*"Sure doll, I have all the time in the world for you,"* Miss. Prissy said in a high pitched tone.

*"Thank you Prissy, I knew you would be here for me. Listen to this and tell me what you think, okay,"* Jewel asked.

*"Okay, I am listening,"* Prissy answered.

*"Here it goes; I went by Conifa's house earlier today; mind you now I called first! Prissy when I got there Conifa was wearing a see through skimpy negligee, and listen to this girl that's the way she dressed our entire visit. She even served me lunch with that outfit on. Don't you think this was a gratuitously poor choice of hospitality?"* Jewel asked Miss. Prissy.

*"Jewel I think that conduct is very rude, downright repugnant and harmful to the eyes to tell you the truth!"* Miss. Prissy answered with a disgusting look on her face, *"I know that was a sight for sore eyes!"*

*"It made me feel very uneasy; I didn't understand why she was dressed like that, and when I ask her she became very defensive,"* Jewel replied.

*"No, honey don't allow Conifa to change the way you feel about anything. You already know something is off about our friend. Don't pay her any attention. That woman probably ran and put that outfit on just to make you think something crazy. You know she is an attention whore."* Miss. Prissy said. After thinking about what Mrs. Prissy said Jewel began to realize that she probably was right about Conifa but what about John's attitude to the situation.

*"I understand Prissy, but listen, when I got home I tried to talk to John about what happen at Conifa's, he got this really weird look on his face. For some reason became defensive too; he took up for Conifa's conduct. He said a person can and should be able to dress any way that want to in their home regardless to who is around."* Jewel answered. *"That's crazy for John to say such ignorant words. Why would he condone her behavior? Maybe he has something to do with her,"* Miss. Prissy said.

*"What do mean something to do with her?"* Jewel asked.

*"Jewel can't you tell there is something going on there with those two?"* Miss. Prissy asked.

*"Something going on, what do you mean? No I don't believe that!"* Jewel answered.

*"There has been talk around town that John has been spotted over that way pretty often,"* Prissy said.

*"What do that mean, what are you saying Prissy?"* Jewel asked.

Miss. Prissy became very quiet, holding her head in her hands she replied.

*"Well, honey babe Dolly and the others believed that there may have been some interactions between those two; I am not saying one way or another cause I don't know the facts."* Jewel wasn't going to listen to this messy conversation. John would never cheat on her with Conifa. If John did cheat, it would be with a young shapely chicks, like the ones in Vegas, not an old has been fart like

Conifa. Jewel didn't want to call Miss. Prissy a liar, but in this case she was sure that rumor got started by one of those old ass gossiping women at church. Miss. Prissy was only trying to give advice. What would Jewel do with this information? She decided that she would never bring it up to her husband; she didn't believe it so why ask him. Jewel didn't want anything to damage the value of her trip; she would pretend that she never heard it until after her trip; then and only then would she confront them both. One way or another she would eventually get to the bottom of what was going on. *"Prissy let's not have this conversation right now! Can we put it on the back burner? I will deal with this nonsense after I get back from my trip!"* Jewel said sarcastically. She was angry, but she wasn't going to make a scene, especially not now. Things have been going so well, now all of a sudden John is supposed to be having an affair with Conifa. Jewel knew that Conifa was always calling John over to check something out on her car, but she never suspected anything.

*"I will not allow my mind to go there about my husband. These women are up to no good, just trying to start something. They can't stand the fact that John and I are happy.* Jewel thought to herself.

*"Sure baby girl, I mean you can discuss it whenever you want to, I really don't know what to believe baby, but I really don't think anything is happening. Let's just have a great time on our trip, alright honey?"* Miss. Prissy asked Jewel.

*"Girl yeah, that is exactly what I was just thinking. People are always running their mouth about something; there is no way I am going to let this shit spoil my trip!"* Jewel laughed, *"It is all stupid, I will talk to you later Prissy!"*

*"It sure is, well alright baby I will see you in a few days at the fly away,"* Miss. Prissy replied.

*"Alright girl, love you and thanks for listening to me,"* Jewel said.

*"By all means baby girl, anytime,"* Miss. Prissy answered.

're

After saying goodbye to Miss. Prissy, Jewel hung up the phone. She didn't want to appear naive but she just couldn't confront John right now; which was by far from the way that Jewel usually handle situation. In the past when she thought someone was trying to get over on her she did things in an intuitive way rather than the right way. She didn't think first before acting or saying how she felt about what was going on. This Southern Belle just reacted; not very often was Jewel affected by opinions of others when she felt threaten or suspected anything foul. In her later years she had soften, especially since she found out that she had Hepatitis C. She was afraid of losing what she thought she had. Jewel decided that she had to be certain there was something to confront him about first. John was a bit uneasy when Jewel returns to the living room. He was sure that Jewel was going to start world war three with him, but instead Jewel came in and gave him a big hug and said.

*"Hey baby, what you doing?"*

John was completely out done, he didn't know what to think or say. He took a deep breath and said,

*"Babe, I am waiting for you. What are we going to do about dinner?"* John was very careful with his response.

*"Umm, I think maybe we will have meatloaf, mash potatoes and veggies. What do you think babe?"* Jewel asked.

*"That sounds scrumptious, just what I was thinking. Now who is going to cook?"* John asked with a big smile. He knew he had Jewel's attention now because she hated to cook.

*"I will,"* Jewel answered. Jewel's answer puzzled John. He thought he knew his wife so well, at this point she had him worried. He knew she had something on her mind, but he couldn't put his finger on it. They both were playing a dangerous cat and mouse game. Neither knew what the other was thinking. John didn't know what to say or do, but he wasn't

going to play this game anymore. John was a little uneasy with eating Jewel's cooking right now, but he figured he better play along, he didn't know what else to do or say to his wife. *"That's fine Jewel,"* he said.

Jewel went into the kitchen to start dinner. She took the ground round from the refrigerator so she could season the meat. All the while she was thinking about her conversation with Conifa, Miss. Prissy and John. *"None of them makes any sense to me!"* Jewel said aloud. She knew that John heard her, but she didn't care.

*"John know that I talk to myself and if he doesn't know now will be the time he will find out!"* She kept talking loudly. She tried to keep quiet; she tried to hold her tongue, but the words kept coming out of her mouth. With every breath, there was a sigh of regret; regretting that she didn't know what was going on; regretting that she couldn't control her emotions. As she prepared dinner tears fell from her eyes as she told herself that her husband wouldn't ever cheat on her with Conifa. She worried that maybe John had tired of her bickering and fussing with him so much. Maybe her jealousy had run him into the arms of Conifa. After dinner, John tried to console Jewel by placing tender kisses on her cheeks; he reach out to give her a hug. Jewel brushed him off saying, *"stop it John!"*

*"Come on babe,"* John said.

When Jewel didn't respond to John's advances, he went to bed without her. Jewel was relieved that John went to bed without bothering her. She didn't want sex tonight; all she wanted right now was to be alone. The situation was too stressful; the only thing in her life worth thinking about was the trip she had planned. She told herself that she would have the most exciting time ever on her trip; she would ignore Conifa and the ladies who made up that lie on her husband. She promised herself to stay away from all the drama as much as possible while she was away. She knew that it would be difficult since how they were traveling together, but some way she just had to make it work. *"This trip is all about solitude in a positive, constructive environment. I Jewel will navigate my life in a direction of quality; I will live my life to its full potential; implementing love and trust."* Jewel had a plan in which she would execute in her way. Her algorithm would step by step come together. When she solved this problem, it would be a job well done. She didn't need help from anyone. With this thought in mind Jewel put away the leftover food, washed the dinner dishes, put the alarm on for the night and went to bed. She climbed in bed beside John, in a matter of minute Jewel was asleep. The following morning Jewel stood looking out her bedroom window; she wondered if it had rained last night. The ground was wet, and the air was damp. She opened the window and took in a breath of fresh air. As Jewel inhaled the crisped air she could easily perceive that it had rain; all of the characteristics were there, the sweet, clean smell of Mother Nature's cleansing. Jewel now knew why she slept so sound last night; she always slept like a baby when it was raining. As she stood in the window, she thanked God for his blessing, for her home and family. Jewel heard John stirring around in the bed; she didn't want to wake him so she quickly with speed and dexterity exited the room. As excited as Jewel was about her trip, she was just as enraged and hurt at the amount of deceit and falsified statements of the women. She wasn't even sure of the veracity of John's statements. Jewel had planned her egress a little more tasteful than this. Nevertheless she would make the very best out of what possibly could be a horrific situation. She totally trusts that God would never put more on her than she could bear. It was a conquering sense of victory for Jewel, to know that she could trust God to see her through it all; to know the enemy was already defeated. She decided to get dressed for the day. Jewel knew what she would be wearing today; she had preplanned everything. She went into her guest room where her suitcases were packed and ready for travel. Jewel decided to wear her grey sweats with a hoodie; she knew her head would get cold on the plane; she also placed a pair of black and grey socks with grey casual sneaker. She always dressed comfortable when traveling and she never over packed her suitcases. Jewel got dressed in their guest bedroom; she checked herself out in the mirror; she loved what she saw standing before her. She was still that Big Beautiful Woman, that caramel statuette. She was ready, smiling as she combed through her hair and put it up in a ponytail. Jewel could smell coffee and bacon coming from the kitchen; John was up, she thought to herself. She followed the sweet smell of coffee down the hallway, through the living room and into the kitchen where John stood naked at the sink stirring his coffee. He looked like a Greek God, his broad shoulder, tight derriere, six-packed chest and muscled legs were screaming, "kiss on me, please!"

*"Good morning honey,"* Jewel said.

*"Good morning, I see you are dress and ready huh babe,"* John asked.

*"Yes babe, I packed my suitcase yesterday,"* Jewel answered.

*"Have you finish packing?"* John asked.

*"Yes, a while ago,"* Jewel said.

*"Am I still taking you to the fly away?"* John asked.

*"Yes babe, how else would I get there?"* Jewel asked.

*"Well, I have no idea if you changed your mind or not, you been acting pretty strange lately,"* John replied.

Jewel wasn't even going to feed into this negativity; it was hilarious; she couldn't believe John even allowed himself to say such an idiotic statement, well on second thought yes she could.

*"My Lord, this man is crazy as hell if he think for one moment that I will fall into this trap; he has another thing coming."* Jewel thought to herself,

*"No, I still need you,"* Jewel calmly said.

John looked at her as if he had seen a ghost, *"you do?"* He asked in disbelief.

*"Yes I do, we will be meeting at the fly away at four p.m."* Jewel reiterated; she had already given John her entire itinerary weeks ago.

*"Okay babe, we will be there on time,"* John replied with softness in his voice. His voice penetrated every nerve and muscles in Jewel's groin; the inner part of her thighs was yielding, readily for his touch, but she couldn't, not just yet. She needed answers, not just made up ones either; she needed the truth. Jewel usually lacked strength when in the presence of John. But today it was a totally different story. She stood tall and firm in her truth. After breakfast Jewel had one last minute errand to run; John had a job to do for the neighbor around the corner, something about an electrical fire in the basement. Jewel thanked John for breakfast by planting a small kiss tenderly on his lips. She secretly didn't want to eat breakfast, but she didn't want to appear unappreciative of his kindness. Jewel would have preferred a cup of coffee and a donut. Jewel remembered back to the time when she had a heated argument with a girlfriend of her sister Stacy. The woman was so wicked she tried to kill Jewel. After their initial argument, the woman pretended to leave the scene. As soon as Jewel wasn't looking, that crazy evil woman put eye drops in her alcohol beverage; now everyone know that eye drops and alcohol mixed together will kill a person.

*"So, now when someone is feeling anger or showing resentment toward me, I always refuse food or drink from them, but how could I with John,"* she thought to herself. The only thing she could do was blessed the food with prayer, asking God to bless the hands that prepared it, to take out all impurities and make it a healthy nourishment to her body. If Jewel didn't trust anyone or anything she certainly did trust God. John kissed Jewel on the lips and gave her a gentle hug and off he went. Jewel followed after him. She needed to go back to Wal-Mart to get another camera for her trip; she could never have enough film and she love Kodak camera's, they took the best pictures. While she was in the store Jewel brought a photo album just for her vacation. Jewel rushed through the aisles of Wal-Mart looking for

last minute things that she needed. Every checkout lines were full to it capacity;

*"It doesn't matter what time of the day anyone come into this store, there was always a long line."* Jewel thought to herself. Jewel decided to go through the quick check line, that way she would get out faster. As soon as Jewel left Wal-Mart she received a phone call from Dolly asking her to stop by Yolanda's beauty shop. Yolanda's was a family owned beauty shop on the west side of Los Angeles. Yolanda's had been in business for three generations. It was one of the most popular beauty shop in Los Angeles that caters to women of color hair. Of course, Yolanda's didn't discriminate or turn anyone away; her shop specialized in hair, nail, facials, and pedicures. Everyone was welcome for pampering and gossiping. When Jewel answered her cell phone Dolly told her, she wanted to give her the itinerary package. Jewel wonder why Conifa gave her itinerary to Dolly.

*" Why didn't she just give me the information when I was over to her house the other day? Oh well, whatever,* Jewel thought, *I will just run over to the beauty shop and get it. "*

Entering Yolanda's, Jewel noticed Dolly sitting under a hair dryer. She walked over where Dolly was sitting and taps on the dryer. Dolly peeped from under the dryer, as always she wore a huge smile on her face.

*"Hey girl, you ready to travel?"* Dolly asked Jewel.

*"Heck yeah, I'm ready,"* Jewel answered.

*"Oh yes, here is your itinerary,"* Dolly said as she gave Jewel a piece of folded paper.

*"I don't understand why you have my itinerary though,"* Jewel said.

*"Conifa asked me to give it to everyone, she said that she had some last minute stuff to get done,"* Dolly replied.

*"Yes, but didn't she say at the meeting that she would give everyone the itinerary package at the fly away? This sure was a big change from what she said the other day!"* Jewel in a denoting way, signifying that Conifa was up to no good as usual.

*"Well, I don't know, but here you go,"* Dolly said still smiling.

Jewel took the itinerary package from Dolly, and said that she would see her later on at the fly away.

*"Don't be late,"* Jewel said to Dolly as she went out the door of the salon. It was almost time to leave for the plane and Jewel was running behind schedule. She rushed along the Blvd hoping that she didn't run into any traffic. She knew if she did it would be a problem; she figured it would just be better to take another route. Dalton was the fastest way to her house, so she made a left turn off Santa Barbara onto Dalton.

*"Yes,* she thought to herself, *no traffic!"* Jewel was home in a matter of minutes. John was already there waiting for her, he had moved her suitcases to the front door;

*"You are running late girl,"* he teasingly said. He knew Jewel loved it when he flirted with her. Jewel smiled at him as she ran up the step to the front door.

*"I know babe, I will be right out. I have to use the bathroom first,"* Jewel said.

*"It's a good thing you had everything ready babe,"* John said to Jewel as she rushed past him.

*"Babe, I always take care of my business!"* Jewel said. Jewel used the bathroom, grabbed her overnight bag, her pillow and blanket. She looked around to make sure she had everything. She suddenly felt as if she was leaving something behind; *"Ah yes, my batteries for my camera, MiPad and cell phone is a must have, I can't leave home without them.* She placed her essential

in a separate bag; they were necessary; she would be nothing without these items. With John's manpower and Jewel's pulling, pushing and tugging they were finally able to get Jewel's travel accessories, and entire luggage set into John's truck. Jewel always said she only took a few clothes when she traveled, but of course, John begged to differ; he said she always took everything in her closet. As they rode along Century Blvd, they held hands. John told Jewel that he was going to miss her. As the couple turned into the parking structure of the fly away, Jewel saw the other women waiting at the check-in window. Everyone was there except for Conifa; John unloaded Jewel's suitcases from the truck and carried them inside the terminal. A few minutes later Conifa arrived; she had at least with ten suitcases; John took the liberty of hauling them all inside for her. John brought the last of Conifa's suitcases inside the terminal, and the group of women's headed for the plane. Jewel kissed her husband goodbye with intense emotions.

*"I will see you in fourteen days babe,"* Jewel said looking deep into her husband's eyes.

*"Yes babe, I will see you in fourteen days, you be sweet, safe travels honey!"* John whispered as he kissed her back dominating her tongue. As they parted ways, Jewel's heart became sad. She turned her head away from John; she didn't want him to see her cry. *"He wouldn't understand,"* Jewel thought to herself as she entered the flyaway. She was deep in thought when the airline attendant called out to her. *"Are you ready to check in?"* When she heard his voice, it brought her back to reality. *"Wait for me,"* Jewel yelled to her friends. *"Girl you had better hurry before you miss the plane,"* Jerry said.

*Yes, I have pre-paid ticket!"* Jewel excitedly said to the attendant.

*"Come on over,"* he said to Jewel with a big smile.

Jewel thought to herself, "Is he flirting with me?

*"What about us?* Miss. Prissy asked.

*"Are you all together?"* The attendant asked.

*"Yes, we are,"* Conifa said.

*"That's fine, step right this way,"* The attendant said.

*"Hold on, let me get my suitcase,"* Jewel said.

*"No, I will get everyone's suitcases,"* The attendant said.

*"Oh, how kind of you,"* Conifa shouted.

*"Why are you shouting?"* Dolly asked Conifa.

*"I wasn't shouting, I only said the man was kind, what is your problem Dolly?"* Conifa asked.

*"I don't have a problem, but I think that you may have a problem,"* Dolly yelled at Conifa.

*"What do you mean by that remark?"* Conifa asked.

*"You know what I mean,"* Dolly replied.

*"Hey come on now ladies; it's not that serious. You shouldn't let everything bother you. You make a huge deal out of everything Conifa."* Miss. Prissy said.

Dolly loved the fact that Miss. Prissy was taking up for her. She rolled her eyes at Conifa and smiled.

*"Who are you rolling your eyes at Dolly?"* Conifa asked.

*"I'm rolling my eyes at your dumb ass,"* Dolly said.

*"Come on ladies, please let us be kind to one another,"* Miss. Prissy said.

*"What do you mean be kind? I think you should tell your friend to be kind. You two stick together like flies to shit. Don't tell me anything about being kind. I have always being kind to you and your friends Prissy!* Conifa yelled.

## CHAPTER SEVEN

## TRUE FRIENDS

Jewel waited for the airport assistance to come and push her wheelchair, she had problems walking long distant, and the Los Angeles airport terminal to terminal wasn't any joke. It was one of the largest airports in the United States, and because of her meniscal tears in her knees she needed help getting to destinations. Jewel kept a bunch of five dollar bills for tipping along the way. Within minutes, everyone's bags were checked in, and they were on their way to the terminal to board the plane. The ladies finally reached Air Jamaica, terminal C246; they searched around looking for places to sit. The seating area was crowded, a lots of people traveling to Jamaica. Eventually they found seats; Miss. Prissy, Dolly, Tara and Conifa sat together and Jewel, Jerry and Brenda G. sat across from them. The plane was scheduled to take off in an hour. With time on their hands, a few of the ladies went to buy snacks and drinks while the others waited. While standing in line B.G. became frustrated at the airport prices and said. *"Damn, this airport food is too freaking expensive! I betcha one thing, the next time I'd bring my own shit; even that heifer ass cashier who sold me this shit knew that price for a soda was too damn high, $3.25, oh wow!"* Brenda G. said loudly.

*"B.G., now you know you didn't have to purchase that soda if you didn't want it, right?"* Jewel asked. After B.G., paid for her soda Jewel had to use the bathroom. Jewel asked the cashier where the nearest bathroom was located.

*"Madam, it's right over there, less than twenty feet away,"* the cashier answered with a smile.

*"Thank you,"* Jewel replied. When she finished using the bathroom, they stopped at a candy store so Brenda G. could get a large bag of peanut M&M's to carry on the plane for later. Once they arrived back to the

seating area, the other ladies were nowhere to be found. Jewel figured that they had gone to get something to drink. It was almost time for the plane to board and Miss Prissy, Conifer, Dolly and Tara hadn't returned back to the seating area. Jewel started worry that the ladies would miss the plane; she questioned the airline agent, asking if she had noticed which way the ladies went. The agent at the desk told Jewel that the ladies had boarded an earlier flight.

*"Excuse me, what did you say, did I hear you correctly, did you say they boarded an earlier flight?"* Jewel asked.

*"Ma'am, those ladies that you were with left about thirty minutes ago,"* The agent replied.

*"How could they have left already when our plane isn't schedule to leave for twenty more minutes?"* Jewel asked the agent.

*"What is your flight number?"* She asked Jewel.

*"It is flight number 5436, to Montego Bay, Jamaica,"* Jewel answered.

*"That plane left early; we announced it over the intercom quite a few times reporting the changes in the time of departure,* the Gate agent said with a sad face, ladies; *I am so sorry."* Jewel was furious; she couldn't believe the ladies would leave them behind like this, especially not Miss. Prissy.

*"You mean to tell me they didn't even have the decency to come twenty feet away and let us know the plane was leaving?"* Jewel looked at Brenda G. and Jerry for answers. *"What in God's name are we going to do now?"* she asked them.

*"There is nothing that we can do, but see if we can take the next flight out!"* Jerry answered.

*"Who would something like this?"* Jewel asked the Gate agent with a look of despair in her eyes.

The agent shook her head and said, "*Unfortunately this happens quite often; however, you are in luck. The next flight to Montego Bay, Jamaica is leaving in just a couple of hours; you can get on this flight. I will even upgrade your seats to first class. Would you like to transfer your tickets now?*" She asked the women.

Jewel took a deep exhalation of air and yelled. "*Oh God, thank you so much! Yes, by all means, please do!*"

"*When all else fails, God is always on time.*" Jewel thought as she and the ladies exchanged their tickets for new upgraded ones. The ladies went back to their seats. They sat there looking at each other in disbelief; searching each other's faces for an answer.

"*Let's not all speak at once, but Jewel I want to know what kind of friends do you have girl?*" Jerry asked.

"*They are all of our friends Jerry and I don't know what kind of friends they are. I am so much more shocked at Prissy's behavioral than the others though. Well, at least we got some great seats in first class.*" Jewel answered.

"*That's true; we did luck out in the seating department,*" Brenda G. yelled, almost squealing her words out. At this point her tone was irritating Jewel. Since the women had to wait two hours, they decided to go get food, just this time they would make sure that they hurry.

"*Excuse me Ms. may I use this wheelchair to assist my friend to get food?*" Brenda G. asked the airport agent?

"*Sure, that's what we have them for, just remember in less than two hours we board.*" the agent replied.

"*B.G. you had my back every since we first met; we were only twenty-one years old, girl that was twenty-one years ago. That's why I love you girl, and I will always have yours. Listen, wherever we go to get food, we have to hurry. Where are we going to get food?* Jewel asked.

*"I hear what you are saying, and I love you too, but heifer just look around, don't you see all these restaurants? All you have to do is just choose one Jewel, it is not that complicated!"* Brenda G. said. B.G. was still angry at the ladies for leaving them, and now she was taking it out on Jewel. She needed an alcoholic beverage and some marijuana to settle her nerve. She loved her cocktails almost as well as her marijuana. She said she needed her marijuana medicine every day, and she didn't give a damn who knew it. *"As long as I got my license from the State of California to smoke this good ole bud, then that's what I'm will do, were her exact words."* They found a small restaurant called Morella that served both American and Italian food, also alcoholic beverages. The women had a bite to eat while discussing their plans for the trip. B. G. only ordered a scotch and soda. After having two scotch and soda the pitch in her voice became higher, elevating upward, extending to the very end of Jewel's nerves. Jewel looked at her watch and said, *"we better get out of here before this girl gets us in trouble."* Jewel said it in a joking way, but the truth of the matter was that she had to release herself from the torture of listening to B.G. go on and on about nothing. Jerry knew how Jewel felt; she never wanted to be in the same room with this girl either; especially not when she had been drinking too much. Jewel and Jerry both loved Brenda G.; she was their friend regardless of her voice. It was just so damn hard to listen to her sometimes. Jerry's personalities brought life into a dark room, and since B.G. had one too many drinks Jerry offered to help her get back to the plane.

*"Well damn, what about me, who is going to push me back?"* Jewel asked Brenda G, while still sitting at the table in her wheelchair. At times like these, she hated that she didn't have her knee surgery sooner. Dr. Prudhoe, Jewel's orthopedic doctor, advised her that she must lose some weight; not only for health reasons but so she would be able to get the surgeries that she needed. She weighted a hundred-and ninety-pounds, the good doctor wanted her to reduce her weight to a hundred-and-fifty-five-pounds; so she needed to lose thirty-five-pounds.

*"Mrs. Dupree you will heal better with less weight to carry around,"* he said.

Jewel had put it off for the last two years. Now that she had lost the thirty-five pounds she planned on having it done in January. But with this trip and all, she wished that she had done it in the summer, now she would be walking and running like the other women.

*"You are going to have to ask that sky caption for help. Take a good look at our friend, she can't help you now, she can barely help herself!"* Jerry giggled. She was so silly at times; that's what made her so much fun to be around. She didn't let too many things bother her; she always had something positive to say regardless of any giving situation. They finally found a nice customer service guy to help Jewel get back to terminal C246. It was a good thing they left when they did because the Gate agent was calling out for them.

*"Where have you all been? The plane is ready for take-off. Come, come to the front of the line Mrs. Dupree, you will be the first one on. "Wheelchairs always go on first!"* she said to Jewel.

Once on the plane, Jewel noticed the plane was almost empty, barely anyone was on the plane with them.

*"What we have here, a chartered plane,"* she ask in a joking way. Although Jewel was joking, it was a strange feeling that they were the only ones in first class. It didn't take long for the plane to fill to its capacity, and they were on their way. The takeoff was smooth; Jewel had forgotten to take her anxiety medicine, which was a must when she was flying. Jewel was afraid of height; the zany bars helped her to relax. It wasn't long before she was asleep. She could feel Brenda G. tugging at her arm, trying to wake her, but Jewel was now in dreamland. When she woke up they were in Montego Bay, Jamaica. *"What a beautiful island this is,"* she thought when opening her eyes. As the plane prepared to land, Jewel glared relentlessly out of her window at the most gorgeous aqua blue wonders of the

're

Caribbean Sea. The bright dazzling sunlight gave forth a glow that glisten each wave that came ashore. It appeared that the heavens and the water met the shore and became one. The great body of water continued as far as her eyes could see, there was no end. The plane flew over Montego Bay, turned around and came back for landing. The huge sign read, *"Welcome to Montego Bay, a vacation of tropical fun and relaxing you will have; this is a small Island in Jamaica, an Island of indigenous people.*

Jewel was told that Jamaica was a beautiful sight to see; a place that if you went once you were sure to go back. *"There were so many different Islands to see. Montego Bay is just one of them; it would take a lifetime to enjoy each one,"* Jewel thought, as she gathered her bags to exit the plane. She couldn't imagine being anywhere right now; she was here, vacationing in Montego Bay, Jamaica. It took Jewel a little longer to get her overnight bag from the compartment above her seat. She made sure to get her bag with her camera, MiPad and batteries from under her seat and caught up to Jerry and Brenda G. at the exit door of the plane. As the ladies waited for Jewel's wheelchair, they hugged each other; jumping up and down in pure joy; they had been successful in getting to Jamaica all in one piece. Brenda G. looked at Jewel and yelled, *"wait a minute helfa, I thought your knees were all fucked up; how the hell are you jumping up and down like this? Oh, so I see, you like Stella, just instead of getting your groove back, you done grew some new knees!"* The women rolled in laughter as they exited the plane together. Once on the ground things looked difference from up there in the clouds, Jewel thought as she entered the Jamaican airport lobby. It was smallest airport Jewel had ever seen. It was muggy and very hot, with no air condition at all. It took the ladies awhile to get through checkpoint. The security was structured to make sure no one escaped captivity if they came through there with anything illegal. Jewel had difficulty getting through checkpoint; a discrepancy with her passport. She looked difference after her weight loss. Jewel told the security personnel, *"I have lost over thirty-five pound, but I don't look that much difference in the face, look at me, I have the same eyes, the same cheekbones and the same smile."* The security finally cleared Jewel, she was able to go through and meet her girlfriends on the other side. Jerry and Brenda G. had gotten a Rastafarian guy to drive them to the resort.

*"Woo wee, ya'll work fast!"* Jewel said as she exited the tiny doors of the airport where the cab driver was waiting with the women.

*"Girl please, this is a cab driver; I don't know what those Italians put in my drink, but it knocked me out. I just want to get to my room right about now. I am tired than a mo fo,"* Brenda G. said.

*"I feel you, I do too; it was really a long flight. I stayed awoke most of the flight; girl, that was too much water for me to go to sleep!"* Jerry said trying to be funny.

*"Are you ready my lade?* The cab driver asked. Jewel loved the sound of the cab drivers voice. She had a dream long ago that one day she would be in this space, and here she was, riding through the streets of Jamaica with her best friends. Life was amazing; she had been blessed with a husband, a son, recently won two million dollars, now she was on this beautiful Island in Jamaica, it was a special treat to be here right now, in this space and at this time in her life. She needed tranquility, she needed peace of mind and she needed to celebrate life; now was Jewel's time.

*"Yes sir, now that the last of our Mohegan's is here. We can go now, come on Jewel with your slow behind,"* Jerry said.

*"I'm here, right beside you girly. I bet you I won't be the one to get left again!'* Jewel laughed. She thought about the other women. She wondered what they were going to say when they met up again

*"Where to Lade?"* The driver asked.

*"Oh sorry, here is the address sir!"* Jewel answered.

" *Oh, so you are going to Sunset Beach, that a nice place mon, how long you stay?*" The driver asked.

" *We will be here for one week. Hey man, I heard about ya'll and that Ganja over here in this part of the world. You know where it is?*" Brenda G. asked.

" *Aye, yes mon, I give you the grand tour of this Island. I can take you everywhere you want to go mon, all you need to do is ask for me. They call me the Rasta Man on this Island. I know where Ganja is; only the best for you lade; Ganja been here all me life, all me fathers life; it was found long time ago growing in grave of King Solomon. It tis here, you want now?* He asked.

" *Hell yeah, I want it now. You sure you not one of the Island cops, right?*" Brenda G. questioned the Rasta.

" *Now is a fine time to ask!*" Jewel laughed. *If he is, we are all in trouble, just being with you. Look Rasta Man, I had nothing to do with this, I don't smoke anything.*"

" *Hell, I don't smoke anything either, don't be leaving me out Jewel,*" Jerry yelled from the back seat of the most horrible looking cab on the Island. The steering wheel was on the opposite side of the car, it had dents on both doors, and cracked taillights; a dented hood and the fool drove like a madman.

" *He drives horribly,* Jerry said to Brenda G. " *which is probably the reason why his car is so damn dented up!*" They were talking about the driver as if he wasn't even there. Jewel wondered why the cab driver wouldn't buy himself a new vehicle. The cab driver drove passed a sign that read seventy-five miles per hour. Jewel had never experience anything quite like it before, this was the ultimate culture shock. She feared for her life. Jewel kindly asked the cab driver to slow down. He told her if he drove to slow that he would get a ticket. " *The people on this Island will run you over; you can't be out here poking around lady! You come to this Island, have fun, you shouldn't ever drive in Jamaica,"* he replied.

*"I will never drive in Jamaica; you don't have to worry about that!"* Jewel replied. Jewel thought she heard a bit of male chauvinism in his voice. She could detect a male chauvinism pig a mile away; John had taught her a good lesson on this subject. She had lived through the first eight chapters. *"Eight years of marriage to John!"* She had also heard that the Jamaican men put their women on a pedestal until they get what they want and then snatched the pedestal from beneath them.

*"Yeah right, who would come over here to drive, the way ya'll drive is totally difference from the way we drive in the states!* Brenda G. yelled, *and by the way what about the Ganja? I am dead serious while ya'll over here talking about learning to drive and shit!"*

*"Mon, I will take you on the way. Not far from the resort mon, not far at all! You just ride with Rasta Man, he will take you there!"*

*"Okay Rasta Man, let jam on it then!"* Brenda G. yelled. She was elated, her first time out the country. *"I am going to have me a ball, high and all! Hey wait a minute, I just rhymed!"* The cab driver drove really fast along Montego Bay's narrow countryside roads, all the while speaking, giving the ladies valuable information on the Island history. He told them he chose this route so the women could see all the beautiful views. From each direction that women could see the beautiful Caribbean Sea. The waves and the clouds met on the shore; the crystal aqua blue sea water danced an electrical rhythm as the waves rescinded to sea. As the women rode along Jewel noticed something very fascinating; it was the most breathtaking view of the countryside she had seen thus far.

*"What is that over on that hill?"* Jewel asked the cab driver.

*"Ah, that place is called the Croydon Plantation; it has nested in those hills o'er Montego Bay since my great father's time. It is a working plantation located in the Catadupa Mountains; they produced some of the world's tastiest fruits and the finest coffee beans you ever had, yes right here in Jamaica. Take a tour o'er there before you leave the Island, you will see. Each delectable fruit will simply melt in your mouth, their specialty is pineapples."* The cab driver said.

*"Wow, this man drive and talk at great speed,"* Jewel thought, but she loved how informative he was, and with-out cost. The information that he gave helped her in deciding some tours to take. She heard Conifa talking about the Croydon Plantation, but she didn't describe it in details. She was sure to take this tour. The cab driver told them about other beautiful tours to take; *"you ladies must take the tour of the Cinnamon Goff Course, and Rose Hall Great House. "Cinnamon Hill Golf Course was built in nineteen-sixty-nine; it stay open year around, and it used to be on a sugar plantation owned by slave masters. Jamaica's past history is still present throughout the golf course. When you ladies tour the golf course you will be able to see it in the forms of gravesites and old homes that has been ruined over the years. Cinnamon Hills is most popular for its lush and lavish landscaping filled with historical sites to see."*

*"Wow that is amazing; I never knew that slaves were kept in Jamaica, I only thought they were in the south,* Brenda G. said, looking puzzled. *"Lord's knows I didn't!"*

*"They kept the slave on this island?"* Jewel asked the cab driver.

*"Yes, they were tortured and killed right here in Jamaica. The slaves were the one that did all the work; they kept the crops and the fruits up for the white man. There is another place that I hope you ladies tour while on your trip. It is called "Rose Hall Great House," the former home of Annie Palmer. The native called her "the white witch of Rose's Hall because each one of her eight husbands died in that mansion."* Jewel looked at the houses and the building along the way; they

were assorted colors of pink, green, blue, yellow-orange, and purple, all separated according to their class;

*"Why are the houses painted such loud colors?"* Jewel asked.

*" We Jamaicans loved us assorted colors; our houses represent the same colors as our flag."* The cab drivers told the women.

*" Oh, I see,"* Jewel replied.

*" There is Sunset Beach Resort over there on the other side of the island, you see it? That is where you will be staying."* The cab driver told the ladies.

*"It appeared to be centered in the middle of the sea!"* Jewel said in excitement.

*" It is; it's an Island in the middle of the sea, sitting all by itself,"* The driver said.

*"Montego Bay is an island sitting in the middle of the sea, all by itself? What in the hell do you mean?"* Brenda G. asked.

*" You see it, don't you lady? Before we go there, we will make one stop for you."* He said.

*" Yeah, okay, thank you very much!"* Brenda G. replied.

*" You are welcome, when we come there; I will do everything for you, okay."* The driver said.

*"Sure, all I want is some Ganja."* Brenda G. said.

*" And that you will get ma-am, only the best for you."* The cab driver said again. The cab driver sped along the coast of the coast until they reached the inland, where all the Rasta's hung out. He pulled up to the Ganja spot. He got out and went across the street to a huge pink building; there a Rastafarian came out; they spoke for a minute or so before he returned back to the car. The cab driver placed a huge sack of Ganja in Brenda G.'s

hand. When Brenda G. looked at the amount of Ganja that the Rastafarian gave her, she couldn't believe her eyes. It was enough to last a year in the states she thought.

*"What the hell is this Rasta Man?"* Brenda G. asked.

*"That's your Ganja ma'am,"* The Rasta said.

*"Ah damn; this entire mountain of Ganja is for me?"* Brenda G. reluctantly asked.

*"Yes, all for you!"* The Rasta said.

In a state of excitation, Brenda G. yelled, *"I sure will, this will last me the entire trip! Do you want some of it?*

*"Ah no, it is all for you lade!"* The Rasta said.

*"So this is the way it is done in the Caribbean's."* Jerry asked.

*"Ah, yes, this the way we Jamaicans do it!"* The Rasta man said with a huge smile, showing all pearly whites.

*"The drive from town to Sunset Beach Resort is only minutes away, we will be there right away!"* the Rasta man told Jewel and her friends. He turned onto a long dusty trail; pineapples and fruit trees grew along the side of the road. Jewel thought for a moment that they were in a forest of fruit trees until the cab driver turned into a huge gated community. *"You ladies have arrived; this is your destination, Sunset Beach Resort! I will help you all out."* He said as he jumped out the right side of the car into the driveway of the most beautiful place Jewel had ever seen in her life. The sun was setting over Sunset Beach, casting a beautiful shivering rainbow which served as a backdrop; it was breathtaking. Its beachfront entrance was a masterpiece, featuring giant hot tubs and tropical gardens; a view of a majestic waterfall in one of the tropical gardens reminded Jewel of her dream of Niagara Falls. The resort/spa was tailored in exquisite contemporary designs. The

're

cabdriver helped the bellhop with the women luggage. At the check-in office the women ran into a bit of a problem; Jerry and Jewel were supposed to share rooms and Tara and Brenda G. were to share rooms. They now had to find out where the other ladies were. The customer service lady walked away, stopped and said something to a tall, handsome man. Jewel couldn't see his face; his back was turned to her. The customer service lady came back, she'd found Tara's room; she gave Brenda G. a master key to get in; once they were all checked in the bellhop carried their luggage to their rooms. Jewel and Jerry's Ralph Lauren designed room was on the first floor; it was idyllic, with an incredible view of Montego Bay finest; they could see the Montego Bay Yachts docked on deck. There was a modern kitchen with stainless steel appliances and all the amenities that they would ever need. Jewel walked over to the window and took in a deep breath of Jamaica's air.

*"I will have a wonderful vacation, under the starlight of Jamaica,"* Jewel thought to herself. With this thought in mind, she yelled from her bedroom window, *"I am here!"* There were a bunch of Jamaican men across the way sitting in the park playing dominoes; they all looked in her direction when she yelled. One of the men motioned with his hand for Jewel to come down. Jewel was excited; she ran from the window thinking to herself, *"the fun is about to begin."* After unpacking their bags, Jewel and Jerry went to check on Brenda G. Brenda G. was a pistol; she didn't take any mess from anyone, and they didn't want her to start a fight with the other women for leaving them behind, not here in Jamaica. Jewel was going to make sure that nothing would interfere with her lavish vacation. This vacation was aligned by God, and nothing would spoil it, not even her so-called friends that left them behind at the airport in Los Angeles, California. Yes, she was angry with Miss. Prissy, but enjoying her vacation was more important to her; she had made it to paradise, which was all that mattered, as well as her peace of mind. She came to Jamaica to rest her mind; to take a mental vacation away from all of her problems in the city and her husband.

## CHAPTER EIGHT

## THE SETUP

The next morning Jewel and Jerry went to Brenda G's room where they found her alone. *"Where is Tara?"* Jewel asked.

*"I have no idea,"* Brenda G. answered

*"Has she even been here?"* Jerry asked.

*"Yea, that heifer been here; her suitcases are in the closet, and her personal things are in the drawers. She has been here."* Brenda G. answered.

*"Oh yeah I see; I wonder where the ladies are?"* Jewel questioned as she walked around the room inspecting everything. She peeped into the closet to see what Tara had brought to wear. Tara always wore beautiful sexy clothes. When that girl went shopping, she brought two of everything; two pairs of shoes, two of the same outfits in different colors. There were clothes in every closet in her home; she lived alone, so she had enough space to accommodate her clothes.

*"How about we go see if we can find the ladies?"* Jewel asked.

*"That sounds good, but please, can we not argue or talk trash about them leaving us, I don't want any hard feelings, we are supposed to be having a great time. We are all here now that is what's important."* Jerry said.

*"You are right Jerry; that is what we all want, right B. G.?"* Jewel questioned Brenda G.

*"I don't know about y'all,* Brenda G. said, *but those heifer's need to be dealt with; what they did is unforgivable; what if there were no other flight, and then what would we have done? I think you both are just a little too passive, you allow others to do things to you and get away with it. Not me, I will fight a mofo that*

*mess around with me. You both are my home girls; I hate it when someone messes with me or one of my dogs."*

*" I understand how you feel, however I feel this is a delicate situation, and we should handle it as such. We shouldn't be on this beautiful island mad at each other. We are too far away from home for that, and we still want to enjoy our vacation, don't we? Why don't we all agree to talk to the women first and see what type of response we will get? It may not be as negative as we think; they may have all been innocent, you know how those women think. Do you ladies agree with me or not?"* Jewel asked. Even though, Jewel asked the women to agree to be civil to the others, she had no intention of allowing Conifa to get away with the way she had been treating her. Jewel wanted answers, and she was sure to get them, just without the help of the other women. Jewel had her own plans on how to get answers from Conifa.

*" Yes I agree,"* Jerry replied.

*"I don't agree, but I will try and go along with this dumb shit!"* Brenda G. said.

*" Look we came on this vacation to have a grand time, and that is what I am going to have,"* Jewel said.

*" So you going to just let them heifers get away with treating you like a lost puppy, huh?"* Brenda G. yelled.

*" I won't say all of that, but there is a way to handle this besides fighting Brenda G,"* Jewel answered.

*" Well my mama always told me to kick a heifer's ass if they came at me in the wrong way. Yall are crazy if you think for one minute that I am going to take crap of those women that y'all so-call friends. Well I want you to know, as long as they respect me, I will respect them, but the minute one of them heifers get crazy, so will I,"* Brenda G. yelled.

*"Let's just calm down, we will handle this as women,"* Jerry answered.

## CHAPTER NINE

## SECRET

John had plans for a getaway with the fellows the minute his wife left. They had very important things to discuss. As soon as he dropped Jewel of at the airport he would go to Las Vegas. There he would meet up with his friends Nathaniel Le, Joe Wright, and Rodney Moore. John had been planning this trip for months; he didn't tell his wife Jewel because he didn't want to hear her mouth. "*All she does is bitch about one thing, or another and quite frankly I am sick of her and her mouth!*" John thought as he drove down interstate 15 on his way to Vegas. He was only about an hour away. Excitement and pleasure were slowly growing in his groin just thinking about the weekend. He had plans of divorcing Jewel, but they were so tied up financially he didn't have a clue how to end their marriage without winding up broke. When he and his wife first got married he was had some love for her. After the first year John started to lose interest in his wife. He was angry with her for not allowing him to get his half of her money, which was the only reason her married her. "*Sure before I married Jewel the twenty million was all hers, but now it belonged to both of us, as well as them million she won at Stateline.*" John thought as he pulled into a gas station to fill his truck up again. His wife didn't want him to spend any of the money. She had promised him that she would split her winnings with him, but so far she hadn't. She did allow him to buy a business, but it wasn't doing very well. John needed money, or his business would go under; he had a plan, but first he had to meet with Nathaniel to put his plan in motion. He wasn't going to spend the rest of his life in misery with his wife. "*I will find a way out of this hell hole I manage to crawl into eight years ago.*" John saw the State Line sign; he knew that he would soon be at the Flamingo Hotel with his buddies tossing shots up. He couldn't wait for all the young ladies in skimpy attire to sit on his lap and give him lap dances. Over the years, he had not been able to do what he wanted to because of

Jewel's bitching, but tonight he would have the time of his life. Just at that moment John's cell phone rings, he answered it.

*"Hey babe, are you there already,"* John asked the person on the other end of the phone.

*"Yes I'm here waiting for you,"* the person on the phone said.

*"What are you wearing babe?"* John asked.

*" I am only wearing my golden brown velvety skin, sweetheart it is all for you."*

*" I will be there in four hours; I just left home babe, keep it warm for me, okay,"* John answered.

*"I sure will; I have been waiting for this night for a long time babe."*

*" I know, so have I, it's been too long without you babe,"* John replied.

*'So tell me why we didn't just get a room together babe?"* the person on the other end of John's phone asked.

*"I told you babe, I got a lots of business going on here this weekend; don't you remember?* John questioned.

*"But we still could have gotten a room together John, what is the problem, why do I need to stay over here alone?"*

*" Come on now babe, I will be there first thing in the morning. I am coming straight to you as soon as I hit Vegas babe,"* John answered.

*"Are you sure John, don't have me waiting for you and you don't show!"*

*"See you soon babe, I can't wait!"* John said.

*" I love you so much John, please don't leave me hanging!"*

*"Damn girl, will you please stop it, I am not going to leave you hanging!"* John replied.

## CHAPTER TEN

## THE WOMEN REUNITES

No one wanted to make a call to find the other women because placing a phone call was so expensive. Jewel decided to call Miss. Prissy; there was no other way to locate the women unless someone reached out. It had to be Jewel, the one that always tried to make sure everything went smooth. Miss. Prissy answered her phone.

*"Hey Prissy, where are you guys?"* Jewel asked.

*"We are down on the beach; did you all just get in?"* Miss. Prissy asked as if nothing ever happened.

*"Yes we did a few hours ago,"* Jewel answered.

*"Okay, I'm happy you all are here, come on down,"* Miss. Prissy answered.

*"Ok, we will be right down, what part of the beach are you on?"* Jewel asked.

*"We are down by the Yacht Golden Sails Club, by the Royalty Express,"* Miss. Prissy replied.

*"Oh, ok, that's where our room is located, we are on our way,"* Jewel answered.

Jewel, Jerry and Brenda G. finally located Miss. Prissy and Conifa. The ladies were relaxing in bathing suits on the white powdery sand on Sunset Beach; Conifa's bathing suit been the skimpiest. Miss. Prissy as always dressed to impress, she wore a two piece bathing suit that covered her body, she was a lady of class and elegant. Tara and Dolly were a few steps away sipping on cocktails; they were being entertained by four impressive and unique Jamaican men; the men complemented the scenery, giving it a spectacular view. Jewel had done her research on Jamaican men and also their women before she left the states. She was aware of their friendly charm; she had heard that the charm of these men had melted many maiden hearts; that they were Casanova's; very dramatic and straight to the point. *"They can be very cunning, looking for American women as a ticket of the island,"* a gentleman in the states once told her.

*"Hi ladies,"* Jewel said to Miss. Prissy and Conifa; *"it look like you are all settled in and having a blast."*

*"Yes we are, I apologies for the mix up at the airport Jewel, but lord knows I thought you all were already on the plane. When I ask Conifa, that is what she told me,"* Miss. Prissy said.

*"The ticket agent said everyone in wheelchairs was already on the plane. I assumed you were one of the handicapped people that got on first. When you girl's went to the bathroom, we all went to get drinks, when we came back people were loading. I am sorry for the mix up ladies, but it wasn't our fault,"* Conifa said.

*"Yeah right, you guys could have checked, you heifer's just didn't care!"* Brenda G. yelled.

*"If you say so, I mean I am not going to argue with you about it. You can believe whatever you want to believe,"* Conifa answered.

*"Conifa you are full of crap and you know it, so just cool it okay!"* Brenda G. yelled in her super high pitched tone; which was the tone she used when she was about to fight; a tone that would make anyone want to run away from the sound of her voice.

*"Ok ladies, come now, there is no need to get upset. We are here; we are going to have a wonderful time, so let's get this party started!"* Jewel said.

*"I am with you Jewel,"* Miss. Prissy answered.

*"Me too,"* Jerry said with a huge smile; *I am going to go and sit with Dolly and Tara is; it is time to get my drink on."*

Jerry turned her attention to the ladies at the bar. She yelled at them, *"Hey, you'll, I am on my way over there, and I need me a shot of something."*

*"Come on over and meet our friends,"* Dolly yelled back.

*"I am going with you,"* Jewel said walking in the direction of the bar. Even though, Jewel didn't drink alcohol beverages she certainly did her research on Jamaica's finest smoothies and non-alcoholic beverages. She had a list of tropical drinks that she wanted to try. First she would try the nonalcoholic Virgin Mary, which is a bloody Mary without the boozes; next she would try her favorite virgin Jamaican margarita; she would try all the ones on her list.

*"How long have you all been here?"* Dolly asked once Jewel was seated at the bar.

*"A couples hours or so,"* Jewel replied.

*"Oh, sorry you all were left behind; girl I was torn trying to figure out what happened back there at that airport. You know we were told that you were already on the plane, right?"* Dolly questioned Jewel.

*"That's what Prissy told us; I would have looked for you all,"* Jewel answered.

*"So you wanted us to miss the plane for you, right?"* Conifa asked as she walked up to the bar to get herself a drink.

*"No one expected for you to stay behind and look for us. When you got your ass on that plane, all you had to do was look to see if we were there. Scan the plane; easily you would have noticed that three Afro American women that you have known forever weren't on the plane. I know better, so stop trying to convince me that you cared Conifa!"* Jewel replied. Jewel was beginning to feel some type of way toward Conifa and her nonchalant attitude about the whole ordeal; it was becoming more unpleasant to listen to her lying mouth. Conifa didn't know that Jewel's emotions were running high at the moment; she was too stupid to know that it would be best for to keep her opinions to herself right now. *"Jewel, don't take your frustrations out on me, whatever your*

*problems are has nothing at all to do with me, I'm just saying,"* Conifa said in a *very sarcastic way.*

It was as if she knew something that Jewel didn't. Jewel didn't take her comments very well; all she could do was leave before she erupted into tiny small pieces and start whipping on Conifa's. She grabbed her drink and walked over to where Miss. Prissy was sitting; Brenda G. followed closely behind her; at the moment, if no one was her true friend Brenda G. sure was. She was there for Jewel; she made sure that everyone knew that Jewel was her home girl, her dog for life.

*"What happened?"* Brenda G. asked Jewel.

*"That woman is getting on my last nerve girl,"* Jewel said.

*"I told you that she was full of shit; you just will not listen!"* Brenda G. said.

*"I know, but I always give a person a chance to fry their behind!"* Jewel replied.

*"Well, I guess her black ass is fried by now, right?"* Brenda G. asked Jewel.

*"If it isn't, it should be, I have so many questions where she is concerned. It will take time to sort it all out, get answers, but meanwhile, I will try and stay away from her,"* Jewel answered.

*"That would be best; I don't want to beat the crap out of your fake ass friend"* Brenda G. replied.

*"What are you ladies talking about?"* Miss. Prissy asked joining in the conversation.

*"Oh, nothing much, just admiring the view,"* Jewel answered.

*"Isn't it beautiful here on this island?"* Miss. Prissy asked.

*"Yes, this is paradise, so romantic; I secretly wished John was here,"* Jewel said as she laid her head back on the lounge chair.

*"Child all these hunks of gorgeous eye candies running around here, please have a good time. John will be right where you left him; you can see him when you get back. He knows you are his bread and butter,"* Miss. Prissy said.

*"So are you saying just because I am his bread and butter I can't think of him?"* Jewels asked.

*"Don't get bent out of shape baby doll, I was just kidding around,"* Miss. Prissy said; she was confused as hell at Jewel's attitude. She didn't realize that Jewel was still upset with her because of the remarks she made about John having an affair with Conifa.

*"I don't see how Jewel is getting bent out of shape Prissy, she has right to want her husband here, he is hers you know!"* Brenda G. snapped at Prissy.

*"It is okay,"* Jewel answered. *"I am going to go up to my room now and take a shower, and get some rest; it was such a long flight. See you ladies at breakfast in the morning.*

*"Don't leave so soon, the fun is just starting, they are getting ready to set up the band. There is a party on the beach tonight,"* Miss. Prissy said.

*"No, I am too exhausted for that tonight girl,"* Jewel answered.

*"Me too, but first I got to get my groove on, I will be up later on Jewel,"* Brenda G. said.

*"Okay, what time you want to meet for dinner Jewel?"* Miss. Prissy asked.

*"I don't know; I have to look at the menu and see. I will call your room and let you know,"* Jewel said as she got up to leave.

*"Wait a minute, where are you going?"* Jerry asked while holding not one but two shot glasses of patron in her hand and a very tall attractive Jamaican man with the other hand. Jerry was working her magic; her friendly personality and charming ways were magnets for men, just as Tara's. Jewel

often wished she still had the charming personality that she use to have but over the years she had changed, became insecure and unsure of so many things. She promised herself that this vacation would help her re-align her life.

*"I am going up to our room Jerry,"* Jewel replied.

*"Ok, but why are you going in so soon?"* Jerry asked.

*"Girl, I am dog tired! You mean to tell me I am the only one tired?"* Jewel questioned Jerry.

*"Yes I guess you are,"* Jerry said with a sly smile, looking over at the handsome hunk on her arm.

*"I will be up in a minute or two; I am going to hang out with Jerry for a while,"* Brenda G. said.

*"Sure girl, you can hang with me and Angel; babe do you have someone for my friend?"* Jerry asked in her drunken voice.

*"They will be at the party tonight, here on the beach,"* Angel said.

*"Ok, I'm gonna grab me a drink and go with Jewel; I will be back later for the party tho. Are they gonna have some of that good ole smoke? I know you know what I'm talking about!"* Brenda G. laughed.

Jewel was just happy to get back to her room and retired for the evening. Her journey, thus far, had been overwhelming to say the least. The distant from Los Angeles to Montego Bay along was exhausting; needless to say she had to deal with the other ladies. Later she would take time and look over her itinerary and the tour packages that Conifa so carefully put together for all of them. Thinking back on the whole ordeal the way that Conifa and the women left her in LA, Jewel needed to make sure that everything was in order, she refuse to be left behind again. She needed to know what time they would meet for breakfast; what time was the tour to

're-

Negril. She took a shower, and slipped into an old worn-out pair of pajamas' her favorites that she wore when carefree and relaxed. Now comfortable in her pajamas she went into the kitchen to see what was in the refrigerator. The Jamaican hostess had thought of everything. In the refrigerator there were fruits to make the best and healthiest Jamaican smoothie such as; "*Otaheite Apple, Star Apples, Sweetsop, Tangerines and Sour Orange.*"Jewel decided to use *Otaheite apple*, she'd heard it has a burst of sweetness to it; it was also known to be a good way of hydrating. Jewel needed hydration; she was quite exhausted from traveling; right now she was in need of a burst of sweetness. She also used the fruit called, "*Star Apple*. A delicious fruit with variations of dark purple to green with a soft pulp flesh core. Jamaican people referred to the star apple as the "mean" fruit because even after they are ripened they still cling to the stem. It offered sweet satisfaction, but the skin is very bitter. Jewel used the pulp in place of milk to make her smoothie. Jewel took a sip of her smoothie; "*It isn't anything like my caramel frappe from Star Bucks. It is healthier though,*" Jewel said to herself as she walked over to the sliding glass door and entered the terrace. She felt a monstrosity imbalance of her nervous system; the feeling from jet lag and the commotion with the women had her upside down both physically and mentally

"*I am going to sit out here for a while girl, I want to see the view and try to relax myself. Girl that plane ride was something else,*" Jewel said to Brenda G.

The terrace where she sat was bordered by colonnades; a platform paved with plants which adjoined the building; it had its own private garden with a waterfall. It was simply beautiful. "*This is a paradise,*" Jewel thought; she looked across the street toward the park, she wondered where all the men went. "*Oh my, Jewel thought, they are still out here, I wonder if any of them saw me changing clothes. Shoot, I was standing right in front of the window. I'd totally forgotten they were over there, oh well, whatever, nothing that I can do about it now.*"

Amidst the swaying palms and shimmering water, there sat Jewel, at an all-inclusive Sunset Beach Resort & Spa in Montego Bay, Jamaica. A resort that had something for everyone to enjoy; including fresh new sparkling restaurants and bars with sleek, contemporary designs; it was a beautiful array of paradise. There was a magnificent Water Park at the resort; it was called Pirate's Paradise; it had slides with twists, turns and rides for all ages. "*My beachfront resort,*" Jewel thought as she sat sipping her smoothie. She looked toward the heavens and whispered, "*Thank you Jesus, thank you!* She was so caught up in the view she didn't even notice patron sipping Jerry had joined her on the terrace.

"*How did you know where I was?*" Jewel asked Jerry.

"*BG. Told me you were out here,*" Jerry answered.

"*Oh, okay,*" Jewel replied.

The geographic location of the resort provided fantastic views of the night sky when it was bright and clear. Through her telescope Jewel could see the Milky Way; there were many other celestial delights in the clear transparent sky that lingered over Montego Bay.

"*What do you have in that cup of yours?*" Jerry questioned.

"*A smoothie, where were you when I was making it?*" Jewel asked.

"*I was in the shower, washing off California!*" Jerry jokingly replied.

"*Jerry and her empty platitudes, she made the most prosaic statements sometimes.*" Jewel thought to herself while gazing at the Milky Way.

"*Do you want to see the Milky Way Jerry?*" Jewel asked.

"*No, the only Milky Way I want to see is that beautiful man that was on the beach!*" Jerry answered. She couldn't suppress her desire for the Jamaican man she met earlier.

*"Child that man probably has ten wives; you know what they say about these men over here. Even Stella got mixed up with a Jamaican man, married him and then found out that he was gay. Now I don't have anything to do with folk's sexual preferences but my goodness, I would have been sick to my stomach. You have to be careful girl, take it slow!" Jewel* said. Even though, Jewel was saying all the right words there were a few studs she seen on jet skis that instantly turned her head around a time or two.

*"What's up helfa's?"* Brenda G. said as she entered the sliding glass doors onto the terrace. She pulled up a chair and sat down. Crossing her legs and lighting up her blunt. She took hit of her blunt and started coughing.

*"This is some good shit! What that damn man was trying to do, kill me?"* She yelled after she finally regained her composure.

*"You better put that stuff down before one of them Jamaican police officer gets you. If they lock you up over here, you won't ever get out; you will be a distant memory! People can say what they want to say about that Ganja and such on this Island, but you better believe the police quell on such behavior; they forcibly put this behavior down! "Yes, Rasta's smoke big Ganja here, but they smoke it up in them hills you see over there, not on Sunset Beach fool"* Jerry said with a serious look on her face.

*"Helfa, where did you hear that shit at?"* Brenda G. asked with a confused look on her face.

*"You better watch cold case files!"* Jerry replied.

*"Cold case files, girl? You are saying the first thing that comes to your mind!"* Jewel said and burst out laughing.

*"I don't know why you're laughing Jewel; it's that reality show that comes on television that them smugglers be bringing drugs across the border into the United States."* Jerry yelled.

"*That show is not called any cold case files; it's something else; I just can't think of it right now!*" Jewel replied.

"*Hey Jewel, when you have the time, I need to talk to you about something, it's pretty serious,*" Brenda G. said. She always wanted to bring up serious conversations when she got high off her so-called medicine.

"*I guess so, depends on what is it that you want to talk about,*" Jewel answered.

"*I think it would be better if we talked alone,*" Brenda G. said.

"*What do you have to say that Jerry can't hear?*" Jewel asked.

"Yeah, what do you have to say that you don't want me to hear Brenda G.?" Jerry inquired.

"*We will talk about it later, it is time for me to turn in; shit I hope this heifer didn't bring that damn man to the room!*" Brenda G. yelled as she got up to leave.

"*Alright, goodnight girl; you are crazy; see you in the morning,*" Jewel answered.

Jewel thought about Brenda G.'s statement for a minute, "*BG. must have wanted to talk about Tara and her looseness.*"

"*I think we are all here to have fun, what happens in Jamaica stays in Jamaica!*" Jewel said loudly as Brenda G. left the terrace.

"*What was that all about?*" Jerry asked.

"*Girl, I don't know, you know BG,*" Jewel answered.

While Jewel was talking, Jerry picked up a few brochures from a table nearby; she didn't want to hear Jewel's lie, saying she didn't know what was on Brenda G.'s mind. Jerry knew better; those two were very close friends and they told each other everything. There were a few serious matters that Jewel was keeping under wrapped until the time was right, and then everyone would know the Southern Bell that she really was. As Jerry read the articles, she mentioned to Jewel about a few nightclub nearby; "*The Pier, oh my here is another one. This one has so much entertainment for us to enjoy. It's called "The Margarita Ville," girl they say that the club doesn't close. These clubs stay open all night here in Jamaica; damn girl, look at these pictures of these skinny girls in this club, they need to gain weight.*"

Jewel looked at a few of the brochures. "*I do see variations through-out these brochures; the girls are rather slim. I wonder why?*" Jewel thought as she turned the pages of the club brochure.

"*Margarita Ville is perfect for anyone looking for excitement and entertainment,*" Jewel said as she glanced through the brochure; *it looks like a lively, fun atmosphere; it says that they have delicious food and fun concoctions. It is only a short ten-minute ride from "Pier One" via a taxi or one of Sunset beaches shuttle buses. I think we should try "The Pier first, what do you think?*"

"*Sounds like a grand idea; let's see what Prissy and the other women have to say tomorrow, if they don't want to come then we three can go alone, you ready for bed?* Jerry asked.

"*Yea, okay, I am pretty darn tired!*" Jewel laughed; *we can do this tomorrow. Girl this is so exciting I don't even know if I can rest tonight. I wonder what kind of day tomorrow will bring.*"

"*We are going to have fun and whole lots of it, that's what kind of day it's gonna be!*" Jerry said in excitement.

"*You are right,*" Jewel said as she closed the sliding glass doors to the terrace. Jewel mind was heavy; she couldn't get the thought that Conifa and her husband may be having an affair. "*If he had to fool around with someone why would it be Conifa?*" Jewel thought while climbing into bed. She would have to confront Conifa; she only had to figure out when and where. Tomorrow she would decide what to do; she would finally get to the bottom of this rumor. Jewel knew that she wouldn't be able to enjoy herself on the vacation with a rumor of deceit hanging over her head. Maybe it wasn't true; maybe Conifa would be nice and tell her the truth. If Conifa was banging her husband she could have his no good ass, but she would have to pay a healthy price for him. Jewel would not allow Conifa to get away clean for ruining her marriage. She had heard that there were a slew of women that thought fooling around with marriage men were okay. Jewel had morals; she would never get involved with a married man, or a man that was in a relationship with someone for that matter. *"And here this tramp is leaving tracks all over the place like she is completely free to do so. The most hardcore part of the entire scenario was that Conifa is still pretending to be my friend; I should have believe it when that woman told me that Conifa had an extreme taste for enema scat sex. She probably was trying all that shit out on my husband."* Jewel remembered back to the evening of her exotic sex party when Conifa was acting as if she didn't like exotic toys when all the time she was participating in enema scat porn.

*"Goodnight Jewel,"* Jerry mumbled as she yarned and turned over for a good night sleep. Jerry had one too many drinks earlier with that Jamaican Rasta. Now she was all pooped out, Jewel hoped Jerry wouldn't have a hangover the next morning.

*"Goodnight girl, welcome to Jamaica!"* Jewel said.

*"Welcome to Jamaica girlfriend and goodnight again!"* Jerry said slurring her words out.

*"Girl, just be quiet and go to sleep with your intoxicated butt"* Jewel laughed.

*"I know I've had one too many to drink, but is so hard to go to sleep,"* Jerry answered. *"I am too excited; what are some of the things you want to do in the morning?*

*"We just discussed this very same thing, do you remember? We are going to call the ladies' first thing in the morning and see if they want to go to those clubs; then get breakfast, and go into town. If we don't get some sleep tonight neither one of us will be doing anything in the morning!"* Jewel said.

*"Girl you act older than me, you know we supposed to be having a pajamas party tonight!"* Jerry said jokingly.

*"Ok drunk woman who tell lies, there will be no pajama party going on in here; we can do that tomorrow night after we rest up. But since you want to keep talking let me talk to you about something that is weighing heavy on my mind. I would tell Brenda G. but I know she will start a fight."* Jewel said.

Sitting up in the bed, eyes wide opened, Jerry questioned Jewel, *"A fight, Brenda G., girl what are you talking about?"* She asked.

*"I have wanted to talk with you about this, I did want to wait until the end of our vacation to bring it up, but it is too overwhelming!"* Jewel said.

*"Lawd child, what the heck is it?"* Jerry screamed.

*"Alright, alright, here it goes, right before we came on our trip I found out from Miss. Prissy that there is a possibility that Conifa and John are involved, like having an affair."* Jewel answered

*"Involved, having an affair with who; what, how and when!"* Jerry shouted.

*"Stop talking so loudly, I don't want the neighbors to hear this,"* Jewel whispered.

*"But how the hell is that possible?"* Jerry questioned.

"I don't know, but I need to talk to Conifa about it. I don't want to ruin everyone's trip. What should I do?" Jewel asked.

"*You better confront that woman right now. And if you don't I will. I knew something was wrong with her, I just knew it,*" Jerry answered.

"*It's surprising to me, I can't believe she did something like this,*" Jewel said.

"*I know you and there is no way possible for you to enjoy yourself with all that crap on your mind, the best thing to do is confront her right away Jewel,*" Jerry reiterated.

"*I know, but the thing that makes it so hard is, I keep second guessing myself about John cheating with this woman. It's just so hard to see him with the likes of Conifa, and I don't want to look like a fool!*" Jewel said.

"*Yeah, it sounds pretty damn strange,*" Jerry answered.

"*It could be something else, I don't know, that's why I have to find out,*" Jewel told Jerry.

"*Yes, you do; make sure you get to the bottom of it; good night girl. You don't have time to be walking around with all that on your mind. If you need some help dealing with her, I got your back. I'm here for you. Brenda G. isn't the only friend that you have on this island.*" Jerry said.

"*Oh my Lord; now why you feel the need to bring B.G. into the conversation?*" Jewel asked.

"*I'm just saying that I have your back, Jewel, but if you must know, it's because you usually go to B.G. when you have a problem, like she is the only loyal friend that you have. I appreciate that this time you confided in me, that's all.*" Jerry replied.

*I appreciate you also Jerry, I know that you are a loyal friend to me. B.G. has been in my life for twenty plus years that's why I confide in her so much. I love you,* *Goodnight girl,*" Jewel said.

"*I love you more Jewel,*" Jerry answered.

## CHAPTER ELEVEN

## REVENGE

After a long exhausting trip John finally made it to Las Vegas; he couldn't wait to get to his room at the Flamingo Hotel. The trip had been a long time coming for John and his gangster friends. They had carefully planned it, and nothing would stop them; they had been working for years to bring Jewel and her friends to their knees. Ralph's Barkmans' companies' assets had been transferred over to his wife Conifa when he died several years ago. Conifa also inherited her husbands' stocks, bonds and investment properties; she had nothing ever again to worry about. Barkmans' Estates dealt with millionaires only; it was one of the most lucrative real estate's businesses in the southern California as well as Nevada. John's and his gangster friends manipulated their way into Ralph Barkman circle of friends and their business venture. They felt that Barkman's Estates was on top of the world, and could afford to invest a few million into their plan of action. After parking John got out of his truck in front of the hotel and took a long stretch; shaking his muscled legs, moving them back and forth. A friendly mannered hotel porter rushed to his aide; he welcomed John and saw to his needs. The porter had smart appearances and great customer service skills.

*"May I take your bags sir?"* The porter asked.

*" Yes, please, "* John said.

*"Do you have your VIP card?"* The hotel porter asked.

*"Sure, here you go young man, "* John answered.

The porter retrieved all of John's suitcases from the back seat of his truck and stacked them on a transporting cart; he then pushed the suitcases inside the hotel. The parking attendant whisked John big Ford f150 away and parked it in the parking garage. He had plans of riding in Nathaniel's'

Bentley the entire weekend. His heart-pounded with excitement at the thought of what was about to take place as he checked into the Flamingo Hotel. His room was one of Flamingos' finest; a blend of modern and vintage furnishings; the chic lighting from the classic Vegas art that centered the huge wall rounded off the vintage meets modern experience. The wood toned floors and chaise lounges added to the elegant atmosphere. Flamingo's signature pink roses were added to the space for a touch of class. The two pillow top king beds were covered with rose's buds pedals. This enhanced John's desire to call his girl right away, but he needed to see his partners first. They were supposed to meet at eight p.m. in the Flamingo's lobby; he took a shower and changed clothes. John was ready to eat, drink, look at the pretty girls and have some fun gambling. John lied to his other business partner who was waiting in another hotel for him. He'd just spoke to her not longer than an hour ago, telling her that he was just leaving home, now he's already in Vegas and off to have fun with his buddies. John didn't care; he was finally running his life, and no one was going to rush him.

*"She will just have to wait,"* John thought as he got dressed in a casual outfit of blue jeans and a Polo shirt. He threw on a pair of vans and off he went. The elevator was too crowded and John couldn't wait to get off. John never liked small, crowded spaces. He was told that when he was a young boy that his childhood rivals use to lock him in the closet. When John reached the lobby the first person, he saw was Ralph Barkman's cousin Joe Wright. Joe Wright was an only child of Ralph's mother's twin sister. The sisters were very close all their lives; after high school they moved out of state and went to separate colleges. In the early nineties after graduating college and getting their degrees they decided on settling back in Los Angeles, their hometown. Moving in the same neighborhood and raising their boys together created an even tighter bond between the sisters. They were even pregnant together, had their babies the same month, three weeks apart. The boys hung out and played difference sports together; the sport they loved

the most was track and field, being an athlete was a gift that God had blessed the boys with. In nine-teen-eighty their twelfth grade year of high school, they were hurt in a car accident on the way home from practice. Ralph had broken ligaments in twenty different places in his right leg; the doctor told Ralph that he would never play again. Joe said it was the coach's fault. He believed the coach was under the influence of drugs on the day of the accident. The coach was the driver of the van that carried the boys from one place to the other. Joe told the police what he suspected, and they did nothing about it. The judge decided not to file charges against the coach. Joe was so torn up over the Judge's decision that he quit the track team. After Ralph healed and was back on his feet, he returned to school. They both finished high school in May of nine-teen-eighty-one with high honors; Joe with a three-point-eight and the Ralph with a four-point-zero. Joe and Ralph were in their early-twenties when they graduated college. The pair started a small business together on the west side of Los Angeles called Barkmans and Wrights Brokerage. They worked together till the day Ralph passed away; at the mere thought of his relative, his close friend passing sometimes still caused Joe to tear up. Joe would always believe that Ralph's untimely death was at the hands of a murderer. Joe swore that one day he would find out who killed his cousin, his best friend. He too believed that Conifa had something to do with it, or she knew who did it. Joe wanted his share of the business after Ralph's sudden death; however, there was a "clause" in the will, a summarized statement that prevented Joe from equally owning half of their business.  The way Ralph had the documents/will/trust accounts setup with the lawyers Joe was left out in the cold. He received a small settlement at the end of the final probate hearing. All those years Joe thought he was an equal owner.  When Ralph married Conifa his personality changed, and unknown to Joe at the time he even removed codes from their national terminals, and NCR which allowed Joe to see the business records and proceeds, their business profits. Ralph had control while Joe's leverage and percentage were reduced to zero; which allowed Conifa to receive commissions on all sales. She had the last say on all transactions, broker loans and hiring and firing. Joe Wright wanted Conifa to step down, but she wouldn't until the blackmailing.

*"One day I promise I would find the truth, I will get what rightfully belongs to me,"* Joe promised himself. Someone had been deceptive, had deliberately and fraudulently changed the document in order to secure unlawful gain to his share. Joe was exceptionally great at smelling a rat and taking over companies when they were at their weakest. Joe would be there to snatch the company before anyone else even heard about it. Now to think that someone did the same thing to him made him angry; yet at the end of the day he couldn't figure out how Conifa outsmarted everyone as she did. Over the years Joe Wright, Nathaniel Le, and John became very close friends, business partners, sharing ideas and making huge investments into Swiss bank accounts on the coast of Jamaica. Jewel had no idea about the guy's dealings. As far as Jewel knew Nathaniel's and John brother-hood relationship didn't go any farther than repairing John's old jalopy and having laughs over a few beers every now and again. Now Joe, a forty-one year old Italian business tycoon was in charge; he was the big boss standing six feet eight and wearing size fifteen shoes. He was a gorgeous hunk of a man. His skin was smooth and silky, as if a caramel sundae dripped over his entire body. He wore a bald-head with a full beard; his teeth were snow white and sparkled when he smiled. John and Nathaniel had to get Joe's approval before they could proceed with any of their investment ideas. He was the master-mind behind all of their dealings, even the fraudulent ones. Joe Wright was the master and chief!

*"All those years I spent working behind the scene with Ralph Barkman is finally going to pay off for me. Now is my chance,"* Joe said as he sat in an oversized chair, in the Flamingo hotel lobby thinking to himself while holding a racing form in his hand. His mind was far away from Vegas; heavy in thought, he was about to embark on a fortune of a lifetime..

*"Hey man, what up homey?"* John asked when he noticed Joe sitting there.

're——

*"Aw same ole thing my brother, what you got going Jack?* Joe asked while showing brotherly love with a hug and a handshake."

Joe had names for all the guys and the girls too. He had a giant personality and a heart of gold until someone crossed him, or he felt as if he had been crossed. Either way Joe Wright was a force to be reckoned with. He loved laughter and fun when it was time for partying, but Joe didn't play when it came down to business; he said that a man should never mix business and pleasure.

*"Where is the rest of the Mohegan's?"* John asked.

*"Man they are in the restaurant; they sent me out here to look for you. Where is your other half?"* He questioned John.

*"Man you know Jewel is in Jamaica,"* John said.

*"I am not talking about Jewel!"* Joe replied.

*"Aw damn man, she over at the hotel,"* John answered.

*"Ah man, how you manage that?"* Joe asked.

*"I am the man boy! I thought you knew by now!"* John replied as he puffed his chest, showed off his muscles.

*"Okay partner, if you say so, come on let join the others, we have a long weekend and lots of paperwork to get prepared, sign and filed. We have to get this stuff cracking if we want to get everything in place before those women get back here!"* Joe laughed.

*"Yeah, I know, you right man, you right, you are exactly correct,"* John answered.

Entering the Flamingo's restaurant where the other guys were seated, Joe and John settled in at the bar. They had a few cocktail before one of the men decided he wanted to eat elsewhere.

*"You know we don't have to stay here, let get out of here and see the Vegas strip. That why this place is called Sin City's, we have got to sin, and besides there are so many other dazzling eateries on the strip. I heard they had the world's top chefs at Masa; which is the most respected Japanese restaurant in the city; over there they use seasons that soak up flavor and character,"* Joe informed the others.

*"Sounds great to me, all in favor say I,"* John said.

*"The I's have it,"* Joe said before anyone could agree. They walked down the strip to Bar Masa. Once inside of Bar Masa, they were seated. The waitress came over to where the men were seated.

*"Hello, what are you all having?"* The waitress asked.

*"We are ready to order,"* the four men said simultaneously.

*"We will have a starter's salads with sides, let me see, ah yes, give me the seafood; red mullet and lavraki in sea salt; I will order desserts later,"* Joe told the waitress.

*"We decided to have the kakavia soup; grilled octopus; crudo and crab cakes,"* Nathaniel spoke for him and the other men. When served, the men said that by far it was the most dazzling seafood dish that they'd ever seen.

*"Alright everyone, let us dig in,"* Rodney said, he had been quiet for most of the evening. The guys finished up dinner and headed for the dance floor. Joe Wright was the first one out on the dance floor; he grabbed the cocktail waitress around the waist and took her out for a spin. The waitress looked at him and smiled, placing her tray of drinks on the table where the other men sat; she gave Joe a quick lap dance.

Rodney yelled, *"get it girl, you better Werk that thang!"*

*"Rodney must have a strong love for Vegas showgirls like I do!"* John thought to himself as he sat at the bar watching the girls clapping their derrieres. *"Wow, look at this one, she is makes beats better than Dr. Dre, clapping that fine*

're—

*ass of hers!"* he said loudly. One of the girls turned toward John and shook her ass in his face. When she bent over an inch from John's face and began shaking her ass, drool fell from John's mouth. All he could think about was, *"if only I could get a taste of her juiciness, it would sure make my night."* Even though, John knew that his weekend was booked up, he would make time for this beautiful woman anytime and any day. After thinking about it for a minute or two John changed his mind; he couldn't get involved with anyone right now. O' girl was over at the other hotel waiting for him to show up; John turned his phone off earlier so if she tried to track him she wouldn't be able to. She would have to realize that he wasn't going to be there with her as they had planned; he would try to make it tomorrow morning before his meeting with the guys. Nathaniel Le found him a big girl; she had a figure like a coke cola bottle. He loved Big Beautiful women. They swayed crossed the floor like magic. Nathaniel suddenly reached down and grabbed a chunk of the girl's jelled ass. She didn't take too kindly to his actions; she slapped the crap out of him and left the dance floor. Nathaniel couldn't believe that the girl hit him. He started to go after her, but decided that it would be his best interest to leave it alone. The guys hung out for a while longer; they all knew that the rest of the weekend was dedicated to the takeover. After a couple of hour of flirting and fun the four gentlemen decided to walk the few blocks back to their hotel. They practically had to carry Joe Wright's intoxicated behind.

*"Stand up man!"* Nathanial yelled at Joe.

*" I am standing up Jack! What you think I am doing, crawling "Jack, Man? Hey, which one of the Jacks are you?"* Joe asked in a drunken stupor.

*"Look guys, all we have to do is get under his arms like this, he can walk!"* John said.

*" Damn right I can walk and don't you motherfucking Jack-O-Ladden ever forget it!"* Joe yelled.

*"Ah man come on now; take a break on all that cussing. We are only trying to help you!"* John said with a firm tone.

*"Yea man, no one told you to toss those shots back like that,"* Rodney said. Rodney, a newcomer to Barkman Realtors, remembers back to the weekend when he first met John. Jewel's stepson Ha-kin had spent the day at the horse races with John when suddenly Rodney appeared out of nowhere; he was stunning and debonair; a charmer, a tall, thin, muscular stallion with an awesome personality. He loved speaking to crowds about God's healing and his salvation/eternal life. Rodney grew up on the south side of Chicago; his parents were both Baptist preachers. For the most part, Rodney lived a good Christian life; only sometimes his gambling would get in his way. Ha-kin had reservations regarding Johns' love for his mother. He noticed the way that John treated Jewel. Even though, Ha-kin appeared nonchalant about the whole ordeal, he was watching out for Jewel; he kept his eyes on his mother's personal affairs. There was no way that he would allow anyone to victimize her. John was misleading Jewel by concealing the truth in order to gain access to her fortune. Ha-kin's friend Rodney was one of the best computer analysts around. They met when Rodney applied for a position as a computer technical engineer at Ha-kin's bureau. After running a background check and getting clearance Ha-kin gave Rodney full domains over the National Immigration and Fraud department. When he brought Rodney on board, he told him that they would become best of friends. Ha-kin's knew that Rodney was a God-fearing man, and had outstanding morals, and would be an asset to him in the business world as well as personal affairs. At the office he insisted that Rodney worked with him on this particular high all profile case; it was important that no one else knew that they were working together, not even Jewel. Ha-kin was going to expose John for the crook that he was, and couldn't take a chance on anyone dropping the ball; it was too dangerous; it was top secret. He figured bringing Rodney on board would give him a greater chance for full recovery, for success. Through all the chaos, Ha-kin had forgotten that he

're

had invited Rodney to join them at the track. However, he was elated that Rodney showed up, it meant that he was interested. Now he could put his plan in motion; they would work together to bring these powerful men down.

*"Hey dude, what are you doing here?* Ha-kin asked.

*"Man, tell me you are joking, don't you remember inviting me?"* Rodney asks.

*"Damn man I definitely did forget. I'm sorry dude. Well, come on sit down, have you picked your horses?"* Ha-kin asked.

*"Yeah man, I stopped up there at the window and got my picks. I am betting on "left foot Suzy," shit Paul Maqsubisha is riding her this afternoon!"* Rodney said with an excited look on his face.

*"Hey, meet my stepfather John Du Pree, John this is Rodney."*

Ha-kin introduced Rodney to John; they spent the rest of the afternoon playing the horses.

The men made it back to the Flamingo all in one piece; once inside they helped Joe to his room, undressed him down to his bare nakedness and left him asleep on the couch. It was payback for all the time Joe Wright called them out of their names. *"When he wakes up in the morning he won't remember how he even got to his room let alone who undressed him,"* Nathaniel laughed. *"He will be asking himself, was it that girl that I was with, did she bring me home, and did we have sex?"* These were questions that the guys were sure Joe would ask himself the next morning. They would never tell Joe that it was them that undressed him. *"Let his big macho ass figure it out for his self. He knows everything!"* Nathaniel said. They only tolerated Joe for their gain, but hated the way he treated them while in the company of his high-rolling partners, calling them hideous names that he'd made up for each of them.

*"Hell, we are men just like he is, and I don't appreciate him calling us names!"* Nathaniel said to each other's one day at a meeting that Joe called at the last minute.

*"Hey partners, I want you guys to meet Rodney from the three blind mice team, he is handling this high profile case,"* Joe Wright laughed as he placed a black folder on the conference table. Joe's actions angered Rodney to no end, but he didn't say anything; Rodney had bigger fishes to fry. There was a time when Joe and John came awfully close to connecting blows because Joe was assassinating John's character. Joe would often speak to John as if he was a kid. Joe didn't have any idea what type of a character John was, but he soon found out that John was a man that no one talked slick too and got away with it. John wouldn't ever tolerate Joe's derogatory statements. He made sure Joe Wright knew how much of a man he really was, all six foot of him rested in his man cave of intelligentsia. They could never be great friends because Joe's egotistical ways got in the path of them ever building a trustworthy friendship. However, Joe Wright would come to know and respect the fact that John had formed an artistic elite group of alliances. After making Joe Wright look like a fool, the men left his room, locked Joe's door and headed for the elevator, on their way to their rooms which was in same hotel, but on different floors. When the elevator stopped on John's floor, he quickly got off, his phobia of small spaces started to kick in. As soon as he entered his stylish Las Vegas room he walked over to the window where he admired the breathtaking view of the Vegas strip. It was an alluring experience for John to see how the city could attract a worldwide network of patrons; he wished he'd thought of that idea. As John turned to leave the window he spoke loudly saying, *"And this is the same city that I married Jewel in, it looks like crap in daylight, boy the shit that a man will do in the middle of the night."* John took shower; towel's himself dry and put on his silk pajamas. Stretching out across the huge bed John laid his head on the soft goose down pillows that layered the top of the bed, giving him a heavenly sense of comfort. When John closes his eyes, the first

thing he saw was the exotic dancer from *"Masa."* Immediately John wanted to go back to the restaurant/night club where he saw the beautiful goddess; he desired to see her clap her ass just once more. He could visualize himself rubbing her ass while taking a juicy bite out of crime. *"Yes,* John thought to himself, *"that should have been a crime, something so breathtaking and with movements like she had."* While thinking about the dancer John fell fast asleep.

When John woke up the next morning, he couldn't remember ever falling asleep. *"Oh my, what time is it?"* He looked at the elaborate antique clock that hung on the wall, giving time to this elegant space.

*"Damn, I was exhausted,"* John thought, getting up from his luxurious bed. It was later than he thought; John had to get moving. Ole girl was waiting for him at the other hotel plus he had to meet the men around noon. John rushed to the bathroom; as usual he did the three most important things while he was in the bathroom, *"Shit, shower and shave!"*

As John stood looking in the closet trying to figure outfit he would wear, he remembered back to the day his wife left for her vacation. After dropping Jewel off at the fly away, John went straight to Nathaniel's condominium in north Hollywood hills to pick his friend up for a shopping extravagance. It had always been a part of John's and Nathaniel's plan; they would get the best of everything. They shopped on Rodeo Drive at Battaglia's; one of the most expensive shops in Beverly Hills. John ended up spending ten thousand dollars for Santoni Italian high-end shoes, and a unique Santoni's watch. He spent five-thousands dollar's for his suit, shirt and tie, and another three-hundred fifty dollar's for a pair of black Rectangular Diamante Sunglasses. Everything that John brought Nathaniel also brought for himself. They decided to buy an entire new wardrobe, *"why not?"* John asked Nathaniel.

*"It's not as we will ever have to worry about money again after the take-over."*

# CHAPTER TWELVE

## SECRETS

John dressed in the Valentino tailored three-piece suit which he purchased the moment Jewel left for Jamaica. After getting dressed he checked himself out from a full-length mirror, admiring what God had blessed him with. *"Cacchio, sono, proprio, carina per essere, "damn I look good!"* John said. He had inimitable sense of style as well as good taste, wearing Valentino's special dark Havana's magnified John swag all the more. Just as John was about to leave his room, his cell phone rings;

*"Hello,"* John answered.

*"Hey man,' there have been a change of plans. I think we should meet over lunch and discuss it."* Nathaniel said.

*"Why, the change?"* John asked.

*"I am not sure, something to do with a locked access code, a password and Rodney.* Nathaniel said.

*"Rodney Moore, what's up with that?" John asked. "Look, tell them we don't have time to be changing plans in the middle of the stream like that. We have too much riding on this!"* He was very angry; he had been planning this for too long to have Rodney Moore emasculate it.

*"I don't know man, ask Joe?"* Nathaniel said. *"He's the one who let that youngster up in our business like this. I told you man that kid was too young! He doesn't have a clue about this sort of dealings, and Joe had the nerves to put him over top secret material like this. Man, he is still wet behind the ears, how in the hell is Joe going to let him run anything? When we first started this venture together, you said it would only be you and I involved. Now look at this load of shit; you got him in on this and he's a stupid Moran's at that! I am telling you man; something isn't right, I smell a rat, a low down dirty rat!"*

John sat back in his chair and took a deep breath; he had to calm himself down before he replied to Nathaniel's statement. He didn't want everything to blow up in his face. He had come too far.

*"Aw, come on man, don't let yourself get all worked up, everything is cool, I will work it out,"* John answered in his usual nonchalant tone. *"I allowed this bit of information to get under my skin for a second or two, but no, I will remain cool, I will stay positive and drive this thing home."* John's thought processes were turning a mile a minute. He had no idea what had taken place, but he was sure to get to the bottom of it right away. John knew that Nathaniel had a short temper, a short fuse which could blow any minute. He didn't want to get Nathaniel upset; he may just start popping caps and kill everyone in his path.

*"I have been the same, you slipping man! You let that fool do the computers, he has the information; how are you going to work this one out? Joe just told me a few minutes ago that we need Rodney Moore; we can't access any of the account information to do the transfer! Do you know anything about this?"* Nathaniel asked John in a sarcastic tone. John was under pressure; getting his plan off the ground was no picnic for him or his fellow partners. Every time they got close to closing the deal, unknowingly Jewel blocked their dealings; now it was Rodney trying his hand at being a boss. There was no way that John would let this twenty-five-year-old kid stop him. John, Nathaniel and Joe Wright had put together a great plan, a way to get everything they thought they had coming to them; they would not leave Vegas without it. John remembered back to the first day he met Joe Wright and Ralph Barkman. Conifa threw a huge charity event for, "Ovarian Cancer Awareness." Conifa invited Jewel and the other ladies to her upscale event. Jewel asked John if he would be her plus one and join her for a night out at Conifa's charity ball. Since John and Nathaniel were working together on John old jalopy truck, John felt that it was no more than right to invite his friend; being polite John invited Nathaniel, and he agreed to come. John and Nathaniel met Ralph Barkman and Joe Wright at the charity ball. They

shared investment stories over cocktails and laughter. Joe was the loudest of all, talking about how he and the women of Atlanta celebrated his forties birthday on his yacht. John knew right then that this man mouth was larger than life; he knew he must feed Joe with a long handle spoon, stay his distant from him. It was an interesting night to say the least.

*"Hey John, can you hear me talking to you? What the hell are we going to do?"* Nathaniel asked John.

*"I will handle it, don't you trust me?" John asked.*

*"Yeah man, I trust you; I just don't trust any of them!"* Nathaniel yelled.

*"I will be there shortly; I have to make one stop first, okay man; sat tight, make sure to keep your eyes and ears opened!"* John said as he walked out of his hotel room to the elevator. He was sure to have phobia trauma now, he thought as the monstrous elevator doors opened. John stepped inside the elevator and pushed the button for the first floor. Each time the elevator came to a stop; someone would get on, or someone would get off. John started to panic; on the fifth floor a distinguished gentleman got on; he took one look at John and asked, *"are you okay sir?"*

*"I am fine,"* John said to the gentleman.

*"You sure, you look awful!"* The man said.

*"Sir, I'm fine!"* John replied, hoping that his answer would quiet the man.

The man turned away from John and started talking to another lady that had just gotten on the elevator on the fourth floor. When the elevator came to a stop on the first floor John was one happy camper. His anxieties were high; he needed to take a Xanax to quiet his nerves. Reaching in his pockets he retrieved his pill bottle and took a Xanax; he would be better soon. John hated pills but sometimes he had to take them. He didn't want to appear out of control and nervous when he reached his child mother's room. He longed to touch her soft tender body and taste her sweetness. He thought

're

of his hands exploring her lengthy legs and thighs, her breast, and her nipples as they rose to an erectile rigid point as he kissed them. He had to make up for lost time. John reached the hotel where the love of his life awaited him. He knocked at the door softly; she opened the door and smacked him across the face. John sure as hell didn't expect this; he started to hit her back, but told himself that he couldn't hit a woman. He knew she would be upset when he didn't show up last night. He could have been honest with her, but he chose not to.

*"Why did you hit me Queenly?"* John asked.

*"You already know why, you son-of-a-bitch. You had me sitting here waiting for you all night long by myself. You turned your phone off, so I couldn't reach you, and you ask me why. You are a low-down-dirty-dog John!"* Queenly yelled.

*"First off woman, I was late getting in; my cell phone died on me, and I left my phone charger at home by accident. So don't come getting on my case before you know what is going on Queenly!"* John shouted.

*"You told me that you were coming here to me John; so tell me why couldn't we get a room together? What kind of fool do you think I am? You are just lying John,"* Queenly said.

*"Babe, I told you that I had a huge convention at my hotel, it's just a bunch of guys shooting the breeze babe. I am going to spend all the time with you as I can when this is all over with; don't you know how much that I love you. I admire you; you are the mother of my child,"* John begged for Queenly to understand.

*" You sure as hell do not act like I am the mother of your child; you lie to me all the time. You told me seven years ago that you made a mistake in marrying that woman. Now look at you! You are yet married to her. You probably have her here in Vegas with you. I am sure that's why you didn't come to me last night!"* Queenly yelled.

*"That's not true, you know how I feel about you; don't start making up shit because you hit me,"* John replied.

*"I'm not making up a damn thing; you have been lying, and I want to know if Jewel is here in Vegas right now!"* Queenly yelled again.

*"Queenly is where she is supposed to be; don't worry about her,"* John answered.

*"So just tell me is everything going as planned John? We have Justin to think about,"* Queenly said.

*"You already know that you and Justin will be taken care off; when you came into my life and got pregnant there was no going back to Jewel. I need you and my son Queenly, I need you babe,"* John told Queenly. The pair argued back and forth the rest of the night. John had a difficult time explaining to Queenly, she didn't believe him because he had lied many times before.

*"Every time you will tell me one thing and do another, just like the last time you told me that lie about your anniversary. Do you remember that, huh, you dirty ass man? You told me that you and Jewel wasn't going to celebrate your anniversary, but you did!"*

*"I don't care what I do for you, it's never enough Queenly, I try everything to make you happy. You are the love of my life babe, that woman don't mean shit to me. It's all about the money!"*

*"That's what your mouth say John, but I'm going to need you to prove it to me. Every time I turn around you are doing some more bullshit, like I said all you do is tell one lie after another. I'm sick and tired of you and your damn wife; I'm tired of your damn friends too. I wished to God you all go straight to hell and burn!"*

*"I will, just wait; I will show you how much I love you even if I have to kill that witch!"* He grabbed Queenly and kissed her lips. She held her man in her arms kissing him tenderly. During their lovemaking session Queenly forgot her anger, she only wanted to taste more of John's sweet nature.

're

## CHAPTER THIRTEEN

## THE CONFRONTATION

The warm Jamaica night air flowed gently through an open window and into Jewel and Jerry's upscale lavish bedroom at Sunset beach Resort. The two women had talked themselves to sleep. The next morning when Jewel got up she made herself another smoothie; she was yet exhausted from staying up late the night before. She wanted to get all the vitamins and nutrient that she could from eating Jamaican fruits. After she had dressed, she walked out onto the terrace to wait for Jerry and her other friends to get up. They were supposed to have breakfast together, and plan their activities and tours. Jewel looked to see if the men were in the park again.

*"There were some good looking gentlemen over there last evening,"* she thought to herself. Jewel was a flirt, but she would never cheated on her husband; she had been a loyal wife, but the way John was treating her now, she sometimes wanted out of the marriage. When she thought of the men, she remembered that she had to talk with Conifa. Jewel dreaded having this conversation, but she would have to do it now; today, if she were going to enjoy any of her vacation. Jewel didn't care anymore; this secret was slowly destroying her mentally. She was not a fake; she didn't even know how to pretend she liked someone; she didn't have a poker face. Every time she and Conifa came in contact with each other they would get into a squabble over the tiniest thing.

*"It has to come out today,"* Jewel thought as she took a sip of her smoothie. Jerry was now up and dressed; she came out on the terrace and sat down. She started right in on Jewel about talking to Conifa,

*"Good morning Jewel,"* Jerry said. She was her old happy go lucky self; Jewel knew that Jerry wanted to finish where they left off last evening.

*"Good morning Jerry,"* Jewel said.

"*So what's up, did you decide what you were going to say to Conifa?*" Jerry asked.

"*Yeah, I did, as much as I hate too, I must do it today,*" Jewel said.

"*So fill me in on what the hell is going on. I know you told me some yesterday, but there has got to be more,*" Jerry said.

"*I think she and John is having an affair; I am not sure, but that's what Miss. Prissy insinuated,*" Jewel said.

"*I know that much, tell me details Jewel,*" Jerry yelled.

"*Okay, so listen to this Jerry; I went over to her house one day right before the trip; just to show her a few things. You know what I mean; well I saw a truck on the next block that looked like John's truck, but I ignored it; I told myself that couldn't have been John's truck. When I got to Conifa's house she was half naked and acted very strange; so I asked her what was going on; she got a nasty attitude about my questions. Later when I get home I spoke to John about it, it and he defended Conifa actions. This confused me, so I call Miss. Prissy to speak to her about it; this was when she told me about the gossip from the women in our circle. She said they were saying Conifa and John were up to no-good.*" Jewel said.

"*Now I see why you feel that way, is there anything can I do?*" Jerry asked.

"*Nothing girl, I will handle it, I just wanted to talk to someone about it; I have to figure out what steps to take myself. We better get ready to go down to breakfast. Did you call Brenda G, was she still asleep?*" Jewel asked.

"*No, I called her; she is up. She has smoked her stuff and is ready,*" Jerry laughed.

"*Girl, you are the cutest when you are joking; let's go,*" Jewel told Jerry.

"*Okay girl, I'm ready to go,*" Jerry said exiting their room. They walked off the terrace, through the garden, and out to the beach area where they all were supposed to meet.

The women met up on the beach; they walked together to Seaside restaurant, an all you can eat buffet. It was uncomfortable for Jewel to sit at the table and break bread with Conifa. The entire time during breakfast Conifa was running her mouth. It upset Jewel so much she had to call her out right away. She couldn't stand the deceit any longer.

*"Conifa, may I speak with you privately?"* Jewel asked.

*"I don't have time this morning Jewel; we have to get to the tour bus by ten o'clock. We are all going zip-lining today. Did you look at your itinerary?"* Conifa asked.

*"No, I didn't, maybe I should have. That's all fine and dandy but we need to talk as soon as you get a chance though,"* Jewel said.

*"What is so important that it can't wait?"* Miss. Prissy asked.

*"I think you already know Prissy!"* Jewel said. Miss. Prissy was acting like she didn't have a clue. She knew what Jewel wanted to talk with Conifa about. Miss. Prissy nonchalant attitude was causing Jewel to become angrier.

*"I said we will talk later, there is no need to start our day off on a negative spin,"* Conifa said as she got up from the breakfast table.

*"Wait a minute now heifer, what is going on, and why the hell is you jumping up like that, you better sat back down before you get dealt with!"* Brenda G. yelled at Conifa.

*"It is none of your business Brenda, and Jewel I have an idea what you want to talk about, none of it is true,"* Conifa said.

*"So how would you know what I want to talk about Conifa?"* Jewel asked as she slowly turned her head in Miss. Prissy's direction.

*"Don't look at me; I have not said a word about nothing to Conifa!"* Miss. Prissy said.

"But, Prissy, you are the only one that I talk to about this issue, how else would Conifa know that I wanted to speak to her?" Jewel asked.

"Honey baby, I have no idea!" Miss. Prissy answered.

""I just want to know what the heifer did to you Jewel, that's all," Brenda G. said.

"Hold on Conifa, I'm going with you!" Jewel yelled. She got up from her chair and followed after Conifa.

On the way to the elevator, Jewel asked Conifa what was the secret; "*what is going on between you and John?*"

Conifa was livid; she couldn't believe that Jewel would even suggest something so ridiculous.

"*I would never have sex with John; I am so surprised that you even think something like that Jewel*" Conifa said.

Jewel didn't believe one word from Conifa's deceiving mouth. There were too many clues, and Jewel wasn't stupid as Conifa and John thought.

"*Jewel, honey can we please continue this conversation after our tour? I promise you I have not been with John. I don't know where you are getting your information, but it's not me. Why would you think this anyway, who told you something so awful?*" Conifa asked.

"*Who told me isn't the point! I will ask you one last time Conifa, are you fucking my husband?*"

"*I told you that I am not, and you are pissing me off talking to me like that!*" Conifa yelled.

"*You are getting pissed off; I have been pissed off ever since the day I left your house; the day you were half naked. The same day my husband's truck was on your street witch!"* Jewel yelled back. Now Jewel was ready to whip Conifa's behind.

*"What do you mean by that?"* Conifa asked Jewel; she had a surprised look on her face. *"Jewel what in the world is you talking about?"* She asked.

*"Witch you know what I'm talking about,"* Jewel said. She was inches away from striking Conifa when the other five women made it to the tour bus.

*"What in the world is going on? You all are not about to fight are you?"* Miss. Prissy asked Jewel.

*"Come on ladies, please wait until you calm down to talk about this situation,"* Dolly said. Jewel was so angry at Conifa, she wanted to beat the crap out of her; she needed to finish confronting Conifa, but it was time for the tour bus to leave, and she didn't want the bus of people to hear what she had to say to Conifa; so she decided to wait until they returned back to the resort. It was a good thing that the bus came when it did; Jewel couldn't believe Conifa; she was such as actress; she could fool anyone.

*"She fooled those people when her husband Ralph died, and she got away with it, she will not do that to me,"* Jewel thought to herself; Jewel was sick to her stomach, but she would have to make the best of her time on this adventure. She promised herself that she would get the truth out of Conifa by the end of the day. Conifa was slick, but there was no way Jewel would allow her to get away without revealing the truth. The women were on their way to Ocho Rios, Jamaica; a town with many waterfalls. The shorelines had one hotel after another, warm sand and turquoise waters. Beyond the shoreline Jewel noticed a rainforest like greenery, which blanketed the mountain's landscape. There was lush tropical foliage as far as Jewel eyes could see. The crystal blue water took Jewel's mind off her problems for a while. As they traveled along the shoreline, the bus driver told the group about the different tourist sites along the way. He said that September was the best time of the year to visit Jamaica. Mystic Mountain

Adventure Park was on their tour; Jewel couldn't see herself zip lining, but it sound like so much fun she would take the challenge and do it. At this point, she would do most anything to take her mind of Conifa and John's behavior. The tour bus turned into the parking structure of Ocho Rias's Adventure Park. The women got off the bus and followed the tour guide to the front gate; here they listen to a session of rules and regulations. After the session was over the women were seated on a huge eighty foot swing. The swing seated three people at a time and would take them up to the top of Mystic Mountain. Jewel, Jerry and Brenda G. sat together; Jewel made sure not to sit next to Conifa for fear of pushing her out into the rain forest. Even though, Jewel was a God-fearing woman; there was only so much she could take. She was so angry with Conifa for screwing around with her husband. Tara, Miss. Prissy and Dolly set together. Conifa sat with another group of women from Canada. The giant canopy swing moved slowly up the mountain, swaying from side to side. Jewel caught a glimpse of Dunn's River through the trees, and tropical gardens along the edge of the mountains. There were huge water-falls and wildlife everywhere; it was one of the most beautiful sites she had ever seen. Once at the top of Mystic Mountain the group of women's got off the swing. They were greeted by group of Jamaican dancers. The dancers circled them in dance while singing one of Jewel's favorite songs by Bob Marley, "*hey little girl over there, you look so sweet,*" their voices were angelic. Miss. Prissy immediately began rolling her hips to the beat of the drums along with the dancers. She had a huge smile on her face; she danced her way into the group of dancers. The crowd was yelling to Miss. Prissy,

"*you better werk what yo momma gave you!*" The yelling and screaming from the crowd caused Miss. Prissy to get down on the ground with her dance moves. She could start a party anyplace, and anywhere. Watching Miss. Prissy dancing, and having fun made the other women start dancing too.

A very attractive Jamaican man that was with the group reached for Jewel's hands.

're—

*"May I have this dance,"* he asked.

Jewel extended her hands. The man took her hand and pulled her to him; he whispered to her;

*"You are a beautiful woman,"* he held her close as they danced. He moved his body up against Jewel's body as if he hadn't had sex in a while. He was full of passion; she could feel his manhood; it was as though his penis was saying.

*"Hey, up there, look down; hey lady, I'm here, see me,"* which made Jewel uncomfortable, but she moved gracefully along, staying in tune with his every move. After the group of dancers finished singing, they said with excitement in their voices. *"Welcome to Jamaica!"*

The ladies joined their tour guide and a few of the Jamaicans dancers for brunch. When they finished brunch the women walked across a twenty-five meter suspension bridge, to an area where they would go through another safety session with the professional zip line tour members. The walk across the suspension bridge caused Jewel's heart to drop in her hand. At this moment, she feared for her safety. The women made it to the other side, and Jewel was able to breathe again. Once the session was over, it was time for some more excitement and adventure; the safety crew members began harnessing the women's for their adventure through the five-mile rain forests. After the seven, women's were harness they were led to the first platform. The crew member told the women he would allow them to go two at a time. Conifa decided she would go it alone; before the crew member could say, *"go,"* she was off through the rain forests. She went so fast, she was out of sight in a matter of moments.

*"That woman is acting very strange, now she has taken off without us once again!"* Jewel thought to herself. It was Jewel's and Brenda G's time to go; the crew member told Jewel to count to three, step out from the platform, and go. Jewel counted to three; stepped off the platform and away through

the rain forest she went, with Brenda G closing in fast behind her. The scenery was a breathtaking view of valleys, rivers, tropical plants, exotic flowers and mountains. Jewel could see an abundance of indigenous wildlife; all different types of birds and butterflies, it was truly paradise for nature lovers, Jewel thought as she came in for a landing on the last platform. When she reached the last platform she could see Jerry, Dolly, and Miss. Prissy as they leaped down. Jewel wondered why they were jumping; little did she know that was the only way she would be able to get back to the big canopy swing, she would have to jump twelve-hundred feet.

*"Why do I have to jump? I can't do this,"* Jewel said to the crew member.

*"Just take a deep breath, and steps out into the air, you can do it,"* the zip-line employee said.

*"Oh lord,"* Jewel said, and took a leap of faith; when she reached the last platform, she felt as if she had left everything inside of her twelve-hundred feet in the air. The women took the eighty foot swing back down the mountain. Jewel was overwhelmed with excitement from her experience with the zip lining adventure; but she was even happier to get off the swing. Jewel promised herself that she would do things like this more often. When she got home, she would let John know how much fun she had zip lining, maybe he would want to do it when they take their world tour. Jewel and the women exited the swing. On their way back to the tour bus, Jewel noticed that Conifa was not with the group of women.

*"Where is Conifa?"* Jewel asked Jerry.

*"I don't know, maybe she is already at the tour bus,"* Jerry replied.

*"Yeah, that heifer left all of us again,"* Brenda G. darn near screamed.

Once they were back at the tour bus, they looked everywhere for Conifa, but she was nowhere in sight. The women asked the tour guide if he had seen Conifa. He told them no, and that she may have taken another bus back to Montego Bay.

*"We will see her down the road,"* the tour guide answered.

With this bit of information, Jewel felt better. She didn't want anyone to get left behind in this unfamiliar place. The drive back to Montego Bay was an interesting one. The bus was quiet; Jewel guessed it was because everyone was all pooped out, or worrying about Conifa no-good-ass. Once they reached the resort, Jewel, Jerry and Brenda G. said their goodbyes to the other women and went to their room. They wanted to get ready for the party at Pier One. Jewel picked her outfit out before the left for Ocho Rias that morning. She was going to wear her sexy black mini dress and her black sandals for more comfort. The ladies took a nap; they needed to be fresh for this evening. As soon as Jewel's head touched her pillow the hotel room phone rang; it was Miss. Prissy, she wanted to know if any one of them had heard from Conifa. Jewel told her no; Miss. Prissy suggested that they all go look for her. Jewel told Miss. Prissy that she was tired and that Conifa was a grown woman, she would be okay.

*"I don't know, maybe we should ask the hotel security if they have seen her,"* Miss. Prissy said.

*"If she isn't back in her room within the next hour, we will go look for her,"* Jewel answered.

*"Well, alright,"* Miss. Prissy replied. Once Jewel hung up the phone she became even more concerned and called the front desk to inquire about Conifa's whereabouts. The woman at the front desk told Jewel that she didn't have any idea where her friend was, but she will put in missing persons if she didn't show up in twenty-four hours. *"Twenty-four hours is too long to wait,"* Jewel thought but decided to check back later. Jewel hung up the phone, and went over to the bed; she sat down and took her shoes off; it had been a long day; she didn't think she would make it to the club if

she didn't get rest; she lay across the bed for a minute to rejuvenate herself, she needed to think. Jewel asked Jerry if she wanted to have an early dinner before their nap. Jerry said yes; Jewel called for room service. Before Jewel could hang up the phone there came a knock at the door. "*Who is it?*" Jewel questioned the person at the door.

"*It's maid service,*" the voice on the other side of the door answered.

Jewel opened the door; it was the maid. Jewel wondered why the maid was there so late in the evening. "*Why are you here so late to clean my room?*" She asked.

"*My little one got sick, and I had to rush home, I am so sorry if I inconvenience you madam, but please may I clean your room*" the maid asked.

"*Oh, it is okay, come on in,*" Jewel answered.

"*Thank you madam; thank you so much! I don't want to lose my job,*" the maid said.

"*What is your name?*" Jewel asked.

"*It is Bebe,*" the maid answered.

"*Do you live close by?*" Jewel asked.

"*Yes, I live in the villa next door,*" the maid answered.

"*I don't have money for your tip, but I would make sure you get it,*" Jewel says. She was sorry that she didn't have money to tip the maid; she only had traveler's checks and credit card.

"*Oh, thank you so much,*" the maid said. Jewel asked the maid for her phone number and address; she told Bebe that she would send her money from time to time to help her out. The maid was appreciative of Jewel's offer to help her. She repeatedly said, "*thank you ma'am*" as she cleaned Jewel in Jerry's room. After the maid left, the concierge came with their food; dinner

're—

looked great. The ladies were served oven roasted herb stuff jerk chicken, fresh green salad with rice and peas. Jerry ordered ginger beer; she said that it sounded interesting. Jewel was sure the herbs that were used on their dinner were grown in this magnificent Caribbean sunlight. They also served goat head soup; which Jewel would have no part of. The smell was horrible; anyone could smell the goat's head miles away. When Jerry tried it, she said it was delicious.

*"Have you ever eaten goat head before soup before Jewel?"* Jewel asked Jerry.

*"No but I like trying new and unusual foods and this is great!"* Jerry answered. When dinner was over, the ladies took a short nap. They slept for an hour or so; immediately after they woke up; Jewel suggested that Jerry called the other women to find out if they were going to Pier One, and if they heard from Conifa. Jerry made the call to Brenda G.

*"Hey lady, where is Tara?* Jerry asked when Brenda G. answered her phone.

*"Was sup with you heifer's? Why you fools leave me all along with this floozy, she took off again with that man she met on the beach last evening. She became very angry when I told her that she couldn't be laying up in here with that stranger; shit I pay for this room too. She told me to tell Miss. Prissy that she would be back later, maybe even tomorrow,"* Brenda G. yelled into the phone.

*"Do you want to come bunk with us? If you do; then come on down, there is plenty of room, and I'm sure that Jewel won't mind; will you Jewel?* Jerry asked, turning her attention toward Jewel.

*"Oh no, I don't mine, not at all. I wouldn't want to be in that big old room all alone. Girl by all means, come on!"* Jewel yelled loud enough so Brenda G. could hear her through the phone.

*"Hell yeah, I am moving in, this heifer can have this room,"* Brenda G. said.

*"Has anyone heard from Conifa yet?"* Jewel asked.

*"Girl nah, that heifer done split; she is afraid Jewel is going to beat that ass,"* Brenda G. said.

*"This is the strangest thing ever; I wonder where she could have gone; I wasn't going to fight her, I only wanted the answers that I very well deserved,"* Jewel said.

*"Yea, but you put some fear in her,"* Brenda G. answered.

*"Maybe so, but I would never hurt anyone. A man isn't worth killing over; however, I did want to push her ass off that swing though,"* Jewel said.

*"I know what you mean, I wanted to help you!"* Brenda G. said with a wicked smile circling the corner of her mouth.

*"I know you did, you love to fight,"* Jerry said.

*"I'm going to get ready for the club, would you be going Brenda?"* Jerry asked.

*"Hell yeah heifer, I'm going to have to find me a Rasta man,"* Brenda G. yelled.

*"Okay then, I will call Miss. Prissy and the others; we need to be heading out soon,"* Jerry answered.

*"Oh, okay then, go ahead and make the call; maybe one of them know where that fool is,"* Brenda G. yelled. Jerry immediately called Miss. Prissy and Dolly's room; no one answered the phone.

"I wonder where those two are," Jerry said.

*"I don't have any idea, on second thought I heard Prissy say something about the Pelican's restaurant; maybe they went to dinner over there,"* Jewel answered. Jewel dressed in her black mini dress, casual sandals and went downstairs to wait for the women. While waiting she took a stroll on the beach where she met a gorgeous man dressed in a police uniform; he walked over to her with a big smile and said, *"Hello sexy woman,"*

're———

*"Ah, thank you, you're not bad yourself,"* Jewel said to the bronzed bow-legged sculpture standing before her.

*"What is your name lady?"* He asked.

*"My name is Jewel, and yours?"* Jewel asked.

*"My name is Hugh; it is so great to meet a beautiful goddess such as you. Where are you staying?"* He asked. *"*

*"Right here at sunset Beach; where you live, and why are you on the beach, have there been a crime or something?* Jewel questioned the Police Officer.

*"No crime, I worked the beach sometimes, just for safety precautions,"* he answered.

*"Oh, I see,"* Jewel answered.

*"Where are you from?"* He asked.

*"I'm from California, Los Angeles County, and you?"* Jewel asked.

*"I live in the Negril, Jamaica. May I have your phone number?"* He asked.

*"I guess so, may I have yours?"* Jewel asked.

*"Yes, by all means take down my number. I would love to meet up with you later. Are you married, or you have a significant other?"* He asked.

*"Yes, I'm married to a complicated mess,"* Jewel answered before she thought about what she said.

After changing phone numbers, Jewel went on her way to find the other women. When Jewel reached the lobby, she saw all of the women except for Conifa.

*"Where is Conifa?"* Jewel asked.

*"The front desk clerk said maybe she went with someone that she met in Ocho Rias; they have not seen her since she left this morning,"* Miss. Prissy said.

Since the women's couldn't find Conifa, they went to the club. The taxi driver dropped them off in front of Pier One nightclub and Restaurant. It cost ten dollars to get into the club. They paid the ten dollars and entered Pier One. It was located on a picturesque Peninsula, overlooking the harbor of Montego Bay. The club's architectural design reminded Jewel of a huge ship with a breathtaking atmosphere. The most spectacular view of the moon and the stars shined so brightly, they casted a night light over Pier One; it was one of the most beautiful thing that Jewel had ever seen in forty-two years. The women danced with hundred of others rocking the night away at Pier One; the dance floor was huge; it sparrow a half mile out into the Caribbean Sea. At times Jewel was afraid that someone would accidentally fall into the sea, especially the drunk girl that kept leaning up against the rope that protected her from going overboard. A circular bar was station in the center of the floor; here Jewel tried many different tropical drinks. Jewel walked over to the window to view the picturesque Peninsula bay; it bordered water as far as Jewel could see. There was a Rasta man on the Pier selling ganja; he came over to talk with Jewel. He asked Jewel for her name.

*"What is your name my woman?"*

*"My name is Jewel, what is yours?"* Jewel asked the Rasta man.

Jewel was a little bit taken back, because the Rasta man said, *"my woman,"* she was nobody's woman; not in California or on this island. She didn't want him to get the wrong impression of her, and think that he would be going home with her at the end of the night. She heard about how bold and strong willed that some of these men are.

*"Oh, they just call me Rasta Rollingman all around here, but my name is Henry. May I sit with you, and keep company with you for a while?"* he asked.

*"Yes, of course you can join me and my friends. They are over there on the dance floor,"* Jewel answered pointing toward Jerry, Brenda G. Miss. Prissy and Dolly. Jewel wanted B.G. to come sit with them since she love smoking Ganja, but when she thought how un-cool that would be with loud mouth B.G., she changed her mind; she didn't want any of them to go to jail in Jamaica. They had lost Conifa somewhere so why push their luck. Jewel thought about her life with John; she didn't want to stay focused on her current situation but thinking of John wouldn't do her any good, she may as well enjoy Jamaica. She took another sip of her tropical drink just as a handsome fellow came over and asked her to dance. The music flowed through the club like mist in the early morning air. She was in heaven as she danced around the pier. Once she and the gentleman stop dancing; she told the man thanks and returned to her seat; the Rasta man was standing there waiting for her return. When she walked up, he reached for her and said,

*"I'm glad you are back my woman."*

*"Thank you,"* Jewel answered.

He offered Jewel a drink; she told him that she would have a tropical drink from the bar. He went over to the bar to get Jewel a drink; meanwhile Jerry, B.G. and Dolly come over to her table with drinks in hand. Miss. Prissy was on the dance floor getting her groove on with two Jamaican men; one had her from the back, and the other one was in the front of her. She was having the time of her life. Dolly came over to the table where Jewel and the Rasta man sat.

*"What are you doing Miss. Lady?"* Dolly asked with the hugest smile Jewel has ever seen on her face. She was the cutest woman, and Jewel loves her smile. Jewel couldn't help smiling herself whenever Dolly smiled; she just had a way about herself.

*"Nothing just having fun,"* Jewel answered.

*"It's a damn shame Conifa left like that, she should have says something,"* Dolly said.

*"Yeah, I wish she has is something, anything at all would have been better than just taken off like that,"* Jewel said.

*"I think she was afraid of Jewel; I mean I would have been afraid too if I was sleeping with my friend's husband, and got caught!"* Dolly said.

*"That heifer knew she was wrong, and didn't want to answer Jewel's questions; that's all, in that order!* Brenda G. yelled.

*"I don't know if that is what she was thinking or not, but she is so wrong,"* Jewel said.

*"Hell, we all know she is wrong, but what does that have to do with it? That helfa is a bitch and that is all, pointblank!"* Brenda G said.

*"She is a handful,"* Jerry said.

*"Yeah, I swear I never liked her, I only put up with her because we run in the same circle,"* Brenda G said.

*I knew we had differences, but I would have never thought she would screw John!"* Jewel said.

*"Have you ever thought, maybe she isn't screwing John, it could be something else?"* Jerry questioned.

*"Like what? I mean, what in the world would they be doing together?"* Jewel asked.

*"I don't know, but they do business together, don't they?"* Jerry asked Jewel.

*"No Jerry, not that I know off,"* Jewel replied.

're—

*"Oh yes they do, I have seen them all together, Conifa, Joe Wright, Nathaniel Le and John, I thought you knew those people hung out together Jewel,"* Jerry said.

*"Nathaniel Le, is that his last name? That name sound very familiar, I thought Johnson was his last name, at least that is what he told me when we dated,"* Jewel said.

*"You and Nathaniel dated?"* Jerry asked with a curious look on her face.

*"Yeah girl, nothing ever came of it, so I never said anything to my friends about him,"* Jewel replied.

*"Oh, I never knew that and I am supposed to be your close friend!"* Jerry said.

*"Oh come on now Jerry, I am sure you have had a man or two that I don't know about. So cut it out, and let dance,"* Jewel said.

The women left the club around four a.m., but just before they walked out the door Tara and her gentleman friend showed up, drunk and full of laughter.

*"Where are you guys going?"* Tara asked.

*"We are going home, that's where. Where have you been all night young lady?"* Miss. Prissy asked.

*"With my friend; we went to his house; he has a beautiful home, and he lives with his brother. Do you want to meet him?"* Tara asked Miss. Prissy.

*"Honey child I have a husband, and a good one at that. There isn't a man alive that can take his place!"* Miss. Prissy replied to Tara.

*"That's right Miss. Prissy, let her have it!"* Dolly said.

*"Are you coming Tara?"* Miss. Prissy asked.

*"Later,"* Tara answered.

*"Ok dear, see you later,"* Miss. Prissy answered.

The women had a blast at Pier One, dancing and, eating great food. The Jamaican men were so nice and friendly. Jewel's friend, the Rasta man called a taxi for the ladies; when they went outside the taxi was waiting for them. Jewel said goodbye to her Rasta man; she got in the taxi with Jerry, Miss. Prissy, Dolly and Brenda G., and back to the resort they went. Tara was left behind once again; she was having the time of her life. The women decided to look for Conifa the next morning; they were all exhausted after their night of fun and excitement at Pier One. Jewel was the first one in bed, but as soon as she got cozy between the satin sheets that were on her bed, the phone in her room begin ring. She answered it.

*"Hello,"* Jewel said wondering who would be calling at four a.m.

*"Hey lady, this is Hugh,"* the voice on the end of the phone said.

*"Okay, but why are you calling so late?* Jewel questioned the stranger.

*"I just want to hear your voice,"* He said.

*"This time of the morning,"* Jewel asked.

*"I just got off work honey, I worked the beach tonight,"* Hugh answered.

*"Oh, okay, so now I'm supposed to understand?"* Jewel asked.

*"Can I come see you?"* He asked.

*"No, I have a roommate and it's the wee hours of the morning!"* Jewel answered.

*"Is your roommate a male or female?"* Hugh questioned Jewel.

*"A woman, why?"* Jewel asked.

*"I have a friend for her, he is a nice guy,"* Hugh said.

*"A friend, we are not going to entertain you or your friend at this hour of the morning, and I think you are being pretty damn rude!"* Jewel said to the stranger.

*"I didn't mean to offend you I didn't realize it was so late,"* Hugh explained.

*"Let's talk some other time,"* Jewel said.

*"Will you be at the resort tomorrow, or will you be out on the tour?"* Hugh asked.

*"You sure do ask a lot of questions Hugh, yes I will be here,"* Jewel answered.

*"Can I call you in the morning?* Hugh asked.

*"Okay, whatever,"* Jewel answered.

*"I can't wait to see you again,"* Hugh said.

*"Bye,"* Jewel said.

*"That was a rather strange phone call,"* Jewel said to herself.

At first sight Jewel thought that Hugh was a nice guy, now she was second guessing herself. *"What man calls anyone at that hour?"* She questioned herself. *He must have thought we were freaks or something. I mean even if I was a freak I wouldn't want to freak with him at first sight. Lord these men, thinking they are God's gift to women. It's our fault though, treating them as if they were babies. I have got to say that man was fine as hell, standing there in that police uniform."*

*"Jewel you better get some sleep,"* Jerry said.

*"I'm, just thinking about that phone call, goodnight girl,"* Jewel said.

*"Goodnight girl,"* Jerry said.

*"You know you are not going to sleep,"* Jewel said..

# CHAPTER FOURTEEN

## CONIFA'S SINS

Conifa's friends didn't know she was the one responsible for killing her husband, and that Joe Wright, Nathaniel Le, Queenly Le, and John had been blackmailing her for years. They were all in on the scheme to take over Barkman's Real Estate Corporation. The men told her that if she did not go along with their plan they would turn her into the police for killing Ralph Barkman, her husband. They sent the women away on an all expense paid trip to New York and Jamaica sponsored by Barkman's realtor, while Conifa and the women were in Jamaica, Joe Wright and the men were in Vegas getting ready for the takeover. Not only were they going to take over Barkman's, they were planning to take every cent that Jewel had to her name. Joe Wright and John came up with the plan to send the women's on an all-expense paid trip. They had to get them out of country; they didn't need anyone around looking, trying to find out what they were up to. Conifa's sins have caught up with her; there was no way out; she confessed to God what she had done. She was ashamed and didn't want her friends to know what kind of person she had become. While she was zip-lining through the rain forest, she cried out to God to forgive her for the things that she had done wrong to everyone. She asked him to forgive her for what she had done to Jewel and her husband Ralph Barkman.

*"Oh God, Joe and John forced me to steal form Jewel; they forced me to steal account numbers and give them to them,"* Conifa had no idea that the men were planning to steal her blind, as well as Jewel. John was supposed to take the money from all of Jewel's account and transferred it into an offshore bank account in the Caribbean. Conifa was told to get the money that John was going to wire to her later that day and invest it in Real Estate on the island in a fictitious name. A name that John had given her to use; if she didn't they would turn her into the police department for the murder of

Ralph Barkman. Conifa told the Lord that she didn't want to kill her husband, but he was beating her all the time.

*"When I was sick with ovarian cancer; he cheated on me with one of my best friends. Ralph would leave for days upon end, not to even look back at me; his sick wife. I had to care for myself; I had to rub the medicine over my sore body because he wouldn't even help me. There were plenty of days that I had to use a mirror to put medicine on my sore blistered vagina; all the while he sat looking at me. He told me if I wanted his help; I had better ask for it; otherwise I could lay there until the rest of my skin fell off."*

"Conifa was heartbroken, and in physical pain all the times."

The last time Ralph left home to be with his mistress for two weeks. Conifa called his cell phone, when he answered it, he told her that he wanted a divorce and that she would get nothing from their business. There was no way that she was going to let him hurt her again ever. She called her friend who was a high power attorney; she asked him to show her a way that she could protect herself from Ralph manipulative ways. He told her what to do. She had a lawyer draw up documents for power of attorney over everything they owned, and she kept the documents in her safe at the bank until she could trick Ralph into signing them. A couple of months later one of Ralph's drunken nights, she conned him into signing the documents. She told him it was for medical bills from her ovarian cancer stay at the hospital. Ralph pitch a bitch about the cost; telling her that she needed to find another source of income to pay her stupid ass bills. The document that he signed gave Conifa power over everything they own. The next time Ralph left for the weekend she didn't say one word; he had already threatened her, she was afraid of him. He stayed away for three weeks; his only call was to tell her that he was filing for divorce when he got back into town. She waited for him, when he came home after his weekend with his mistress; Conifa gave him a piece of a poisonous plant, one that would eventually cause his heart to stop. She purchased a plant call Conium which is highly toxic from the Nathaniel Le, who dabbled-in medicine. Conifa took her time, and mixed it in Ralph's toss salad; she watched him eat every single drop of his salad. Ralph's death came in the form of paralysis; his mind was wide awake, but his body couldn't respond. Conifa watched his respiratory system shutdown. The ingestion of this plant was fatal; Ralph took his last breath. Conifa remembered Nathaniel's question when she asked for the plant. *"Why do you want it?"* Nathaniel asked.

*"I wanted to kill my husband; I'm just kidding, not really though, she laughed, I need it for my yard; I'm going to plant it right alongside my creeping Charlie's to keep the bugs away,"* Conifa said.

*"You wanted to do what with it?"* Nathaniel asked with a wicked smile. He figured that Conifa wanted the plant to do something dangerous with it, but a course she was not going to tell him. Nathaniel decided to put it on the back burner for later. He would wait and see what she did with the plant. It was not long before Ralph died suddenly. Nathaniel knew immediately that Conifa had something to do with Ralph's death; he and his friends start terrorizing her. When Joe Wright found out about it, he started his blackmailing plan. Conifa released her zip line hooks, falling into the rain forest, and killing herself. Her body was mangled; wild hungry animals had gotten hold of her body overnight. The corners couldn't make-out who she was; the crew members found her identification in her fanny pack. Then and only then were the authorities able to tell who she was, and where she was staying. They called the resort to inform her family or friends of her death; they said when she fell; she died on impact; she didn't suffer much.

*"The lady felled in the rainforest. We have searched everywhere trying to find out who she is; countless hours for any information leading to the where-about of her family, or friends. The only information that we've come up with is the address to the resort, an airline ticket, and a few other personal things that were in her purse. A few photos, car keys, hairbrush,"* the officer said.

're—

## CHAPTER FIFTEEN

## THE MASTERMIND

Meanwhile, back in Los Angeles Ha-kin was getting himself together to travel to Las Vegas, Nevada. He was going to make sure that John and the other men got what they deserve, and it wouldn't be his mother's hard earned money. His friend Rodney Moore was waiting for him at the Flamingo hotel in Vegas. The FBI and the immigration officers were on high alert; staked out in the adjoining room of John's. In route to the airport Ha-kin received a phone call from his best friend Rodney Moore telling him to hurry, that the men were getting restless and he couldn't hold them off too much longer. Rodney said that John wanted him to come to his room right away; he wanted the password to the accounts.

*"I had the security password changed before I left for Vegas, and no one can access the account without the new password,"* Rodney told Ha-kin.

The FBI's had been looking for Nathaniel Le and his sister Queenly Le for quite some time. Now they would transport them back to the Caribbean to stand trial for embezzlement, and a long list of other charges including the murder of Nathaniel and Queenly's grandparents for their money. They were on the most wanted list; they had been running from the police for nine years. The FBI would take John Dupree and Joe Wright straight to prison when they belong. Ha-kin had been watching the five criminals for years, ever since John and Nathaniel started together Ha-kin could tell something wasn't very right; he started to poke around in Nathaniel's path and found out that Queenly Le was his sister. He also found out that everything that they were telling Jewel was all lies. When he saw Queenly Le son Justin in the park with John that day, he knew that was their son. *"He looks just like him,"* Ha-kin thought as he watched them play. Ha-kin kept quiet; he didn't want to hurt his stepmother, but when he overheard them talking on the phone about the takeover, he had to come up with a plan. He and his friend Rodney staged a huge fight between them making

're

it seem like they had become enemies and Ha-kin fired Rodney from his position at his company. Rodney waited six months and then went to Barkman Real Estate Company seeking employment; Joe Wright hired him. Joe took Rodney under his wings. As soon as John found out about him hiring Rodney he had a problem with it. John told Joe right then and there not to bring Rodney in, but Joe didn't listen. Ha-kin's and Rodney plan was in action. John was having the thrill of his life spending Jewel's money on Queenly Le and their son Justin. Ha-kin played along with everything;

*"I am Head Executive and President of foreign affairs; what would make them son of bitches think for one moment that I'm going to allow them to fuck my mama?"* Ha-kin thought to himself. He would make it in time to put a stop to what John and the other men were up to. About twenty minutes later Rodney called Ha-kin's cell phone again.

*"Hello, what's up man?* Ha-kin asked.

*"Ha-kin, these fools are on one. They want me to come right now with the password. I can't hide forever,"* Rodney said.

*"First off man you are not hiding, they just don't know where you are, keep them busy, don't go to them whatever you do!"* Ha-kin said.

*"Okay, things are going to go just like we plan, don't you worry one bit. We're going to take care of mama,"* Rodney said.

*"I'll be there in another twenty-five minutes; meet me at the airport; terminal twenty-nine. I'm flying on Delta Airlines. I have the FBI and the immigration department already in place at the Flamingo hotel. Make sure John and his crew stay at the Flamingo; don't let them leave man. Tell them that you are held up in traffic, and you will meet them in John's room in one hour,"* Ha-kin replied.

*"One hour?"* Rodney asked.

're

*"Yeah, just to throw them off for a while, and then I will have time to get there before they figure out things are all bad. I can't wait to see the sons of bitches faces,"* Ha-kin said.

*"I know, neither can I! They been talking all of that foul crap, now let's see what they have to say for themselves,"* Rodney said.

*"I got this; I will see you in a few,"* Ha-kin replied.

*"Alright man, see you when you get here, be safe up there now you hear!"* Rodney answered.

Ha-kin couldn't wait to bust these guys. If he hadn't figured out what they were up to, his poor mother would have lost everything. *"John Dupree had his eyes on my mom's money from the word say go."* Ha-kin thought as he hung up the phone and walked toward his plane. Ha-kin wasn't on the plane thirty minutes before he was landing in Vegas. When he got off the plane Rodney was there to pick him up from the airport just as they plan.

*"Hey man, didn't I just speak to you ten minutes ago,"* Rodney laughed as he hugged his friend.

*"Yeah man, that was pretty damn fast,"* Ha-kin answered.

*"Now let's get to work before these thugs get away free,"* Rodney said.

*"Naw man, they are not going anywhere. I called ahead; they got the hotel surrounded right now, I didn't want to take any chances. That damn Joe Wright, Nathaniel Le and John Dupree are some slick one, or so they think,"* Ha-kin laughed.

*"Yeah, he is, always telling his fucking business to everyone. Conifa beat me out of my inheritance. I am so tired of people fucking over me; I am going to get everything that belongs to me! Blah, blah, blah, is all he does!"* Rodney said mocking Joe Wright.

*"I know, it is all over now, it's all over,"* Ha-kin said as they drove up to the Flamingo Hotel. The guys went inside; there they met with the FBI and the men from the immigration department. They had to make sure that John Dupree, Queenly Le, Joe Wright and Nathaniel Le were where they were supposed to be. John had bought Queenly over to his room; she had been bitching so hard; he figured it would be better just to bring her. He didn't want his goon friends to say anything to her, especially not Joe; John was jealous of his mistress and the mother of his only child. He loved her with all his heart; he would let nothing stand in the way of them living a long and happy life.

Rodney called John on his cell phone and asked, *"Hey man, I had been waiting in the lobby, where you guys at?"*

*"What the hell do you mean where we at? We have got to get this thing moving so we can all collect,* John laughed, *" but seriously man, come on up, we are waiting for you!"*

*"I have everything with me,"* Rodney said.

*"You damn better have everything; look how long we have been waiting! I don't have any more time boy!"* John yelled.

*"Okay, all right, I will be there in a second. I am on the elevator coming to the ninth floor right now!"* Rodney yelled back at John.

The FBI's and the immigration police were already on the ninth floor; they were in the adjoining room. Rodney knocked at John's door; as soon as he knocked John opened the door and snatched Rodney inside. John checked Rodney's pocket for his wallet. John was looking for the security password to transfer the stolen money into the foreign account, so Conifa would be able to withdraw the money and take care of business in the Caribbean.

*" What's up man? Why are you all in my pockets?"* Rodney asked John loudly.

*"Man you know why I'm in your pockets; I think you are trying to pull a scam or something. Grab him Nathaniel! Man why are you not on your job? Come on; help me so we can get this shit over with!"* John yelled to Nathaniel.

*"Hey man, let go of me! I can give you this shit; you don't have to wrestle me down for it. I'm a part of this plan too; I want my share just like you do!"* Rodney yelled, as he felled into the adjoining door. He wanted the police to hear him. It was their clue to let the FBI know that Rodney needed help and was in trouble. When the FBI's heard the commotion next door in John's room, they burst through the double doors with guns drawn and the men and Queenly under arrest.

*"I will read you your rights,'* the federal agent said.

*"I don't need any rights read to me, just let me call my lawyer sir,'* John said to the detective.

John gave Ha-kin and Rodney an evil eye as he spoke to the officer.

*"I can't believe this punk ass kid took me down like this. Man I'm going to kill you and yo mama; you mother fucker you!"* John thought to himself. He couldn't believe this was happening. He thought he had everything figured out, but what he didn't see was Ha-kin coming.

*"I knew that boy was up to something!"* John said.

The Immigration officers put handcuffed on Nathaniel Le and Queenly Le while reading them their rights; they were placed under arrest. *"Do you see what you have done now Joe? I told you man, I told you, but you wouldn't listen to me! You had all them big ass ideas, now look at what you have gotten us all into,"* Nathaniel yelled at Joe Wright.

*Whatever you do man don't panic, it is going to be okay. Whatever they think they have will not hold up in court, do you remember our lawyer's phone number?"* John asked Nathaniel.

*"Yeah, I remember the number; I will call as soon as we get to the police station,"* Nathaniel replied.

*"Make sure you tell Joe to keep quiet, he is the one with the big fucking mouth,"* John told Nathaniel. He was trying to whisper to Nathaniel, but Queenly started screaming and crying so loudly John became nervous and couldn't finish getting his words out. He was worry about Queenly. She was screaming and crying to John about their child.

*"Oh my God John, what are we going to do about Justin? John please help me; don't let them take me back to the Caribbean! I will never get to see you or Justin again; please help me baby, please,"* Queenly crying to John.

*"Don't worry babe, it's going to be alright. I will make sure of it, don't talk to anyone. Do you remember the lawyer's phone number? Call him and get him to post your bond. Call yo mama-nem, and tell them what's going on. I know that they will take care of Justin for us. We gone be alright babe; you'll see!"* John shouted to the love of his life. It hurts him so much to see Queenly in handcuffs.

The Immigration officer told John to be quiet, but John kept talking, ignoring the officer's command.

*"Don't you dare tell me to shut up? I'm a grown ass man, not your puppet! Queenly, I got you baby, please don't worry; I will never leave you.*

*"Save me babe, please save me! You said nothing would happen to me and our son! You told me that we were in the clear, and now look at us; we are in trouble! I love you baby, what am I going to do without you? I don't want to live without you John!"* Queenly yelled.

John had to figure a way to save her, and him from the wrath at hand. He decided the first chance he got he would call Jewel, try and explain to her what a terrible mistake he had made. He would tell Jewel anything she wanted to hear, as long as it kept Queenly out of jail.

*"I love you Queenly!"* John yelled; he watched the immigration officers take Queenly and Nathaniel through a block of double doors until they were out of sight. Even though, he was thinking as fast as he could, he didn't have enough time to come up with a plan for Queenly. The officers hit him across the back with the club for talking, and told him to shut the fuck up.

*"My son needs his mother!"* John screamed at the officers.

The officer threw John to the floor and put his knees in John's chest to pin him down. When the officer threw John to the floor, the sound of him falling was that of a lumberjack tree in the forest; it echoed the room. The FBI told John that they had been watching him and his friends for some time. They knew about the blackmailing, the murder and they knew all about his plan. After the officers had got John and Joe Wright in handcuffed, they would transport them to the Las Vegas city jail, there they would stay until trail. Joe Wright didn't put up a fight. He did everything the officers asked of him. He thought that he could talk his way out of it all; he tried to con the officers by saying;

*"I'm so sorry sir; I had no idea of what was going on. I'm just here for a convention; these are my friends, they will tell you that I know nothing about whatever you guys are talking about; may I call my lawyer sir?"* He asked the officer. He had no clue that the police knew all about him, they knew every case that he ever had.

*"No, you will have your chance to make one phone call after we get you booked in,"* the officer told Joe Wright.

Joe Wright didn't like the officer's answer one bit, he didn't like anyone telling him what he could or could not do. He had a plan for this officer; he wasn't going to spend eternity behind bars.

*"I don't understand why you thought you would get away with this John; me and my mama are not fools!"* Ha-kin said to John as the policeman lead him and Joe Wright away in handcuffed.

John looked at Ha-kin and Rodney with hatred in his eyes. He told them that he would bring them down off their high horses if it were the last thing he ever did. He swore that this was not the end. As the police officers took the men away, the officer turned to Ha-kin and Rodney and said;

"*We need to finish the investigation down at headquarters; can you come down in a few hours?* The lead investigators will want to speak with you."

"*Yes we will be happy to assist you all in any way possible!*" Ha-kin answered.

The CEO of the Flamingo Hotel helped to bring things to an end by allowing FBI to listen in on all of John's and his friends conversations. The police officers thanked Ha-kin and Rodney for helping them bring down the criminals. They have one more to get which was Conifa Barkman. They would apprehend her at the resort where she was staying at in Jamaica. Ha-kin was elated; he grabbed his buddy around her neck and gave him a man hug and said, "*Thanks, man, I knew you would stand beside me. I love you Rodney; you are just like a brother to me!*

"*I love you too Ha-kin, you are my brother, and Jewel is like a mother to me. There was no way that I would let them sucker's getaway with that little scheme of theirs. They didn't know that every time they touched that computer, their information would remain there. Getting information for a programmer like me is a piece of cake,*" Rodney proudly said with his chest high in the air.

"*I know Rodney, thank you again brother, let's get out of here, go and grab a bite to eat before we head to the police station,*" Ha-kin replied.

"*Okay, sounds like a great idea; all that commotion, I'm starved!*" Rodney answered.

"*I need to call my mother right away,*" Ha-kin said.

"*Maybe we should let her enjoy her trip one more night? It is all going to blow open in the morning, might as well!*" Rodney answered.

*"No, she is still in the present of that evil woman; I want mama safe, away from that woman!"* Ha-kin replied as he dialed Jewel cell phone number.

Jewel didn't answer; his call went straight to voicemail.

*"I wonder why mama isn't answering her phone,"* Ha-kin said while dialing her again; he got her voice mail once more. Ha-kin decided to call again later that evening. Jewel could be in danger; he must warn his mother.

Ha-kin and Rodney stopped at a fast food place on Vegas Blvd. They placed an order for burgers, fries and a drink; something quick, they didn't have the time to relax in a restaurant setting. There was information that the FBI still needed from them. Ha-kin had turned over all of the tapes that he and Rodney had to the proper authorities. There were just a few more loose ends to tie up, and then he and Rodney could blow Vegas and the crooks with it. Ha-kin hoped that the investigators threw the book at each one of the men for what they were trying to so to his mother. After eating their burgers, the guy's headed downtown Vegas to give the FBI the last bit of information they needed to fry John and his demonic friend's rear ends. On the way Ha-kin tried calling his mother again, still no answer.

*"I wonder where she is,"* Ha-kin said.

*"You know the reception is terrible in Montego Bay,* Rodney said. *She will be all right John; we didn't come this for something bad to happen to her now. Just call her in the morning; allow her to have this last night of excitement!"*

*"Yeah, you are right; I worry so much about mama. She has been the only person true to me since I can remember. She took me in and raised me just like I was her own. She is my mother just as if I was born into her! I will try and wait till morning; no promise, but I will try,"* Ha-kin answered.

*"I know brother; I know,"* Rodney said as they walked into the Las Vegas Police Department.

Once inside the police station, they were offered a seat and a cup of coffee. They both refused. They just wanted to get on with their life. The investigator began the interrogation; the officers asked them the same questions over and again.

*"So when did you first notice your stepfather betrayal?"* The FBI asked Ha-kin.

*"Not long after they got married sir. I knew something was off when they came home from their honeymoon. My mother was always full of laughter; she loved to joke all the time. One day I came by to visit and she appeared super depressed; from that point on I kept a close eye out for her,"* Ha-kin told the investigator.

*"And you?"* The investigator turned his attention to Rodney.

*"A few years ago, yeah that's about the time Ha-kin asked me to help him,"* Rodney answered. The investigators asked lots of questions; when they were finished they told Ha-kin and Rodney; *"well we guess that about seal it up guys. If we need you will call you; but you are free to go. If you hear anything about that woman Conifa Barkman, make sure to call us immediately."*

*"We are leaving for the island in a few hours; we have to meet up with the international police in Montego, Bay. They are the only ones that can arrest Conifa Barkman,"* Ha-kin stated. He hoped that the information they offered the FBI would be enough to placed John Dupree, Joe Wright, Nathaniel Le, and Queenly Le in the electric chair; after the interrogation was over, John and Rodney were on their way back to Los Angeles. They had a long night ahead of them. Their bodies were tired from all of the excitement and chaos. One great thing for sure they would leave all of the ugliness, betrayals, lies and deceit in the city of sin. They wanted nothing to do with those people ever again; it had been a long journey for he and his dear friend Rodney; all the guys wanted to do now was go home and get rest, but Ha-kin was worried. He was still worried about his mother; he wanted to know how Jewel was doing over there in Jamaica. Ha-kin remembered back when he was a little boy; how Jewel stuck by him when his father

went away to the Army, and never came back. His father married a woman from South Carolina, and had four children of their own and two stepchildren that the woman had from a previous marriage. Ha-kin's father would every so often send him a few dollars when he was back in elementary school. If it had not been for Jewel, he would have been in a foster home, and all alone. It was now time for him to give back, and take care of his step-mother. As he drove down the Vegas Blvd. toward the airport, he thought of how loyal Rodney had been to him and his mother. He had always wanted to have a brother as cool and supportive as Rodney. Ha-kin remembered the days of going to school alone with no brothers or sisters, but now he had Rodney Moore by his side; this made him feel great. He looked over at Rodney; "*My partner,*" Ha-kin said to Rodney.

"*You are my partner, and my friend,*" Rodney said.

"*Now mama will be able to get on with her life,*" Ha-kin said to Rodney.

"*Yeah man, that was all bad. The marriage I mean,*" Rodney said.

"*Yeah, I hated when mama met John. I knew something was up though man; I couldn't understand why Nathaniel would introduce mama to his friend if he wanted her,*" Ha-kin said. "*It appeared to have been a game all along man,*" Rodney answered. "*It was, they both were after mama's money; and that child of theirs, "Justin," what's going to happen to him?*" Ha-kin asked looking puzzled. "*Man, I don't know,*" Rodney answered. "*I sure as hell hope mama don't decide to adopt him the way she did me. You know Queenly's people are all going to jail the minute the FBI find them,*" Ha-kin said. There was a heap of traffic on Vegas Boulevard because people were in town for the "Tyson," fight, and different conventions. Ha-kin decided to drive home with Rodney instead of taking the plane. He and Rodney could make in two hours. He merged onto the fifteen freeways and headed north. He wanted to get home so he could contact his mother, and let her know that the police had arrested John and his friends.

## CHAPTER SIXTEEN

## THE TRUTH

Jewel awakens to an impeccable ocean view; it had the most ultimate exotics sunrise that stretched across the cliff of Montego Bay; the clean ocean breezed it way into her room. As far as Jewel could see were exotic escapes, which nestled among lush gardens, and thatched roofed villas that perched on the ocean's edge. There were couples jogging on the beach's white sand; they jogged up the stairs and down the other side, disappearing into the cove. Jewel also noticed a group of people equipping themselves with the diving mask, and all sorts of device; she guessed they must be preparing themselves to go snorkeling in the aqua blue ocean. Jewel watched as the snorkeler moved farther out into the sea, and disappeared into the aqua waters. Jewel could see the world from a better view; this was the most relaxed she had been since she arrived in Montego Bay; it was an authentic experience of gloriousness. Jewel remembered the call that she received in the early a.m. from the policeman that she met on the beach. She decided to give Hugh a call. She was interested in him, and she wanted to know more about him.

*"Why not; after-all John is carrying on with Conifa. I may as well have some excitement in my life also,"* Jewel thought to herself. Jewel took a timeout, she had to collect her thoughts, and plan her day. First she would take a long luxurious bath, and afterwards, have breakfast on the terrace. She wasn't ready to see or talk to the other women. She had to get herself together. She ran her bath, and filled the tub with favorite Channel body wash; once the tub was filled to its capacity, Jewel undressed, and got into the tub of bubbles.

*"Oh my goodness, this water feels so great,"* Jewel said to herself; as she slides her body deep into the water. As Jewel gently stroked her body, she secretly wished that instead of water, her body was covered with a tall, dark chocolate Rasta she met on the beach last night.

After Jewel had finished with her bath, she put on a sexy colorful summer dress that she bought at Macy and a pair of purple sandals. Jerry and Brenda G. were still fast asleep. Jewel decided to wake them up.

*"Ladies, hey lady, it's time to get up, the rooster has crowed!"* Jewel jokingly said as she pulled the covers of her friends.

*"Stop it helfa,"* Brenda G. yelled.

*"First off, I am not your helfa and second it is almost 9 o'clock. I'm going to have breakfast on the terrace, what about you all?"* Jewel asked the women.

*"We will have what you are having,"* Jerry said while taking a long stretch.

*"I'm going to call room service now. You ladies might want to get up!"* Jewel yelled at the women's again from the living quarters of their huge room.

*"Okay, already, we are getting up,"* they said simultaneously.

Jewel walked over to the in-house phone; she dialed room service; when the person on the other end said hello, Jewel replied;

*"Good morning sir; I would like to order room service, please."*

*"What would you like to order?"* The man on the other end asked.

*"I'm ordering for three; I will have the ackee with saltfish and the bammy bread, and for my girlfriends I will order the Jamaican patty, made with Lobster. Make sure to fry the Lobster with the pastry crust,"* Jewel told the man on the phone.

*"Alright madam, will you be having breakfast on your terrace, or in your room?* He asked Jewel.

*"On the terrace sir,"* Jewel answered. She wondered why he asked her where she would be eating.

*"Ok madam, I will be sending your order right up,"* he said.

*"Girl what was that you order?"* Jerry asked Jewel.

*"Cow's foot for you and Brenda G;"* Jewel answered. She waited to see their reaction. She knew that this information would be explosive; Jewel laughed to herself at the thought of B.G and Jerry eating cow's feet.

*"Hell naw now helfa; you done went to damn far! There is no way that I will be eating anyone's cow foot today!"* Brenda G. yelled.

*"I was just kidding; you ladies are having fried pastries crust stuffed with Lobster; this delicious recipe can also be made with chicken, fish or vegetables. I know what you girls like, that why I ordered this specialty for you. Jerry you like your food spicy and B.G. you like yours mild with a hint of spice; this dish can range from mild to spicily depending on what is used to prepare it. I am having the Ackee, which is a fruit that is similar to scrambled eggs when fried, with salt fish. The salt fish and ackee cooked together make an incredible meal, especially with fried bam-my bread. They say the bam-my bread is at it is best when made with cassava flour,"* Jewel answered.

*"Girl where and how did you get all that information about the food over here?"* Jerry asked Jewel.

*"I did my research on the food, as well as the men,"* Jewel laughed.

*"Well girl, it all sounds delicious,"* Jerry said.

*"Yeah, and I can't wait to try it heifer!"* Brenda G. yelled.

*"So ladies, after breakfast what are your plans for the rest of the day? I'm thinking about spending some with Hugh and find out what he is about,"* Jewel said.

*"Who the hell is Hugh, are you trying to be like Tara now?"* B.G. asked.

*"Hugh is the guy that I met on the beach last evening,'* Jewel answered.

*"Oh yeah, the guy you met on the beach, he is handsome,"* Jerry said.

're

*"He called me right after we got here from Pier One this morning. He wanted to come up to our room; I told him it was too early, and that I had roommates. Now I want to see him though. What do you all think?"* Jewel asked.

*"Girl, please go see the man, have all the fun you can, don't allow nothing, or no one to hold you back!"* Jerry said.

*"Yeah heifer, go have you some fun, show John that you still have what it takes!"* B.G. said.

Jewel laughed at B.G.'s comment; as the women were chatting, someone knocked at their door. *"Who is it?"* Jewel asked.

*"Room service,"* the voice on the side of the door answered. Jewel opened the door and found the most gorgeous man she'd ever seen in her life standing there, she instantly felt as if she had known him her entire life. He had golden bronze skin, dreadlocks wearing a white baseball cap, white sandals, turquoise green silk shirt and white see-through linen pants. The ocean breeze from an open terrace window caused his pants to dance against his thighs, causing friction within Jewel's anatomy. His shirt clung to every muscle in his chest; Jewel could have sworn she saw him his chest and arm muscles. He smiled at her and extended his hand.

*"Good morning,"* he said.

*"Good morning,"* Jewel said.

Jewel took his hand; an electrifying shock of excitement rushed through her body. Jewel could feel confidence in this extraordinary man by the touch of his hand. He stood in the doorway, looking deep into her eyes; Jewel's body felt as if it was slowly dissolving into the floor. He had to have known that he was causing an arousal within her. Jewel looked away from him, and down at the floor. She felt a sudden attraction to this man. She wanted to keep him for the rest of her stay in Jamaica. She couldn't

're

explain her feelings if she tried. She was overwhelmed and nervous at his presence.

*"And a lovely morning it is beautiful. I have you ladies' breakfast, may I come in?"* The man questioned Jewel.

*"Yes, please do,"* Jewels answered, her heart was accelerating, she started to have anxieties; her mouth was warm with saliva.

*"Where shall I put your trays of food?"* He asked.

*"On the terrace, right here on this table,"* Jewel said as she walked outside to the buffet table that sat in the middle of the garden. When she walked away, the man watched her hips as they swayed from side to side. When she looked over her shoulder, he was standing there admiring her body, which caused a burning fire inside of Jewel.

*"Enjoy your meal,"* the man said as he leaves the room. Jewel watched him as he walked away; his backside was firm and tight. She wanted to follow after him; she wanted to know who he was, and where he lived. She told herself if she ever saw him again; she would tell him how she felt. She wanted to tell him before he left, but she was embarrassed about the way she was feeling, and she didn't want the women judging her. Jewel didn't know why she was so attracted to him, but he gave her butterflies in the pit of her stomach.

*"What is the matter heifer?"* *You look like you seen a ghost are something!* B.G. said in a teasing manner. Brenda G. would make a certain chuckling sound when she thought something was funny, and Jewel couldn't stand the sound at times, and this was one of those times.

*"What make you ask me that question Brenda?"* Jewel asked.

*"Girl, we all saw how you were acting with that man, don't try to play us!"* Jerry laughed.

*"Whatever, he was fine though; yes there is something about him!"* Jewel replied.

*"Sometimes instant attraction is the best thing, at least you know it's real,"* Jerry said.

*"I know, I wished I could see him again, I wonder if he works here every day?"* Jewel asked.

*"Well, the only thing I can say is if he is for you he will be back. Hell anything is better than that half of a man you have at home, no good son of a heifer's!"* B.G. said. The women sat down at the breakfast table on the terrace and began eating their breakfast.

*"Wow, this pastry lobster crush is great,"* Jerry said

*"Y'all know that concierge man look like he felled straight out of heaven, and Jerry it is called a fried pastry crust, stuff with lobster,"* Jewel said.

*"Whatever, it is to die for!"* Brenda G. yelled.

*"Okay, girl, you don't have to yell!"* Jewel answered. The women enjoy their breakfast; everything was delicious. Jewel's cell phone had been turned off since last evening. She made sure of it because her signal was roaming off the tower in Jamaica. She would have to pay a high cell phone bill if she hadn't shut it off. She would call Hugh from the land line phone in the room, but as soon as she thought about it the land line phone ringed.

*"Hello,"* Jewel answered.

*"Hello honey, how are you feeling?"* Hugh asked.

*"I'm great! Are you okay now?"* Jewel asked.

*"I'm good right now, but if you allow me to come see you I will be even better,"* Hugh answered.

*"Maybe, I was just thinking about you,"* Jewel answered.

*"When is a good time honey?"* Hugh asked.

*"It's okay if you come over here?"* Jewel answered.

*"I'm on my way sweetie,"* Hugh replied. The women's poured Jewel a small glass of wine to help her loosen up. It had been years since Jewel drank anything that contained alcohol, but this was a special occasion. Jewel sipped on her wine; it was just what she needed. Jerry got up to leave; she said she was going down to Miss. Prissy and Dolly's room to see if they heard anything from Conifa or Tara.

*"I will be right back,"* Jerry said to Jewel and B.G.

*"I don't know why you worry about them heifer's. I bet you any money them bitches wouldn't be worried about you!"* Brenda G yelled.

*"Okay, so what, I worry about people; when I will find out something, I will let you know,"* Jerry said.

*"Let me know as soon as you do, I will turn my cell phone back on for a couple of hours.* Jewel answered.

*Okay, I will. Are you coming with me Brenda?'* Jerry asked.

*"No, I have to get my head bad first,"* Brenda G. said.

*"You're going to be here all by yourself,"* Jewel said. She was hoping that B.G. would go with Jerry.

*"Doesn't she see that I'm about to have company; my goodness she is one noisy chick!"* Jewel thought to herself. Since Jewel wasn't going to have any privacy, she decided to call Hugh and ask him to meet her on the beach. As soon as she dialed his number B.G. told her that she was going to take a walk on the beach. Jewel hung up her cell phone. She wondered why it took B.G. so long to get the hint. *"What was her problem?"*

Brenda G. finally left; Jewel freshened up, turned on some Jamaican music that she had pre-recorded, and sipped more wine to relax. There was a knock at the door; she opened the door and invited Hugh inside. They chatted for a while, asking questions, and getting to know each other. Jewel found out that they had several things in common; they both were Christian, and they had some the same aspirations. Hugh had two children's; a son and daughter. He had never married and had been a police officer for twenty years. He asked Jewel if she would go out with him after he finished work later that day. She said yes, and they made a date for six p.m. He wanted to take Jewel into town and buy her a gift before they went on their date. He said he didn't want her to forget him while he was away at work for eight hours. Jewel and Hugh went into town to do some shopping. In the town, Jewel met a beautiful young lady named Samaria, who worked in one of the small boutiques in the marketplace; she was a beautiful sweet girl with high cheekbones and slanted eyes. When Jewel saw her, she thought to herself; *"wow, she is so pretty; she looks so much like me; she could be my daughter."*

Samaria was very polite and offered to help Jewel shop for gifts in the tiny boutique where she worked. Jewel was pleased to meet her they exchanged email information during their conversation. Samaria said she wanted to come to the states when she finished high school, and go to college. Jewel wanted to take her under her wings, and help her come to the United States. She wanted this beautiful young lady to be successful in all of her dreams, and the goals that she had set for future. Jewel told her new found friend that she would do whatever she could to make it happen for her. Samaria was elated; she told Jewel that she was happy to have met her. She showed Jewel a picture of her mother. Jewel and the young woman's mother look like they could have been sisters.

*"This is why you look like one of my children, you and my daughter could have been twins,"* Jewel said to Samaria.

*"Ah yes, I thought the same thing as soon as you walked into the store. I said you looked just like my mother; that is why I wanted you to see my mother's picture,"* she said to Jewel in excitement.

*"Wow, what a coincidence,"* Jewel said to Samaria. Samaria was full of life; she was happy; she started dancing around the store; when Jewel asked how she learn to dance the way she did, she laugh, and said,

*"Come, come, I will teach you!"* She taught Jewel a few of the Jamaican steps to the dance that she was doing;

*"You have to do it like this. There is a little hop to it when you dance; that is the way we do it here in Montego Bay; now let me see you do it!"* She said to Jewel. Jewel tried but couldn't get the steps. She thanked Samaria for being such a great host,

*"You are beautiful, make sure that you contact me when you are in the states,"* Jewel said to Samaria. They hug goodbye, and Jewel and Hugh continued on their way. Hugh was such a gentleman, when they reached his car; he opened the door of his car for her. He paid for everything and bought her tons of gifts. Jewel was infatuated by this handsome hunk of a man. It was rare to find an American man that treats his women like this. They seemed afraid of a strong black woman; Jewel thought as she sat down inside of Hugh's car. The traffic in town was terrible. The taxicab drivers were driving one-hundred miles an hour; one cab driver bumped into a woman that was crossing a very narrow road, and kept going. The woman managed to get up and walk away without being hurt badly.

*"They stopped for no one,*" Jewel thought to herself, *what in the hell, how can they drive like this without killing someone?"* As Hugh drove through town, he decided to take Jewel for a ride along the coastline of the Caribbean; he was so romantic; he turned to Jewel and asked her;

*"My lady, will you take a trip with me up the coast?*

're

Jewel would never have rode off into the sunset with anyone, but today here in Jamaica, she felt like living a little. She had been pinned up in her emotions lately; now, today all she wanted to do was be happy. She told the handsome man that wanted to spend time with her that she would love to hang out with him. *"Yes I will go with you, just make sure to take care me,"* Jewel said and laughed.

*"No worries my babe, I will take great care of you,"* Hugh said with a smile.

The Streets of Montego Bay was narrow; there were people traveling on foot in the street. Hugh did all that he could to avoid hitting the pedestrians as he drove through town. In a matter of minutes they were out of the small town, and riding along the coastline. The coast of Montego Bay was a beautiful sight to see. There were layers of verdant mountains with rolling country sides and rain forests. The pair came up on an underwater cave. Hugh asked Jewel if she wanted to go for a swim. Jewel told him that she never learned to swim but that she wanted to go closer so she could get a better view of the beautiful cave that bellied the steaming rivers of Montego Bay. After visiting the cave, they climbed the rock and sat atop gazing longingly at the dimming sunset over the bay; as the whales gathered together to mingle for the night. It was the most romantic getaway Jewel had ever experienced; she didn't want it to end, but it was getting late, and Jewel was ready for Hugh to take her back to Sunset Beach, to her room and her friend.

*"Can we go back now,"* Jewel asked Hugh.

*"Anytime you are ready, my love,"* Hugh answered.

Hugh took another route back to the resort; he wanted Jewel to see the other side of the island. During the drive, they came upon one of the most beautiful home Jewel had seen since she had been on the island. Hugh told her that the home belong to Annie Palmer, the White witch of Rose's Hall.

"*They named it "Rose's Hall because the woman that used to live here killed all of her husband's. The natives say the house is haunted. Would you like to go inside and see it?*" Hugh asked.

"*Yes, I would, I have heard so much about that place. Didn't she have slaves also?*" Jewel asked Hugh.

"*Yes she did, she was an evil woman,*" Hugh answered.

"*That doesn't matter to me, I'm used to evil women,*" Jewel replied while giggling.

"*You are, why is that? As beautiful as you are, you should only be around beautiful people!*" Hugh said.

"*Yes, you are right; I was just having fun with you,*" Jewel lied. She didn't want to talk about it anymore. It would bring her spirit down; she didn't want the images of John and Conifa having sex together on her mind; this was a special mini getaway, which she was going to enjoy to the fullest.

"*Will you take me closer, please?*" Jewel asked Hugh. She wanted to get a closer view of Rose's Hall.

"*Yes honey, I will take you to the front entrance,*" Hugh answered.

Hugh drove up the hill to Rose's Hall; he wanted to get as close as he could so Jewel could get a better view of the mansion.

"*Would you like a tour?*" Hugh asked.

"*Yes I would,*" Jewel replied.

Hugh paid the entrance fee, and the old lady allowed them to go through an iron double door that made a loud squeaking noise when they opened it. The inside of the mansion was that of antique and gold. There were sculptures and artwork from all over the world. The floors were made of jade turquoise stone, and the walls were gold. There were many rooms; all sizes. The back of the mansion edged the hillside, overlooking Montego Bay, Jamaica. They stood on the patio while Hugh told Jewel all about the history of Jamaica.

"*Look over there that is the Marina!*" Hugh said with excitement in his voice.

Jewel could see the Marina; huge ships were docking, and passengers were unloading.  As they stood on the huge patio of Rose Hall, Jewel could see other homes that edged the hills of Montego Bay's Ocean. She wondered how someone could live so close to the edge like that. She would never be able to sleep at night if she lived there. After touring Rose's Hall, Jewel asks Hugh if they could head back to the resort.

"*Can we go back now; my friends are waiting for me. We have more tours to take before our date tonight,*" she smiled and said.

"*Yes lovely lady, I will get you back safely, I want you to be comfortable at all times,*" Hugh replied. On the way back to the resort she thought of Hugh, she wondered where he lived, and if he was married, she wanted him, and she wanted him badly. She figured she felt this way because she was vulnerable; the rejection of her husband John was hard to deal with; she needed to feel love again, to be held by a strong pair of arms. When Hugh reached the resort, he pulled into the parking area; he turned off the engine; he got out of the car, and walked around to the passenger door and opened it. He took Jewel's hand and helped her out of the car; he gently pulled her to him and said. "*It was such a lovely afternoon; I will see you tonight babe.*" He leaned in for a kiss before Jewel could answer. He kissed her full on the lips. His mouth tasted like peppermint candy, oh so sweet to Jewel. He parted Jewel lips with his tongue and kissed her passionately. Jewel returned his kisses. As she kissed him back, she could feel his manhood rising to the point of explosion. She was also at the height of her sexual peak. She had to stop herself before she pulled her clothes off right there on the pavement. Jewel felt like a teenage girl in the backseat of her young lover's car.

*"I can't wait to see you again?"* He said.

*'That will be fine; I will be here for four more days; I loved being with you, and the mini getaway was so sweet Hugh,"* Jewel answered.

*"Ok, see you at six o'clock,"* he said.

*"Yes honey, I will see you then,"* Jewel answered.

*"I can hardly wait,"* Hugh said in excitement.

Jewel skipped barefoot across the white sand to her beachfront room; she was in heaven; *"Could this be her dream man?"* she asked herself. She wasn't looking for a relationship with anyone, but it was something about the men on the island. Jewel wondered if she was just plain horny or was she lonely for her husband; whichever she was going to do whatever she wanted to do while she was here, and she made sure to bring condoms just in case. When she went home, she would only carry away her memories. She came to have fun and enjoy herself; that's what she was going to do. She thought about being with Hugh since she first met him on the beach. Of course, she had a deeper attraction for the concierge but Hugh was here right now, and he was a beautiful spirit. It was her time to be happy. If John and Conifa wanted each other, they could have each other. She would give him a divorce as soon as she got home; sure she loved John, but Jewel would never be with the man that cheated on her and she knew about his cheating. That was just not who she was; she was a loyal, caring, trustworthy loving woman, not a woman to be walked over like a doormat by John. She would show him who the boss was; *"Just you wait and see John Dupree; just you wait and see. Jewel is back!"* She thought as she turned the key to her door, and let herself into her resort room. Just as Jewel opened the door to her room, her cell phone starts ringing. It was Jerry.

*"Hey girl, you and B.G. need to come down here to the lobby right away!"* She yelled through the cell phone like a mad woman. It was unusual for Jerry to be so emotional and the yelling is what Brenda G. does; the sound in her

voice made Jewel very uncomfortable. A million thoughts ran through Jewel's mind; she was afraid of what it could be.

*"What is it? Here I come, but where the heck is B.G.? I don't know where she is, I just got back to the resort Jerry!"* Jewel answered, she was confused. Jewel turned around, running through the terrace, and out onto the beach. She saw B.G. walking along the shore about a half mile down the beach. She yelled to Brenda G., but she doesn't hear her. Jewel ran as fast as she could down the beach to where her friend was. Her knees hurt with every move that she made; she stopped along the way and sat on a huge rock. She yelled for B.G., *"Hey Brenda; B.G. come quickly; something is terribly wrong,"* Jewel yelled to her friend. B.G. waved to her and asked, *"What? What the hell is the matter?"*

*"Come quickly, Jerry said something is wrong; I don't know what!"* Jewel yelled.

Brenda G. walked with dexterity, making two steps at a time; by the time she reached Jewel she could tell that something awful had happened.

*"What happening homie?"* Brenda G. asked, looking curious.

*"I don't know, but Jerry and the others are in the lobby waiting for us,"* Jewel answered.

*"In the lobby, I bet you any money it's about that damn Conifa's ass,"* Brenda G. replied. Jewel and Brenda G. run down the beach toward the resort. Jewel was out of breath from running. She was in no shape for all this recreation she thought to herself. They reached the lobby where the other women were sitting in tears. Jewel hurried over to Miss. Prissy, who was so shaken up she could barely sit still; Jewel hugged her around her neck and said, *"Please tell me what happen."*

*"Oh baby, it's terrible, just so horrible; I'm leaving here, I can't take any more of this!"* Miss. Prissy replied. It tore Jewel up to see one of her closest friends in so much pain; she wanted to hold her trembling body forever. She

're

wanted to protect Miss. Prissy; but how could she? No one was telling her what happen.

"*What is going on, what the hell is going on?* Jewel asked again.

Just at that time a host of Jamaican police officers came in with the manager and the CEO of the Bay's resort. Each one of them had the look of death written on their faces, and they were walking straight toward Jewel.

"*What are the police doing here?*" Jewel questioned the women; but they only shook their heads, and said they couldn't believe any of the things that had just happened.

"*None of what things, what has happen?*" *Okay, forget it; just let me ask these officers!*" Jewel said. She was becoming angry with the women for not letting her in on what was going on. To Jewel's amazement Hugh was one of the police officers that were on the scene. He walked over to her and said, "*I just barely met you, and I have to bring you this horrific news. I'd just dropped you off when the news came over my car radio about your lady friend. I was close by the resort, so my sergeant told me to come here right away. I had no idea that I would be speaking to you again so soon, and certainly not with this kind of information. I 'm sorry to say, but this lady, your friend, was found dead in the rain forests. We think she committed suicide, and the reason we think this is because all of her safety hooks on her zip line were open. It has taken our Police Department all this time to figure out who she was and from where she came. One of the crewmembers that work in the rain forest found her passport, and itinerary with her travel and hotel information this morning, not far from where her body was found,*" Officer Hugh said.

"*Is there anything you can tell us that would help us figure out why this tragedy happened?*" Another one of the officers asked Jewel. Jewel was in total shock; she couldn't believe what she was hearing. The officer was talking to her, and all she could see at this point was his mouth moving. She couldn't hear anything else. Dolly Madison took a hold of Jewel and said,

're

*"Jewel will you please answer the officer. Hold on sir; I think she is in shock!"* Dolly said through tears and anger. She was angry because the police was questioning Jewel, and she felt Jewel was in no shape to be interrogated. Jewel regained her composure and began to speak, but her words were coming out slowly, and at a blur. *"Conifa is dead, huh, what do you mean?"* She asked Hugh. When Jewel asked the question, her eyes opened wide, and she screamed at the officers. *"Conifa is dead!"* Jewel yelled, *"what the hell is going on, why on God's earth would she commit suicide?"* Jewel started feeling guilty; their last words were that of pure hatred. Jewel didn't know if she should tell the officer about the argument between her and Conifa. She thought about it for a minute, knowing that she didn't do anything wrong, and if they found out about the argument later they would be suspicious of her intentions. She decided it would be best to tell the truth; before she had a chance to open her mouth with a comment her cell phone ringed again. This time it was her son Ha-kin. Jewel was so happy to see her son's name appear on the caller ID. When she answered her phone Ha-kin could tell right away that something wasn't right.

*"What's wrong mama?"* He asked.

*"Oh my God Ha-kin, it is a mess here! Conifa is dead!"* Jewel said loudly.

*"Conifa is dead? What do you mean she is dead mama? How did she die mama?"* He asked. Ha-kin knew that anything could have happen. There were just too much greed and evilness going on; someone was bound to get hurt; he didn't wish death on anyone, but as long as it wasn't his mother, he was okay.

*"She committed suicide Ha-kin. I don't know what to do,"* Jewel said as she walked to the other side of the lobby of the resort.

*"What do you mean by you don't know what to do mama?"* Ha-kin asked.

*"I found out that she and John was having an affair, and we had a terrible argument right before we went zip lining just before this happened. The police*

*want to know if I know anything to do with it; what should I say?"* Jewel asked her stepson Ha-kin.

*"Mama, tell them the truth as you know it. Don't sugars coat anything; everything is going to come out in a matter of days. It wasn't your fault; I will come to Jamaica, and fill you in on everything. I will take the next flight out mama, don't you worry about a thing. I love you mama!"* Ha-kin said.

*"Ok, I love you too honey, but what do you mean everything is going to come out in a few days?"* Jewel inquired.

*" It is a long story; it will take too much time to tell you on the phone mama, plus I need to get to the airport right away. I'm bringing Rodney with me. See you in a few hours mama. Keep your head up, pray mama, pray!"* Ha-kin said as he hung up cell phone. He didn't want to tell Jewel anymore; it would hurt her too bad. He needed to be there in person. Jewel hung her phone up and put it in her pocket; she walked back over to the officers. She had to speak with the investigators. There was no way that she would blame for that woman's death she thought to herself as she approached the policeman. The policemen were standing in the lobby conversing about Conifa's death when Jewel walked up to them. She went over to the lead investigator and asked if she could speak with him. The investigator said yes. Jewel told him what transpired between her and Conifa at the rainforest. She told him that she believed that Conifa was having an affair with her husband John. She told him that she confronted Conifa about the affair just before the zip lining tour, but Conifa denied it all, and they got into a heated argument, nothing else. The investigator looked at Jewel with a raised eyebrow, as if she had something to do with it. Jewel wasn't about to allow him to intimidate her. She kept speaking, letting him know that she was innocent of this crime, the only thing she was guilty of was not realizing that Conifa wasn't her friend before now. She blamed herself for being so passive, for allowing John to treat her this way. She knew something was off with their marriage a long time ago, but did nothing about it. As Jewel was speaking

're—

to the investigator, Hugh walked over; he wanted to protect her, but he didn't know how. He was unsure of what was going on; he couldn't jeopardize his position on the police force to help a complete stranger. He had just met Jewel; she was so sweet, she couldn't have done something so terrible; he thought to himself as he moved closer to her. *"It's okay sir; I will take over from here; this young lady has been through a lot,"* Hugh said to the lead investigator.

*"Okay, I think I have what I need, go ahead,"* the investigator told Hugh.

*"Take your time and tell me everything, I'm here to comfort you,"* Hugh whispered to Jewel.

*"I just told the sergeant, investigator, or whoever he was, that I believed my friend was having an affair with my husband, so I confronted her. That was no reason for her to kill herself. I didn't threaten her or anything. You remember when we were together, and I told you that I knew evil people. She was who I was speaking of; I just didn't want to spoil our getaway with that type of conversation,"* Jewel told Officer Hugh.

*"Can we please keep that information our secret for now, at least until this case is over?* Hugh asked.

*"Yes of course, but weren't you on your lunch break or something at that time, I mean when we were together?"* Jewel asked Hugh. She wondered why he didn't want anyone knowing that they were together earlier. Conifa killed herself yesterday according to the police; them being together today had nothing to do with Conifa's death.

*"Yes, but my private life is just that, my private life. However, I do want to help you all that I can,"* Hugh answered Jewel. Hugh hoped that by him mentioning that he was there to help her; she would shut her mouth about them being together. He didn't want to have anything to do with her if she was a murderer. He had to get clearance first, as soon as he got back to the

police department. He would run a national background check on her; he had to make sure that she wasn't a big time criminal. He had worked too long to become a policeman to allow someone to cause him to lose everything.

*"So when you told your friend you suspected that she and your husband were having an affair, what did she say?"* Hugh asked. Jewel was now skeptical of giving answers to Hugh because he was acting so strange, and different from the sweet man that took her on a tour of Montego Bay. She didn't know if he was ashamed of her, or protecting his job. Either way she was careful how she answered him.

*"She said that it was all a lie,"* Jewel answered. The sergeant walked over with a phone in his hands and gave it to Hugh. Hugh took the phone and walked away. He needed to talk in private, away from the noisy crowd of women and officers; Jewel watched him as he walked to the other side of the lobby; she watched his every move. Hugh facial expressions changed as he was conversing with the person on the other end of the phone. He turned his back to Jewel so she couldn't see his expressions. When he turned around facing Jewel, he looked straight at her; he nodded and shook his head in disbelief. Jewel wondered what he was talking about, and to whom. She could sense something else had come up; she didn't quite know what to expect at this point. Everything was starting to look like a set-up to her. Hugh walked back over to Jewel and said, *"This suicide is much more complicated than any of us realized; there is a huge problem; there is so much we don't know. Will you be able to stay for a few extra days, so we can get to the bottom of it all?"* Hugh asked Jewel.

*"Why, yes I guess, but what now? What is going on?*" Jewel questioned Hugh.

*"There have been some new leads in this particular case. It is so much. We will have more information to share with you all a bit later. Just please don't worry, and hang tight for now, that is,"* Hugh said.

*"I will try and contact you later on,"* Hugh said to Jewel as he walked away to talk with the other investigators. The officers gather their things to leave. When Hugh walked passed her with one of the investigators he ignored her. She could tell they were friends because of the way they both looked her up and down, and then looked at each other and smiled. They acted as if they had secrets between them. At that moment, Jewel wasn't sure if she ever wanted to talk to Hugh again. Jewel and the women sat in the lobby in a daze, looking at each other. They were confused and hurt at the same time. *"She had so much to live for; why would Conifa kill herself?"* Jewel questioned her friends.

*"We don't have any idea why she would kill herself Jewel; it is so horrible!"* Miss. Prissy said.

*"I know I said some hurtful words to her, but why would that make her go and kill herself?"* Jewel asked.

*"I don't know; it is all so crazy, like something out of a horror movie!"* Dolly said.

*"With that heifer, doesn't any of this surprise me,"* Brenda G. yelled.

*"Well, it sure surprised the hell out of me!"* Jerry shouted, and lowers her head as if she was praying. Jewel sat with her hands clenched together in an emotional state of alarm, and fear at what had taken place; *"and here in Jamaica of all places,* she thought to herself. *Now what would they do? How would they get Conifa's body back home? She had no one to care for her; she had treated her friends poorly."* Jewel was trying to figure it all out. *"What was it that Ha-kin had to tell her? What was so important that he would fly half way around the world to tell her? This has to be a nightmare! May I wake up now dear lord?"* Jewel asked. She silently said a prayer for Conifa.

*"That is the same way that I feel; as if I am having a nightmare; some of that nightmare on Elm street bullshit. That is why I never liked Conifa; that bitch will*

*fuck up a wet dream. She brought her dizzy ass way over here to kills herself. Man that done mess up my high!"* Brenda G. yelled loudly.

*"It is a nightmare, but try to be more sympathetically Brenda,"* Dolly said.

*"I am, but being sympathetic got my nervous system of key; it's compromising my style heifer. I don't like shit compromising my lifestyle,"* Brenda G. said.

Once Miss. Prissy regained her composure, she said, *"poor Conifa, why would she kill herself over something so petty? There has got to be more to this story!"*

*"Because she is a petty and a conniving ass heifer; killing herself probably was as easy for her as it was screwing this woman's husband,"* Brenda G. yelled.

*"Please stop being cruel B.G.,"* Jewel said.

*"I'm nice but Jewel you are way to kind; I mean that woman was trying to mess up your life,"* Jerry said.

*"We don't know the entire story; let's just wait and see what happens,"* Miss. Prissy said.

*"The story, what story? The story is that she is a no-good ass person who isn't woman enough to stand up to the shit she had done,"* B.G. said.

*"I feel so sorry for her family,"* Jewel answered.

*"Girl don't be sorry for that trash, she has been screwing around with John,"* Jerry answered.

*"I just can't believe she could be so evil,"* Jewel replied.

*"Well believe it, that heifer did it and took the easy way out!"* B.G. answered.

*"Killing herself couldn't have been easy Brenda G."* Miss Prissy answered.

*"Well that's what she did, damn heifer!"* B.G. replied.

're—

## CHAPTER SEVENTEEN

## HA-KIN AND RODNEY MOORE

Ha-kin and Rodney were on their way home from Vegas. They would take a plane from LAX instead of Las Vegas, Nevada's airport. It would be simpler than leaving Rodney's car in Vegas, and coming back for it. The takedown went well; Queenly Le and the rest of the crooks were behind bars where they belonged. Ha-kin and Rodney was elated to be leaving Vegas. It had been a long battle for them; all the hoops that they had to jump through to bring those men down, and all of the time he watched John abusing his mother was over. As he drove down the highway, he wondered how he would tell his mother that her husband was a fraud and that he didn't love her. How would he tell his mother that John had a mistress and an eight-year-old son? Ha-kin's heart was heavy with sorrow and pain for his mother Jewel. His only comfort was that he knew he would always be there for her; he would comfort her in her time of need. He was confident in knowing that this part of her life was over. Jewel was a strong woman; she would bounce back. Ha-kin relaxed in positive thought that everything would be all right; he pressed the accelerator picking up speed. He was ready to blow to the city never to look back. The city of sin could have all of his dirty dealings to themselves. Ha-kin cell phone ringed, it was a call from the Vegas Police Department; Ha-kin answered his cell phone. *"Hello, is this Ha-kin or Rodney?"* The voice on the other end asked.

*"This is Ha-kin,"* he answered.

*"Investigator Simian here, I have some news for you. Are you sitting down?"* He asked Ha-kin.

*"I'm on interstate fifteen; I'm on my home,"* Ha-kin answered.

The investigator told Ha-kin that Joe Wright was killed in a tussle by one of the investigators.

*"He was what?"* Ha-kin asked.

*"What happened?"* Rodney asked Ha-kin.

*"Hold on a minute man, I'm trying to hear the man. It is the Vegas detectives,* "Ha-kin told Rodney.

*"Man put the phone on the GPS system so I can hear,"* Rodney said, but Ha-kin ignored him.

*"Yes, one of the investigator's was trying to get the information from him and he reached for the investigator's gun. Investigator Raul wrestled with Mr. Wright for his gun back. The gun went off killing Joe Wright with a single gunshot to the head. It was already bad enough, now we have another death on our hands to deal with,"* the detectives said.

*"Ah man, sorry to hear this, but those guys have to get what is coming to them. All of those rotten seeds that they have planted has finally grown up and took him out of the game,"* Ha-kin said.

*"Yeah right, yet it still is a damn shame man; I get sick of seeing these senseless deaths. I have no idea why folk think that they can get away with breaking the law!"* The detective said.

*"You are right; some would never learn, but thanks, Detective for letting us know. At least now we won't have to worry about him getting out, and stalking us for revenge in the future,"* Ha-kin said.

*"No, you won't have to worry about that at all, he won't be returning anytime soon. Well, take care; if we need you will we be able to reach you at this number?"* The detective asked Ha-kin.

*"Yes sir, all means, anytime you can call me!"* Ha-kin answered.

*"Sounds great, have a safe trip home, and thanks again for helping us bring this case to a close,"* the detectives replied.

Ha-kin hung up his cell phone and turned to Rodney, who was waiting impatiently for an answer and said,

*"Man, guess what Joe Wright has done; he tried to take the investigators gun; the gun went off and killed the fool."*

*"Ah, no man; come on now, he didn't do something that crazy!"* Rodney said with a questionable look on his face.

*"Yes he did," the detective; just told me,"* Ha-kin said.

*"Damn man, that man was crazier than we thought, and we went up there just the two of us with that David and Goliath type shit; like we were invincible; we are lucky to be alive. We were blessed to get out of there!"* Rodney said.

*"You are right man, only by God's grace! I have got to get in touch with mamma, she needs to know what is going on,"* Ha-kin said. He was getting anxious again. His mother was not answering her phone; he tried again. Ha-kin knew that Joe Wright had been in prison prior to meeting Jewel for fraud and extortion; this would have been his third strike. He would rather kill himself than go back to prison for the rest of his life. Ha-kin remembered over-hearing Joe Wright making a statement to Nathaniel Le about a person spending their life in prison; Joe Wright said that he would rather be dead than live in prison for the rest of his life.

*"He meant every word of it,"* Ha-kin thought to himself, as he drove up interstate fifteen. He tried several more times to reach his mother, but she wasn't picking up her phone.

*"What the hell is going on? Why isn't mama answering her phone? I hope those Jamaican police officers haven't done anything to her,"* Ha-kin told Rodney as he turned off interstate fifteen onto the Interstate ten freeways. He was less than an hour away from home when he tried calling her again; this time she answers. *"Hey mama, how's everything there on the island?"* Ha-kin asked Jewel.

*"Honey, she left us in the rainforest; she went ahead of us,"* Jewel screamed into the phone.

*"Calm down mama, please calm down. I can't make sense of anything that you are saying; can you please start over?"* Ha-kin asked his mother.

*"I know that I told you this before Ha-kin, but she committed suicide in the rainforest baby. She killed herself, and the police over here think that I had something to do with her murder!"* Jewel yelled.

*"What? Don't worry mama; I will take care of everything. You just hang tight, and try to stay calm; I told you that I was on my way there. Rodney and I just need to grab a few things for the trip,"* Ha-kin told Jewel. He finished his conversation with his mother just as he parked in the driveway of his house.

*"I'm home now mama; Rodney and I are going to grab a few things and head to LAX. We will be on the island in about seven hours. I will talk to you soon, okay mama. I love you!"*

"*I love you too mama,*" Rodney yelled into the phone. He had to be there for his mother. He didn't want the Jamaican police to frame her for something that she didn't do. He would not allow anyone to pin Conifa's death on his mother. Ha-kin and Rodney wore the same size clothing, so they pack a few things from Ha-kin's closet to wear for the Jamaica trip. There wasn't enough time drive to Rodney's house to get clothes and make their flight. They only needed clothes for a few days; Ha-kin and Rodney made it to the airport just in time to catch the next flight to Jamaica. After checking in with their pre-paid tickets, Ha-kin made an important call to the Vegas investigator that was handling Joe Wright and John's case. He needed to tell them about the situation in Jamaica. He asked the investigators to place a call to Jamaica, and let the detective over there know what was going on in the states. *"Tell them this entire thing tie's together; let them know that Conifa Barkman is at the center of it all. Will you please fax them all of the information.*

're—

*Make sure that they know that Jewel Dupree had nothing to do with any of this mess. It was all a set-up. I know you all call them once before, but my mother is scared out of her mind. Tell them everything, my mother thinks they are trying to implicate her in that woman's death,"* Ha-kin said to the investigator.

*"We will, there is no sense in what these folks did. We will get on it right away,"* the investigator promised Ha-kin.

*"Thank you sir, I appreciate your promptness, my mother doesn't have the first clue as to what's going on. She is caught up in a net of lies, and deceit, all started by Conifa Barkman, Joe Wright, Nathaniel Le, and his sister Queenly Le. Oh let's not forget my stepfather the master-mind John Dupree. I want them all brought to justice. I am sorry to say, but it's a good thing that Joe Wright ended his life, better off for the environment!"* Ha-kin told the investigator. Ha-kin had become enraged at what John and his gang of hit men's were doing to his mother. Ha-kin and Rodney flew out of the Los Angeles airport to Montego Bay on the next plane. Rodney was right beside his friend for backup. He had John and Jewel's best interest at heart. He would stay with Ha-kin until this thing was over. They travel non-stop five hours to Jamaica, once the plane landed Ha-kin and Rodney went straight to Sunset Beach resort; where they found his mother and the other women on the beach talking. They were chatting about the whole ordeal that had just taken place several hours earlier. When Jewel saw Ha-kin, she ran to him crying; he held his mother tightly.

*"Have you ladies had any sleep?"* Ha-kin asked his mother.

*"Just a little bit last night, it was difficult though,"* Jewel answered.

*"You will have to get some rest mama,"* Ha-kin said.

*"I know, maybe later,"* Jewel answered her son. She had forgotten all about her date with Hugh last evening. She wondered if he even called her. She looked at her cell phone. She had five missed call from Hugh; knowing that

he thought enough of her to call her again made her feel better. Ha-kin lead her away from the other women; consoling her, telling her that now he was here, and he would let nothing happen to her. He took Jewel away so he could try and calm her down meanwhile Rodney stayed with Miss. Prissy, Dolly, Brenda G. and Jerry. Rodney told the ladies the rest of the horrific story. Ha-kin and Jewel walked down the beach a ways to talk about what happened. As they were walking, Tara and her Jamaican friend walked passed them; Tara yelled to Jewel and Ha-kin. *"Hey Jewel, is that Ha-kin with you?*

*" Yes it is, where have you been girl?"* Jewel asked with tears in her eyes.

*" Why are you crying Jewel, what happen, why is Ha-kin here?'* Tara asked.

*" I came to take care of my mama,"* Ha-kin answered.

*"Your mama can take great care of herself, can't she?"* She questioned Ha-kin, but her eyes were fixated on Jewel's face. Tara could sense there was something terribly wrong. Ha-kin wished that Tara would go about her business. He wanted to try and calm his mother broken heart; Jewel was worried about where Tara had been for the last twelve hours. She was sick to her stomach at all the horrible things that had occurred in the last twenty-four hours. The thought that something had happened to Tara made it worst; at this moment she was happy that Tara was safe.

*" Yes, mama can take care of herself, but there is some earth shaking stuff going on that mama, and I need to discuss. Can you please go over there with Rodney and the other women? They are right over there; do you see them?"* He asked, pointing his finger in the direction of the group.

*"Why is Rodney here?"* Tara asked Jewel.

Jewel tries to inform her about what was going on, but broke down in uncontrollable tears. She couldn't get the words out. She fell to the ground and held her head in her hands; she was mumbling something that Tara couldn't understand. Tara turned her attention back to Ha-kin; Ha-kin told her once more to go to Rodney, *"He will explain,"* Ha-kin said. He walked away with his mother holding onto his arms. She was an emotional wreck; Ha-kin could barely control her. He sat his mother down and began explaining everything to her. Jewel was in total shock and disbelief at the horrible accusations that were coming out of Ha-kin's mouth.

*"No, no, no, I don't believe any of this! He couldn't have; I know John better than that boy!"* She said to Ha-kin. She took off running down the beach. Ha-kin ran after his mother; he caught up to her and brought her to a shaded area on the beach. The furnishing where they sat was that of maple veneered plywood which anchored eight oversized chairs; the area was layered with miniature palm trees and tropical plants; it was beautiful, serene and tropical. A quiet place, Ha-kin thought, *"here I will bring peace to mama's mind,"* they sat down, and Ha-kin began to tell her more about the entire situation. He yelled to Rodney and the women; he motioned for them to come to him. *"Come over here everyone, let me fill you all and at the same time. It will be too much to keep repeating."* Everyone came over to the shaded area on the beach where they sat down to listen to what he had to say. There was anticipation and in their faces. So much had happened; they couldn't imagine what was next.

*"What is going on?"* Tara asked.

*"I'm afraid to ask him anything, too much shit is happening for me; now what?"* Brenda G. asked. *"She must not have heard anything that Rodney told them,"* Ha-kin thought. *"She is always high of that stuff she calls her medicine."*

*"Please hurry and tell us, we are all on edge; this is too much for me, and now Ha-kin is here with more information about Conifa. That's why my husband wants me to come home. He has already gotten me an exchange ticket. I don't want to leave you all, but I am going home to my husband,"* Miss. Prissy said.

*"Okay, this all began when my mama first married John. I hate to tell you this mama again, you're such a beautiful woman, and mother to me, but I have to tell you the truth,"* Ha-kin told Jewel.

*"I don't think I'll be able to hear it again Ha-kin,"* Jewel answered and began tearing up. What he had to say was too difficult for her to understand or comprehend. There was a large dark empty hole in the center of her heart; she knew it was all true, why else would Ha-kin come all the way to Jamaica if it weren't the worst case scenario.

*"What did those bastard do?"* B.G asked again.

*"Mama, right after you and John got married I overheard John talking on the phone to Nathaniel Le. They were talking about the day that he introduced you to John; John was laughing and joking about it. Now me being a man, and all, I wondered why Nathaniel would introduce you to John when he wanted you for himself. I remembered how Nathaniel used to chase after you like a dog in heat. I was happy when you turned him down. I always thought he was a con artist, out for no good. He was no good for any woman and especially not you mama. I also thought that it was pretty strange for a good man to be putting women down as he was doing; a real man don't do something like that. I know some men will play those sorts of games; I did everything I could to catch him and Nathaniel off guard, they were pretty damn slick. Out of curiosity I bugged John's cell phone; I listen to his calls. A while later I overheard them talking about all those million that your father left you and that you won in Vegas. He said that you were trying to keep all that money for yourself, and you were trying to shut him out and that he was going to get every dime from you. Later they came up with a plan to steal it from you, and take Conifa's company at the same time. Joe Wright found out that she killed her husband and started blackmailing her. John also has a mistress mama, name Queenly Le, who is Nathaniel's sister. As a matter of fact mama you know her, she works at Dr. Borene's office. She also has a son by John who is seven years old; the boy's name is Justin Dupree."* Ha-kin's mouth was open to say more words when Jewel interrupted him,

*"Now you wait a damn minute, what did you say? Now you are talking crazy boy!"* Jewel yelled at Ha-kin and threw her cup to the ground.

*"I know it hard to hear mama, and it is very complicated, to say the least, but you must let me finish,"* Ha-kin said. *I have been following them for years, and I watch everything that they did. Conifa and those guys set up this trip through Barkman's Corporation just to get you all out of town. Conifa was supposed to invest the money here in the Caribbean after they stole it from you; she didn't know that they were planning on stealing her company as well. Rodney and I followed them to Las Vegas right after you ladies left for Jamaica. They were all arrested by the FBI right there at the Flamingo Hotel. The immigration police expedited Nathaniel Le and his sister Queenly Le back where the hell they came from. The authorities have been looking for them and their parents for nine years. They had warrants for their arrest. While we were on our way here the Vegas investigators called me and told me that Joe Wright had been killed. He got into a scuffle with one of the detectives, he was trying to take the officer's gun; the gun accidentally went off shooting him in the head, and killing him. This would have been Joe's third strike; he would have spent the rest of his life behind bars. I'm so sorry mama, but it is the blessing that this evilness has come to an in, and you didn't get physically hurt in all of this bullshit."* Jewel was so angry at John for deceiving her; she knew all along that he was cheating on her with someone. He was so slick she could never find out whom he had been cheating. Jewel have been overwhelmed with guilt believing that because she blamed Conifa for coming between her and John that she killed herself; now she finds out about Conifa's plot and that she killed her husband Ralph. Even though she felt that Conifa got what she deserved, it still brought tears to Jewel's eyes. Jewel sat on the beach crying wondering how John could be so evil, how he could treat her so mean and cruel. She had given eight years of her life and everything that he ever asked of her. This was her thanks for being a great wife; well he could just rot in jail for all she cared at that moment.

*"I knew something was going on between those two, but had no idea what. I couldn't see John with her sexually though; Conifa and John, I mean,"* Miss. Prissy told Dolly.

*"Yes, it's sad, but it is better that Jewel know that it wasn't her fault that Conifa killed herself,"* Dolly said.

*"I guess we better get ready to go up to our room Dolly; we have to pack all our things again. It is so hard to believe that this has taken place honey baby; can't anybody tell me that this isn't a horror movie!"* Miss. Prissy said.

*"Yes Prissy, I am coming; I want to say goodbye to Jewel first,"* Dolly told Prissy.

*"You ladies are leaving: that's too bad; I have to stay until this situation is cleared up,"* Jewel said.

*"It won't take long girl you will be okay. If you need us to stay, we will,"* Miss. Prissy and Dolly told Jewel. They did not want to leave her in Jamaica to deal with the death of Conifa all alone, but Jewel's son Ha-kin and Rodney was here. They would take care of her; knowing this was the only thing that made Miss. Prissy feels better about going home. Miss. Prissy's husband Prof. Henry Tolbert didn't want his wife to get caught up in any danger. He told her to come home right away.

*"No go ahead Mrs. Prissy, I'll be all right; my boys are here; you go ahead home. I'm so sorry for this nightmare that Conifa, John and the rest of them created. Thanks for your concern, you are a good friend. What time is your flight leaving in the morning?* Jewel asked Miss. Prissy.

*"I believe it is at eight-thirty Jewel; I need to take another look at the reservation that my husband called and got for Dolly and me. Well, okay then, give me a hug; best wishes girl on everything going smooth tomorrow at the police department. Will you be coming home after your visit to the police station?* Miss. Prissy asked Jewel.

*"Truthfully I wished I could stay here, and never go back to the states. If I go home I will only have noisy people asking me tons of questions, and have folks looking at me with pity and shame in their eyes. Besides I have met someone that is nice; why shouldn't I finish my vacation and spend some time with him? I was supposed to meet up with him last evening but I forgot. I hope he will call again,"* Jewel said to her friends.

*"Yes honey child, and a gorgeous hunk he is,"* Jerry said as she wiggled around trying to get up from the sand. Jerry fell backward; she had a shot glass of Patron in her hands. When Jewel told her that it was too early to be drinking she blamed it on Conifa's death. Dolly walked over to where Jewel was sitting in one of the oversized chairs. She bends down and hugged Jewel around the neck; she spoke softly into Jewel's ears saying;

*"I hope you know that I love you, you are a beautiful woman; Jewel I admire you; this doesn't determine who you are, nor does it defines your path. I will see you at home. You had better take good care of yourself,"* Dolly said, and she smiled a smile that Jewel loved so much.

*"I will be fine, don't you Miss. Prissy worry about me. Brenda G. and Jerry are here. I have enough back up power,"* Jewel said as she looked over at B.G. She laughed when she thought of Brenda G.

*"That girl is a fighter; she would never allow anyone to bother any of us,"* Jewel said.

*"Damn right, I got your back Jewel, yours too Jerry!* Brenda G. yelled.

Jewel's cell phone rings, she looked at the caller ID? The call was coming from John. Jewel's heart felt as if it suddenly stopped; she was frozen in time; the ringing of her phone got louder and louder. Just as Jewel goes to answer the phone Ha-kin pulled it away from her.

*"Don't answer it mama, there's no need to talk to that man. How much does he have to do to you before you get enough?"* Ha-kin said as he put the phone in his pocket.

*"Please give me my phone back, I will not talk to him Ha-kin,"* Jewel told her son. Ha-kin gave the phone back to Jewel; as soon as he did it begin ringing again. This time Jewel answered it. She told John to stop calling her, and never to call her again. John begged Jewel for help; *"Jewel, this is John, babe please don't hang up. I know Ha-kin done told you a bunch of lies. I need you baby, please help me. These people have set me up. It is a hold bunch of lies baby. Something about embezzlement, fraud and murder."*

*"John, I loved you for eight years, and for eight years you have cheated on me. You have a child with some girl; you were going to let them people kill me for you to get my money. No more lie's John; it's over! You go straight to hell! Make sure you take the rest of your fraudulent friends with you!'* Jewel yelled through her cell phone at her husband.

*"But bae, they gave me a bail. It's a million dollars, please bail me out; then we can straighten this entire thing out. It is all lies baby; hey baby can you hear me? I love you babe!"* John yelled, *please don't leave me in here Jewel, you are all I got bae!"*

*"John, how could you? I gave you my life, and this is the way that you treat me?"* Jewel asked.

*"I will be here for you Jewel, anything you want; just please bail me out,"* John begged.

*"Who are these people that would make you wanted to turn your back on me this way John?"* Jewel asked.

*"I didn't baby; those folks are nobodies; they just want to blame someone. Ha-kin and that boy Rodney has everything twisted. They think it was me; I don't have any idea what they are talking about. I love you and only you baby,"* John said.

're——

*"Stop lying John, just stop it!"* Jewel yelled through the phone.

*"Mama, just hang up,"* Ha-kin said.

*"No, I will finish telling this sorry bastard what I feel about him,"* Jewel said.

*"But mama, he is making you so upset, please just hang up the phone,"* Ha-kin told his mother.

*"Please don't listen to him baby, he has something against me,"* John said.

*"You put yourself and so many others in harm's way; no John, I will not listen to you ever again!"* Jewel said and hung up. John called her back again; Jewel didn't answer his call. Ha-kin came over to his mother; he hugged her and said,

*"Good job mama, good job."* After Ha-kin had told the women the full story, their heart was broken; they couldn't believe that their trust, love and friendship had been compromised by Conifa's greed. Miss. Prissy wished that she had never met Conifa, or introduced her to her friends.

*"What are we going to do now, will we be going home early, or do we stay?"* Jerry asked Jewel.

*"I haven't made up my mind yet, I know that I have to stay here until the investigation is over,"* Jewel said.

*"Oh yes, I forgot all about that, all this damn commotion,"* Jerry said.

*"I know child, it's a tragedy,"* Tara said. She had been quiet; she was relieved that Jewel had found out about Conifa, but she wasn't ready to go home. She wanted to spend more time with her Rasta-man. She had been sitting there with the women listening to the entire ordeal trying to figure out how she would make her get away. She wasn't about to spoil her vacation because of this nonsense.

"*That woman, lord that old ass heifer is too much!*" B.G. said while shaking her head and looking very disgusted.

"*When will you guys be going back to LA?*" Jewel asked Ha-kin and Rodney.

"*I need to get back by tomorrow evening; would you like to leave with me at that time?*" Ha-kin asked his mother.

"*I'm not ready to leave right away, but I guess so if these policemen will be done asking me questions,*" Jewel answered her son. Secretly she wished that everyone would get the hell away from her; allow her to meditate and find her path. She knew that they all loved her, so she didn't make a fuss.

"*What else could they need though; they have everything from the beginning to the end of those guys plan of action. I mean what else could Jewel tell them?*" Miss. Prissy asked.

"*I have no idea, but I will not leave this island until I find out. They will not be coming to the states looking for me for murder. I need to sign the necessary papers to clear my name,*" Jewel said.

"*Mama, before you leave I will make sure that all is well. You won't have to worry about anything,*" Ha-kin answered. Jewel could not say a word at that moment. She was becoming overwhelmed again. Tears flowed from her eyes like a river; she had no control; she dried her eyes, but the tears started again. She wanted to run away, to hide from the embarrassment that she was feeling, and her friend's sympathetic eyes looking at her in pity. The silence was bothering Rodney, he spoke up and said;

"*Yes, Mrs. Dupree; we are going to take great care of you and the other women. That's why we are here; this has been a tragic situation for each of us. Jewel your heart is broken I'm sure, but I promise you it will get better.*"

"*Thank you Rodney, we need all of the protection we can get, considering all the mishaps that have happened to each of us,'* Dolly said.

're

*"You know that is right, I don't even know if I want to stay here, I leave for one night, come back and people are dead,"* Tara said.

*"Maybe that's a good reason for you to change your ways. Maybe if you had been here you could have help save the heifer!"* B.G yelled at Tara.

*"Brenda, do you have a problem with me?"* Tara asked.

*"Damn right I have a problem with you, and I always have because you are disrespectful, and I don't like it,"* B.G. answered Tara.

*"You are crazy if you think for one minute that I am going to allow you to talk to me that way anymore. I am telling you right now to stop it! This is my body, my life, and I can do what I damn well please with it!"* Tara yelled at B.G. She had gotten angry at Brenda G; it was about time. Brenda had been on her case for a while now.

*"Come on ladies, we have enough problems, we don't need anymore!"* Miss. Prissy said.

*"It wouldn't have made any different if she were here or not, Conifa killing herself was bound to happen; stop being mean Brenda,"* Jewel said to Brenda G.

*"Yes there is nothing that anyone could have done to save any of them folks, they were all evil,"* Miss. Prissy said.

*"Thanks, Miss. Prissy and Jewel. It means a lot to me that I have friends that are true to me. I won't be staying here with you all. I am going to my friend's house until my vacation is over. We have big plans, the next time you all see me I may be married. He had everything a woman could ask for; he has three houses, a yacht and five cars. He has three children, but no wife or girlfriend,"* Tara said as she rolled her eyes at Brenda G.

*"Heifer please, that man is probably coning you. You sure are silly to be a grown ass woman; why the hell would you think something so stupid? Haven't you heard*

*about these Jamaican men? I mean I am not trying to come down on you; I like you, but I just don't understand you!"* Brenda G. yelled.

*"Brenda, you just need to shut your mouth; everything that comes out of it is foul, ignorant and inconsiderate! I don't have any more time for this crap, I'm leaving. I hope you ladies have a safe trip home. My honey and I are off to have some fun. Hey, wait a minute, what about the trip to New York? We all have to cancel that ticket right away. I will change mines from Shadow's house,"* Tara said.

Shadow was the man that she had been hanging out with since they had been on the island. Shadow walked over to Tara and asked if she was ready to go. Tara got up from the sand to leave the beach with him; Miss. Prissy asked Tara for the man's address and phone number.

*"Give us his phone number and address Tara. It is not safe for you to wander off like this with strangers. We don't want anything to happen to you baby girl,"* Miss. Prissy said.

*"Oh madam, I will allow nothing to happen to my queen, I love her. I will always take great care of her,"* Shadow said to Miss. Prissy. His answer made Tara smile and blush like a school girl. She looked over at B.G. as if to say, *"see I told you so!"* It was a good thing Brenda G. didn't see the way that Tara looked at her. It would have been more fussing back and forth between the two of them.

*"Maybe not, but we still need those digits,"* Jerry said.

*"Just give us the number and be on your way,"* Miss. Prissy told Tara and the man once more. Tara asked Shadow for his number; he gave it to her. Tara gave the phone number and address of the man to Miss. Prissy.

Miss. Prissy put the information in the Fanny pack that she kept attached to her waist. She made sure not to lose anything. Jewel said goodbye to Tara; she held her head in the palm of her hand and prayed. She prayed that Tara would be okay; she asked God to protect her with his shield of protection. Tara hugged everyone and ran off down the beach hand-in-hand with her new love. When Jewel looked up again, Tara had disappeared into the sunset. All she could see was Tara's white linen dress flowing with the wind; it looked like a kite in the distance cloud.

*"Now that I have Tara's information I feel better; she sometimes caused me to worry. I swear that girl can meet a man wherever she went. I'm not mad at her that is what she supposed to do; she still young at heart. So who is leaving in the morning with me?* Miss. Prissy asked again.

"Not me, I don't think we should let that heifer screw up our trip. She has screwed up everything for everybody else; which is enough for one bitch to do!" Brenda G yelled.

*"Brenda, that is downright insensitive for you to say such a thing! Do you have any compassion for anyone besides yourself?"* Miss. Prissy asked. Brenda's condescending ways was getting the best of her.

*"Hey Ha-kin, how in the world did you find out about all of this again? This shit sounds like a horror television show!"* B.G said.

*"Like I told everyone I have been on to these guys for a long time. I couldn't tell mama for fear that she may be too afraid to stand up to John's evil and manipulative ways,"* Ha-kin said.

*"Wow, I don't see how you kept all of this to yourself for so long,"* Jerry said.

*"In our line of work it is mandatory silence, on the job and off,"* Ha-kin said to the women.

*"Top secret and everything; wow Jewel you have an awesome son,"* Dolly said. She smiled and rolled her big baby doll eyes toward the sky; she was doing some harmless flirting.

*"Yes I do; I have loved him since he was five years old; since I first laid eyes on him. I remember the first time I met him; he was the cutest little boy ever. He was*

*passionate, loving and caring back then and he haven't changed one bit in all these years. Ha-kin I love you; you have always treated me so well,"* Jewel said to her son, as she hugged him around his neck. Ha-kin blushed and smiled at Jerry, who was staring at him like he was a piece of cherry pie that she wanted to eat, but Jerry knew better than to mess around with Jewel's son. Ha-kin was off limits to any of Jewel's friends. Jewel told him when he was eighteen years old not to let her catch him flirting with her friends; that it wasn't acceptable at all. It didn't matter what she said, he still flirted with Jewel's friends behind her back; he just didn't ever take it any farther. Ha-kin had a thing for older women. Jewel's friends were always checking out him out from a distant. Ha-kin was a respectful young man; he told his mother that he wasn't ready for a serious relationship; he wanted to enjoy his young years without wife and children. He said that when he got married it will be for life; he was still a young man. Jewel knew that when he got married he would love his wife and children because he knew that family was the most important thing in this world and that he would always protect them. Today he proved just how much of a man he was. Jewel was happy to have him in her life. Now that Ha-kin was here on the island rescuing Jewel and her friends from Conifa and her evil gang of friends, Jewel had a greater appreciation for him and his friend Rodney. She looked at her son with admiring eyes; she was so happy that he saved her life and her fortune. John had planned her demise; not only did he plan her demise, he had a son and a mistress; he was leading a double life. Her husband never loved her at all.

*"No matter what you tried to do to me John Dupree, God had my back. It didn't work out the way that you wanted it to. I pray that you get everything that you have coming to your no-good ass!"* Jewel said quietly to herself.

*"Mama is you alright? You are awfully quiet,"* Ha-kin said.

*"Yes my child, I'm alright now, thanks to you and Rodney for obeying the voice of God and saving me from that evil man."* Jewel answered.

're

## CHAPTER EIGHTEEN

## CONIFA'S LETTER

The sun was setting over the Caribbean Sea; this horrible day had slowly come to an end. The women decided to have dinner and turn in for the night. It had been the second most horrific day Jewel had ever encountered. She needed to rest her mind, her body and her soul. Tomorrow would be another stressful day for her. She would have to go to the police station to answer more questions. Her life was spinning out-of-control, but she would hold back the rivers of tears that lingered behind her eyes. She was going to remain strong through it all. Even though she didn't want to believe that John was behind it all; and was in jail, looking at life in prison for trying to defraud her, she knew that it was all true. Some way she would have to start a life all over; at this point she wanted to get away from it all. She didn't want to go back, but she didn't want to tell the others her plan. She wasn't ready to do damage control. As she was thinking about the situation, she drew a box in the sand where she was sitting. At this point she felt as if she was inside the box, and couldn't get out. Ha-kin came over and sat on the sand next to his mother. Jewel told him that she was ready to get food and turn in for the evening. *"Do we order room service for dinner, or do you all want to go to the Hoping Crab restaurant on the beach?"* Jewel asked the group.

*"Let's eat at the restaurant, I heard they had fantastic food, and besides, I want to sit down in a nice relaxing setting."* Ha-kin answered. They all agreed to eat at the Hopping Crab where they would be in a comfortable environment. Jewel didn't have an appetite, so she only orders a salad. Jewel looked around for the concierge; the man that brought them breakfast earlier this morning, but he wasn't there. She figured maybe he didn't work the evening shift. She wished that she could see him again before she left the island. There was something magical about him that brought Jewel to her knees at first glanced upon his face. She wondered who he was. She

silently asked God to allow her to see him once again. She wanted to make sure that she wasn't fooling herself; the way that she was feeling about this stranger made her feel a little uneasy. Hugh was nice, but to Jewel the concierge man was a spirit from heaven. Ha-kin looked over the dinner table at his mother; he asked her if she was alright. *"You awfully quiet mama, what are you thinking about now?"*

*"Ah, just wondering about a few things; tomorrow will be rough for me,"* she said. She didn't want the group to know that she was dreaming about the concierge; a man that she'd only seen for a brief second. She had made one huge mistake by marrying John in a hurry; she didn't want to hear anyone saying that she was making another one so soon.

*"It going to be okay mama; in the morning Rodney and I will go and represent you. We will stand with you. When it's all over we can all get on a plane and go home,"* Ha-kin said.

*"Thanks honey, I will be glad when it's all over so I can breathe again,"* Jewel said.

*"I feel you on that Jewel; this nightmare will soon be over,"* Miss. Prissy said.

*I'm finish with my dinner; I've eaten all that I can; the food was excellent,"* Miss. Prissy said to Dolly and the others.

*"I am going to my room so I can finish packing; unless there is something else that you all want to do; it is still early. Are you ready Dolly?"* Miss. Prissy asked Dolly.

*"Yes I'm ready, I going to hug and kiss everybody goodbye right now; I'm sure y'all will be asleep when we leave in the morning,"* Dolly answered. Dolly and Miss. Prissy got up from the dinner table; hugged everyone and said goodbye.

*"We will see you all back in Los Angeles. Good luck Jewel and be safe honey baby!"* Miss. Prissy said as they exited the dining room.

"Take care, see you all at home," Dolly said as she turned around for the final time; waves and blew kisses at Jewel and the group. After dinner, Ha-kin and Rodney walked the women's to their room. Brenda G. stopped by the front desk to let the clerk know that Tara had left the resort. She wanted to give the clerk the keys to the room; she told the clerk that she didn't want them charging her for the nights that they didn't stay in the room. Brenda G. gave the clerk the keys, and they all go to Jewel and Jerry's room. Once they got to the room, Jewel made drinks for everyone; they had nightcaps on the terrace. While the group sipped wine and Jamaican beer, discussing what they would do the following day, Jewel cell phone ringed. Jewel looked at the phone but she doesn't recognize the number, so she didn't answer it; simultaneously Ha-kin's cell phone ringed. When Ha-kin looked at the caller ID, he recognized that the call was coming from the police department there in Jamaica. Ha-kin answered the call. When he got off the phone, he told everyone that the investigators wanted to come over to Jewel's room tonight. This worried Jewel, she wondered if they were coming to arrest her for Conifa's murder. Ha-kin could see the worried look on his mother's face and said,

*"Mama it is going to be all right. The investigators said that they have something very important to show you."*

*"Something important like what though?"* Jewel asked.

*" I don't know mama; we would have to wait until they get here, and then we will be able to find out,"* Ha-kin said.

*This all sounds pretty mysterious to me,"* Jerry said.

*"Hold on peoples, we will have to wait it out! Let's not speculate; we know that no one here has done anything against the law, right?"* Rodney asked as he looked from one person to the other.

*"Yes Rodney is correct, let's just hang loose, we will find out soon enough why they are coming at this time of night,'* Ha-kin told the group.

*"I don't know about this shit, but I know it had something to do with that heifer!"* B.G. quietly said. Everyone turned and looked at B.G.; no one could believe that she whispered her words. The group looked back and forth at each other and started laughing. It was hilarious to see Brenda G. in a state of fear. She was high as a kite and didn't want the police to question her. Just at that moment someone knocked at the women's door; Brenda G. took off running into the bathroom. Brenda's actions caused Rodney and Jerry to laugh out loud; it was so funny they couldn't stop laughing; *"Sssssh,* Ha-kin said. They stop laughing, and Rodney went over to the bathroom door and asked Brenda G. to come out. *"Girl come out of there, you are going to cause these people to think we are up to something!"* Rodney yelled to Brenda G. through the bathroom door. *"They don't want me! Why do I need to come out?"* Brenda G. politely asked. *"I will tell them that you are in there if you don't come out!"* Rodney said. *"All right fool, I'm coming out!"* Brenda G. whispered through the bathroom door to Rodney. She had gone into the bathroom and hid her marijuana; she came out of the bathroom smelling like a ton of perfume. Rodney, Ha-kin and Jerry laughed again at Brenda G. Jewel was too nervous to see anything funny at the moment. Ha-kin went to the door and opened it. There were four officers; they stepped inside the room two at a time. Ha-kin offered them a seat at the table. Two of them sat down, while the other two stood close by the entrance. Ha-kin offered them a beverage, they declined. One of the investigators motioned for Jewel to come over; he said that there was something that he wanted to show her. Jewel nervously walked over to the investigator; she sat down at the table. The investigator took a plastic bag out of his briefcase; he carefully laid the plastic bag on the table; he put on a pair of gloves; he handed Jewel a pair of gloves to put on; she took them and put them on; he then reach into the plastic bag and pulled out a piece of paper, and gave it to Jewel. He asked Jewel to read it loudly. Jewel took the piece of paper and began reading slowly while everyone waited in anticipation. The letter read:

're—

*"Dear Jewel," If you are reading this letter, I want you to know that I am so sorry that I wasn't woman enough to tell you exactly what was going on face-to-face. I want you to know that I never wanted to hurt you. I am afraid that Joe Wright, John Dupree, Nathaniel Le, and Queenly Le's people are going to kill me; they have been blackmailing me for years. Joe Wright found out that I poison Ralph with medicine that Nathaniel got from across the border. Those few times when you saw Nathaniel come into the doctor's office, he was coming to bring the medicine to his sister Queenly Le; she then gave it to me. She is the person that stole your keys that day at the office. I overheard her and John laughing and talking about how dumb you looked when you were looking for your keys. They said when you were looking for the keys; Queenly had given them to John to take next door to Mike Master's Key shop. John was having copied made for Queenly. John wanted Queenly to be able to come and go from your home as she wished, but only when you Jewel wasn't around. John came to the doctor's office that day to see Queenly, not you; that is why he didn't have time for you. They also have a son; his name is Justin Dupree. He is seven years old and he looks just like John; if you don't believe me, go to her parents' house in Compton. That is where Queenly and their son are living right now. The address is twelve forty-four one- hundred-twenty-Third Street. I am sorry for killing Ralph, but he treated me terribly. I had to get rid of him, now he won't be able to beat another poor sick woman. You make sure to watch out for John because the morning that you were sick, and didn't know why; well it was because John used the same plant in your food that I gave to Ralph; he was trying to kill you, but for some reason you didn't die. My ovarian cancer has returned, and I only have a year to live; I don't want to fight anymore; I don't want to cause you anymore heartache. I want you to know that they are planning on taking everything that you have, before I allow them to destroy us both I rather end it all, right here, right now. With me out of the way, you will have a chance to save yourself from what they are about to do. I have no answers for what I have done; I can only ask that you and God forgive me.*

*Conifa Barkman;*

Jewel could not believe that she was reading a letter from Conifa Barkman; a letter that she had written just before she died. *"When did she have time to write this letter? When did she plan all of this?"*

Jewel's emotions were crashing everywhere; she was relieved that Conifa took time to write a letter to say sorry. At least this would clear her name, but there was a part of her that was angry as hell at this woman. If Conifa hadn't already killed herself she would choke the life out of her right here in front of these investigators!

*"How dare her!"* Jewel said loudly.

*"We are very sorry for all that you have been put through Mrs. Dupree; hopefully this will bring you some closure; this case is over. You are free to go home whenever you choose to. We will handle the rest; here are copies of everything for your records. You may need them farther down the road,"* the investigator told Jewel." Jewel took the paperwork; she would put them away somewhere safe. *"Thank you for everything,"* Jewel said to the investigator.

*"Thank you so much for clearing my mother,"* Ha-kin told the investigator.

*"Thanks, you all did a great job,"* Rodney said.

*"Yes they did,"* Jerry said.

Brenda G. was quiet for the first time; she has nothing to say. Rodney and Jerry couldn't wait until the investigators left so they could tease her because she hid in the bathroom. Brenda G. walked outside to the terrace; she was having no part of them teasing her. She walked out to the beach and sat down in the sand. The investigators got up from the table; they shook everyone's hands as they exited the door.

*"Have a good night,"* the investigator said.

Jewel was still in shock at what she had just read in the letter from Conifa. Even though Ha-kin had told her everything; she just didn't want to

're-

believe that this woman could be so damn evil. Conifa had sat in her house and pretended to be her friend; when all along she knew about the troubles that were brewing and she said nothing.

*"What type of a person does something so terrible?"* Jewel questioned herself. She doubted her choices of friends, she had made so many mistakes in choosing who she hangs out with, she was afraid of her thoughts at the moment. Jewel thought back to the time when she and Conifa went go to Yolanda's together to get their hair whipped up. They have so much fun, and all the time she was pretending. Jewel wanted revenge, but she knew that God would not like it. Ha-kin knew his mother was sad at the turns of events that had happened. He wanted to do something to make her feel better, so he asked Jewel if she want to go home right away.

*"There's no reason to hang around mama, everything is over now. We can all go home; what do you guys say?"* Ha-kin asked.

*"I'm not ready to go back to California, I'm going to enjoy my vacation, and I'm sick and tired of running around in circles by other people. I'm staying right here on this island until I'm ready to go home,"* Jewel answered Ha-kin.

*"No I don't want any more of this, I'm ready to go home Jewel. We can come back when the time is right. Is just too much confusion right now, I wouldn't be able to enjoy myself,"* Jerry said.

*"I don't want to stay, I think I will go back with the fellows, I don't want to get busted over in this mofo,"* Brenda G. said.

*"Mama is you sure you want to continue your vacation, why don't you come home in the morning with us? Please mama!"* Ha-kin begged his mother.

*"No Ha-kin, those people have taken too much of my life already, they will not get another moment of it. I'm done living my life under the thumb of others. I came here to have fun; right now all I feel is anger, resentment and fear. Fear that my life is closing in on me, and I can't stop it from happening. I know she confessed to*

're

*all the wrongdoing, but I'm still very angry, I don't want to go back to all those ugly memories,"* Jewel told her son.

*"It looked like I won't be able to change your mind, so how about if we all go home and renovated your house for you? We will clean out all of John's things, wipe away his memory from every wall, every corner; when you do come home everything will be brand-new. What do you think mama?"* Ha-kin asked.

*"Yes, that sounds like a great idea,"* Rodney Moore said. He was looking at Brenda G. he wanted to start with her, but decided to wait for a while. It was the nicest he had ever seen Brenda G.'s personality. She must be afraid; he thought to himself.

*"Yes I would help,"* Jerry said. *I will do whatever I can to help my friend. She has had enough misery, she don't need any more. The minute she gets home, the entire-neighborhood will come asking questions. You know how fast bad news travel."*

*"I can stay there for a while and help. I don't have anything else to do with my time right now. My grandchildren are out of the country until December third, so I will be free as a bird. I will work with this heifer right now,"* Brenda G. said as she pointed to Jerry.

*"That is fine; you all can do what you want. I need a break from this rat race that was created by John and his crew. I will be all right, I just need to process all this information, and there are too many folks around for me to do it. I will keep in touch with you all,"* Jewel said.

*"We understand Jewel,"* Jerry said.

*"Okay mama, so how long do you plan to stay over here?"* Ha-kin asked. *"For the entire two weeks; there is no need for the New York trip now that everyone is leaving. I love Jamaica, I will stay here on this island,"* Jewel said.

*"She will be okay if nothing else Jewel is a strong ass heifer. She knew what she wanted and she wants to stay in Jamaica,"* Brenda G. said.

're

"*That has already been decided Brenda. All he is asking now is when his mother is coming home,*"Jerry said.

"*I know that, and I want to know to, but I'm not going to make it sound like I don't trust that she is okay enough to handle her own business!*" Brenda G. yelled. The group looked at each other and said, "*welcome back Brenda G, now that the police are gone you are a loud mouth badass!*"

"*No, I'm not a bad ass; I just say what's on my mind!*"Brenda G said.

"*Rodney, are you ready to go; wait, how about we spend one last night on the beach before we leave? We don't have to stay long, just have a few drinks. I want to celebrate mama's freedom. Then afterwards we can all say our goodbyes. We need to get to the airport early in the morning. Ladies, I'll make sure that your flights are taking care. I will handle everything, don't worry about anything,*" Ha-kin said as he bends over and kisses his mother on the cheeks.

"*Why don't we just go up to Ha-kin and Rodney's room after the beach party Brenda?*" Jerry asked. *That way we can all leave together and won't have to wake Jewel so early in the morning.*"

"*That's cool with me; they have two adjoining rooms; we can sleep in one and the guys can sleep together in the other one, right guys?*" Brenda G. asked Ha-kin and Rodney.

"*I'm cool with that, just so you know, here's the room number.*" Ha-kin said. "Oh, okay thanks," Jerry said as she took the piece of paper with the room number on it from Ha-kin and put it in a pocket.

"*I'm not cool with it, I'm not sleeping with Ha-kin,*" Rodney smiled at Jerry in a flirtatious way.

"*Thank you Ha-kin for the key,*" Jerry said, smiled at Rodney.

"You are welcome," Ha-kin answered

## CHAPTER NINTEEN

## JEWEL FINDS LOVE

Jewel got up from the table and walked away from the group; she needed time to think, and she needed the time alone; she walked down the beach. When she looked back she could see her son in women joining her. She stopped walking, went back and told each of them that she needed time and space by herself. Ha-kin looked at his watch; he began speaking to his mother in a quiet tone saying," *listen mama, it is eight already, can you please not go too far away? I do want to spend my last hour here with you.*"

"*I won't go to for, just down the beach away. There are people out; nothing would happen to me I will be back in a few minutes son,*" Jewel answered.

"*You sure you don't want us to go with you?*' Jerry asked.

"*Yeah heifer, you can't leave me, I'm your road dog,*" Brenda G. yelled.

"*You are too scary to be someone's road dog, look at how you ran when the police officers came into the room. I wouldn't want to be anywhere with you, and something is happening. You will be the first person to run,*" Rodney jokingly said to Brenda G. He sure did love to push her buttons, and he knew which ones to push.

"*Shut up Rodney; it is all good homie; go ahead and take your walk. We will be right here when you get back,*" B.G. said as she sat down in the white sand and lit her joint. She took a long drag of it and started coughing.

"*Killed her dope,*" Rodney laughed.

"*Go ahead mama we will be here, I trust you are okay, have a nice enjoyable walk; don't do anything I wouldn't do,*" Ha-kin said in a joking way.

*"Okay honey I'll be right back,"* Jewel said as she walked away. She went down the beach toward the nightclub. There was a beautiful Jamaican music flowing in the air. The music made Jewel want to dance. The song that was playing was, *"Hey pretty lady over there,"* Bob Marley. Jewel knew the song, so she sang along as she walked further away from the group; she turned around to see if she could still see them. They were sitting in the sand tossing up drinks. She didn't care, she couldn't drink and besides she didn't want to drink. All she wanted to do was get away as far as she could from them all right now. As she continued her path along the ocean, she came upon some laid-back Rasta's lying in the sun. As she passed, they spoke to her; Jewel looked at them and kept walking. She didn't want to be rude, but there were no words that she could speak, her thoughts were all over the place. She entered a stone column where she sat down for a minute to collect her thoughts; she picked sea shells from the sand, and threw them into the ocean; when she did she thought of John. *"How could he be so different from the man that she married all those years ago? How could I fall for a man like him?"* She questioned herself. She had no answers; she got up from the stone wall and began walking towards a beautiful uniquely designed home that she saw in the distant. The home was sitting on a private acre of land gently edging the ocean. As she moved closer to the beautiful home she quietly whispered, *"At this point anything beautiful will help me take my mind off John, and all the chaos that I am facing."* She marveled at the rich mahogany wood and the French doors of the home. As soon as she thought about the beauty of the huge French doors, she thought of Conifa and the time that she made a mistake and went to Conifa's house instead of going to Starbucks. She remembered how nasty Conifa treated her when she heard that Jewel have been to her house. Jewel also remembered the time when Conifa was dressed in a skimpy outfit; she remembered all of the ugly words that came out of that woman's mouth over the years. She remembered her exotic toy party and the way that Conifa pretended that she didn't like the toys; the put-downs and the manipulations that she had said and done.

*"How could she kill Ralph though?* Jewel questioned herself.

Jewel quickly left the home and walked back down the stairs to the beach; she didn't want any more memories of Conifa right now. She loved Ha-kin so much; she knew everything he just told her was all true, but she didn't want to admit it to herself. She strolled about a mile farther down the beach; kicking her feet and the white sand as she move farther and farther away. Ha-kin was very worried, but he didn't want to hover over his mother, so he stayed behind and let her go her way. Jewel laid there in the ocean crying her eyes out. The water was so clear that she could see the fish swimming around her; which gave her some peace of mind, but the thought of John and Conifa kept reappearing. Thoughts of her mother's prayers came back to her. She could hear every word that her mother said. She decided to pray; she remembered the words that she told herself before she came on the trip, then it all became clear to her. God had already prepared her for this; she remembered when she had the dream of her standing at the bottom of Niagara Falls. In her dreams, the water spewed out of heaven, washing away all her fears. God had placed Ha-kin in her life for this reason; he had put Miss. Prissy and the other women's in her life for support. She remembered the first day that she met Miss. Prissy and Dolly. That day Jewel and Conifa were at Fox Hill Mall shopping for Christmas presents when Conifa noticed the ladies.

*"Hey ladies what are you doing here? Are you buying something for me?"* Conifa asked in a joking way.

*"Hello Conifa, how are you?"* Miss. Prissy asked.

Dolly never spoke to Conifa; she only waved her hands in her direction. Jewel wanted to get John a Rolex watch. When the ladies saw her looking at the watch, Dolly made a comment saying, *"wow that is beautiful, you must love whoever you're buying it for!"* she said with a big old smile. The minute Jewel saw her smile she felt closeness to Dolly; just as if she'd known her all life.

're——

*"Sometimes you meet a person that makes you feel so comfortable it feel like you have known them forever,"* Jewel thought as she introduced herself to the ladies.

*"I was going to introduce you ladies Jewel,"* Conifa said. Miss. Prissy came over and took a look at the watch; she said,

*"Oh, my, that is beautiful, how much is it?"* She asked her Jeweler.

*"Oh, the cost is about forty-five-thousand dollars with the taxes,"* the Jewelers answered.

*"That's a little too rich for my blood!* Miss. Prissy replied.

*"Mines to,"* Jewel said. *I was just looking ladies,* and she laughed. They all exchange phone numbers and the rest was history. The Lord brought Rodney to Ha-kin for this reason and this reason alone. There was nothing for her to fear; or was there? She raised her head to heaven and yelled out to the lord. *"Oh my God, please help me, show me the way, how to start again. How can I ever trust again?"* Jewel shouted loudly across the ocean into the heavens above her.

At that moment, a voice came out of nowhere and said, *"you can start right here with me right here and right now, come take my hand. I will take you for away from your troubles. I will care for you always my sweetness,"* the voice said.

Jewel looked up into the sweetest face this side of heaven. It was the face of the concierge; he who brought breakfast to Jewel and the women room earlier that morning; the one that Jewel searched for at dinner. Jewel couldn't believe that he was standing there on the beach, looking down at her. He was reaching for her hands; She remembered the attraction that she felt for him the minute that she opened her bedroom door.  She had wanted to pull him inside and keep him forever. Now was her chance, *"what would she do?"*She thought to herself.

"*Take my hands honey,*" He said

Jewel reached up and took his hands. He pulled Jewel's body from the water; she wrapped her legs around his waist as he carried her onto the sand. He gently laid her down, and kneeled down besides her, looking into her eyes with intensity; as he caressed her fingers and stroked her hair. He asked her if she was alright. Jewel took a second look at him, nodded her head, and said, "*Yes, I'm okay, thank you.*"

"*Will you take a chance with me, baby?*" He asked Jewel.

*No playa, I don't even know you!* Jewel said.

"*I'm no playa, I'm strictly here for you and only you my sweet lady,*" the stranger answered.

"*Why not take a chance that God sent this man to help me. It is all too coincidental; God had to plan it all. It had to be God who sent Rodney into Ha-kin's life to help us; now I believe it's you lord sending this man to ease some of my pain. I know it is the Lord father, God.*" Jewel thought to herself.

"*This will be my last night here on this island I think, but I will be happy to spend time with you,*" Jewel replied.

"*You have made me the happiest man on earth.*"

He reached for her hands, placing her hands in his they walked up the beach towards Ha-kin and the women.

"*What do we go from here?*"He asked.

"*Where do you want to go?*" Jewel questioned.

"*I have a beautiful place that I want to show you; will you come with me?*" He asked.

"*Where is this beautiful place?*"Jewel asked.

're———

"*It is my home you can see it from here,*" he said with excitement in his voice.

"*Oh really where is it? I can't see it,*" Jewel replied.

"*Look up there; the home with the huge French doors!*" He said pointing up to the hill where Jewel had spent so much time with Hugh earlier. "*Wow, I went by that house when I was on tour yesterday. Do you live there?*" Jewel asked.

"*Yes my love, I grew up there on Jack's hill, of course, the home is too large for one person. I don't need eight bedrooms six bathrooms, maid quarter tennis court, spa and a pool, but is the smallest home that I own; not to brag, but all my accomplishments are firsthand. I had to work for everything that I have, and my parents taught me Godly morals. My parents died years ago, leaving their estate to me; most of the properties you see up there all belong to me. My father was half Indian, and Jamaican; my mother was Jamaican. My father's parents were well-connected entrepreneurs. When they passed away, my dad became soul owners of all of their estate here in Montego Bay. We own one-hundred acres of luxurious hotels, including the Peninsula; which is a whirl of glamour all of his own. It used to be located on Munson hill. It was a sugar plantation which we later grew coconut, pimento's and other spices there. The Peninsula was home to me for quite a few years until we moved to Jacks hill. I had a vision for my new domain; we started redevelopment of luxurious cottages and complexes on the hill. We built homes and shops for the native of Montego Bay. I was dedicated to my dreams and work tirelessly to turn them into reality. We celebrated the renowned hill, and open its doors to the world of tourists,*" the man finally stopped talking and took a deep breath.

"*So I guess that makes you a wealthy man,*" Jewel said.

"*I'm okay, not hard up for anything but you baby,*" he said.

*"Are you a player, because I'm not a loose woman, but damn baby you're fine,"* Jewel said under her breath. The word hard up," caused tension in Jewel's groins.

*"You are charming; thank you for saying that. It must feel great to have whatever your heart desires,"* Jewel answered.

*"You are charming also, don't you think so?* He questioned Jewel.

*"Yes sometimes, I do, why do you ask?"* Jewel asked.

*"I don't know, I sense a tiny bit of sadness in your eyes, when I try and make eye contact with you, you look away. I think you're the most beautiful woman I ever seen,"* he said.

*"You are very nice,"* Jewel said as she looked him in the eyes for the first time. What he said was true about her, she was insecure and now she was also vulnerable; she had to be careful. If she hadn't been insecure, and afraid of growing older she wouldn't have married John. She rushed into marriage too soon; she also remembered how upset Ha-kin was when she broke the news to him about her getting married. When Ha-kin heard the news of their marriage he asked, *"but why Mama; you don't even know him well enough to go and marry him.*"Jewel was upset at Ha-kin for getting so involved in her personal life. She never appreciated anyone trying to tell her what to do. He wasn't the first to try either and he would be the last. There was something different when this man told her about herself. For the first time in life she wanted to listen. *"Was she in love at first sight? Or was she so torn up inside until she was trying to escape reality? She would soon find out."*

*"May I ask you a question?"*

*"Yes of course,"* he answered.

*"I hope I'm not too forward, but the first time I saw you were when you came to my room. My question is why do you work as a concierge if you're wealthy?"*

"*That wasn't my job, only went to see you again. I am the owner of this establishment,*" he said and smiled. His smile was an electrifying masterpiece. It sent Jewel's mind and body traveling into places unknown; it touched parts of her body that had never been touched before without hands, causing her great emotional stimulation.

"*Jewel collected her emotions, and said to the strange man; wait a minute, you aren't the concierge? Now you have me confused as hell. Why would you do such a thing?*" She questioned the stranger. "

"*Well, if I would have told you then, would you have felt the same way about me?*" He asked.

"*Maybe I would have, why wouldn't you just be honest?*" Jewel asked.

"*Well when women find out that I'm rich, they look at me with different eyes. I am disgusted with women's that only want me for my money, but you are so beautiful. I had to try for the sake of the passion that I felt in my heart for you. When I left the room I wanted so badly to come back and tell you how lovely you are. I noticed you when you exited the taxi your very first day on the island; as I waited for my limo you passed me by, your beautiful fragrance caught my attention. I couldn't get you out of my mind. When my limo came for me, I told him to go away, and I came to you, but you and your friends were talking. I didn't want to interrupt your serious conversation, so I went about my business. I just happened to be in the restaurant when you call for your breakfast that morning. I was having a conversation with the head chef. I asked him to allow me to bring your food. I hope and pray that I didn't overstep honey,*" he said with a serious look in his eyes.

"*How did you know which room, I was in?*" Jewel questioned him. She was so sick of the games that people played. "*Why can't people just tell the truth?*" With all the craziness going on in her life right now, she sure as hell didn't need more drama. Jewel was unsure of this man, but there was something about him that melted her heart. Besides him been attracted, he was a

're—

charming individual, he was a reflection of love, compassion, and kindness all rolled up into the statute of muscles. He didn't even have to open his mouth to capture Jewel's heart. He had only said a few words, but each syllable sang a sweet melody to Jewel's ears; captivating her inner soul.

At that moment time stood still. She had to look away from this Casanova before she made passionate love to him right there on the beach. "*When you and your friends were getting your room keys, I came over to speak to you, but you ladies were having a conversation about something that sounded pretty serious. You didn't see me, but I heard the desk clerk tell you which room you were in. I also heard you when you gave the chef your room number. Beside I am the owner, I know just about everything that goes on around this resort, who comes, and who goes,*" he answered. Jewel listened to all that the man had to say. She could understand exactly what he meant. She was going through the same thing right now. Her money was the only reason why John married her. She knew how this sensitive loveable man felt; it was sad to think that a person had to watch out for predators like John and the women's that were only after his money. She decided that she would join him for a tour of his home. "*It is okay, but before I go anywhere, I need to go back and let my son and my friends know my whereabouts,*"Jewel said.

"*Yes sure baby, where are they,*" he asked.

"*Down the beach a ways,*" Jewel answered. They walked together; parting the white sand with their toes, as they move swiftly along the shores of Sunset Beach. The shoreline of Jamaica was calling out to them through the waves that came rushing inbound. All along the shore, Jewel saw some of the most beautiful Caribbean attractions for the tourist to see. Jewel wanted to pretend she was a mermaid and swim out to sea, disappearing into the deep blue waters with this gorgeous man that she had just met. They walked past the Royalton White Sand Resort; it was beautiful as well. Everywhere Jewel look was gorgeous, the hotel sat on a hill; it had a variety of decorated rooms and suites. The stranger started to tell Jewel

're

about the Royalton White Sand Resort; he said that once upon a time it was a place that was used for slave trading. The white man would have auctions selling Negroes slaves. White slave owners would come from miles around to purchase slaves. Sometimes a slave would try and get away by running into the villa; when the slave master would bring the slaves back, they would chop off their feet to keep them from running away again. Sometimes they would hang them from a tree in the forest. This man had so much history on Jamaica; he offered to tell Jewel more, but it was getting late. Jewel figured if she didn't say anything they would walk up and down the beach all night long. It was miles and miles long; there was no end to the waters. She looked up at the tall man; she admired his swagger. He was a trophy that she had found on the beach; everything a woman could ask for; he was from heaven, sent to her by God.

"*May we go back now?*" Jewel asked the man.

"*Yes, of course, we can go right away!*" The man answered.

"*Thank you, I don't want my son to worry about me,*" Jewel said.

"*By the way what is your name beautiful?*" he asked.

"*My name is Jewel; Jewel Dupree,*" Jewel answered.

"*I don't even know your name, and I'm leaving with you. I must be in love! What your named kind sir?*" Jewel asked looking up at the man with admiring eyes.

"*My name is John; John Osterman,*" the stranger answered. Jewel looked into the stranger's eyes, she found comfort in him, and he was from heaven, a gift from God. She was happy that she'd met him.

The End:

The Suitcase volume two is coming: I hope you enjoyed your read;

jmanuel49@yahoo.com

# THE SUITCASE

In a world of confusion, heartache and despair we are sometimes faced with obstacles that we don't have a clue what the outcome will be. We hold on to faith and believe that things will work out. As for myself now on radiation treatment for staged three liver diseases from hepatitis C, suspected infidelity from my spouse, and if that wasn't enough, here came old menopause. While sitting in my office chair one night I dialed my husband's cell phone number, and once again it went straight to his voice message. I heard his voice greeting playing Biggie Small, "baby give me one more chance," over and over again. This time he had been away from home for two weeks. I hung up the phone; I couldn't stomach hearing the recording anymore. I said to myself this would be the last time that I would be disrespected. I crawled from bed and got dressed, got into my car and drove to the lawyers' office and filed for a divorce. The words of a young wise man name Lamar whom I met years ago came to my mind as I signed the divorce papers, "if you don't mind, then it don't matter." Today I decided to pack all of my challenges into a suitcase and take a mental vacation; I have chosen not to allow my challenges to control my life anymore. Through-out my life I've had many challenges unfortunately this was the most complicated one. I pray that the suitcase help you find peace, serenity, and above all the love of God. The Lord didn't intend for us to have a marriage of despair, instead he wanted us to have a happy and contented marriage of love, mutual respect, understanding, and trust; a marriage that endures the test of time. It isn't easy but it can be done if we trust God to give us what we need instead of trying to do it on our own. Wait on God to fill your heart with the love of a spouse that will last in love forever. I rushed into marriage for fear of getting older and living alone. It is better to live alone than have of marriage of infidelity, lies and manipulations. Your time will come, whatever you do wait on the Lord.

Ruby Manuel

**THE CHARACTERS IN THE SUITCASE ARE**

**A DISTINGUISH INFLUENTAL GROUP OF**

're—

**MIDDLE AGED WOMEN**

**IT IS A STORY OF TEARS, PASSION, INSERCURITIES,**

**MISTRUST AND DEADLY LIES.**

**FOLLOW THE DIALOGUES AND**

**JOURNEY OF THESE WOMEN**

Palmdale, California

Copyright@2014 Ruby Manuel

ISBN 978-312-37703-5

The Suitcase is dedicated to my young cousin Reggie Jermaine. He was murdered in 2014; exactly one month after our family reunion. I love you Reggie, your smile was infectious! *R.I.P. Reggie, we will always love you; may your smile travel wherever the suitcase go.   September 11, 2014 an angel went home; @25years old;

Made in the USA
Las Vegas, NV
21 January 2022